POISON'S DANCE

POISON'S DANCE

BEYOND THE TALES BOOK THREE

TRICIA MINGERINK

Sword & Cross
Publishing

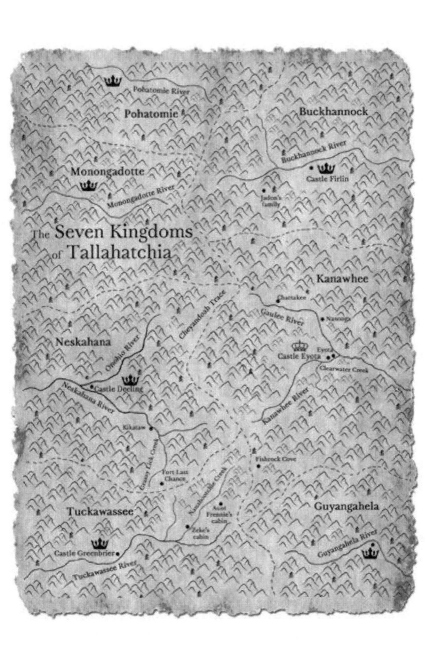

CHAPTER 1

ALEXANDER

High King Alexander flexed his fingers on the canoe paddle and stared at the rushing river ahead. The Gaulee River roared with the late spring runoff, the rising sun glinting pink and gold in the white, thrashing crests of the water churning over and around boulders. "I can't do this."

In the prow of the canoe, Daemyn Rand, Alex's manservant, bodyguard, advisor, and friend, glanced over his shoulder, the fringe on his buckskin shirt swaying with his movement. "You've improved a lot since last year. Don't worry. I'll step in if we start floundering."

"And we'll be here to fish you out if you capsize." In the canoe next to them, Princess Rosanna, the girl Daemyn was courting, and her bodyguard Isi Degotaga were both wielding paddles and appeared far more relaxed in their canoe than Alex was in his.

Princess Rosanna swayed in time with the current, the fringe on her buckskin shirt swishing in the light breeze. Blue beadwork created patterns on her shirt while a long, black braid swung down the center of her back. Isi's curls were tied back with a bright red ribbon, matching the red beadwork on her pale yellow linen shirt.

Beyond Rosanna and Isi, Captain Degotaga, the head of Princess Rosanna's bodyguards, and Zeke, Daemyn's nephew, were also keeping pace in their canoe. Other canoes filled with guards, both Alex's and Rosanna's, spread out along the river, keeping watch.

Alex swallowed, his heart throbbing in his throat. He wasn't ready for this yet. He'd been going down the Gaulee with Daemyn, Rosanna, Isi, Zeke, and the guards ever since they had returned from that disastrous visit to Pohatomie the previous fall. Shooting the rapids first thing in the morning wasn't Alex's favorite thing to do. But, he tolerated it since it was what everyone else loved to do.

As he was learning, that was how friendship worked sometimes. Daemyn would have preferred to live a quiet cabin in Buckhannock, but he stayed at Castle Eyota out of loyalty to Alex. Rosanna, Isi, and Zeke had all moved to Castle Eyota out of loyalty to Daemyn.

Compared to that, Alex could manage to brave this river a couple of times a week.

And, more than that, the trip to Pohatomie had shown him that he was pathetically unskillful when it came to survival. Alex was not a capable person. He had been raised to be the high prince a hundred years ago, in a time when the Seven Kingdoms of Tallahatchia had been prosperous and—mostly—at peace. He'd had to do nothing besides sit in Castle Eyota and be regal.

But after the curse that had caused Alex to sleep for a hundred years, he had woken to a Tallahatchia splintered by war.

In this Tallahatchia, being skillful was more prized than

being regal. To be the high king this Tallahatchia needed, Alex had to be stronger. More skillful. More capable.

That meant he needed to steer this canoe and shoot those rapids. It would prove he could be just as capable as Daemyn and Zeke and all the rest of Daemyn's many, many, many relatives.

He had to do this. He couldn't keep putting this off. He'd gone down this river many times, first in the center of a canoe, then in the prow. Daemyn and Rosanna had talked him through exactly what he had to do.

Daemyn flicked his paddle, sending a shower of droplets at Alex. "You'll be fine. I wouldn't be sitting in this canoe if I didn't reckon you could handle this."

Alex let out a long, slow breath. Daemyn thought he could do this. It would be fine. The Gaulee wasn't running dangerously high as it had earlier in the spring. Now, the higher water smoothed out some of the most dangerous sections of rapids. This was about the safest time of year to tackle this river.

"All right." Alex dug his paddle into the river. Now or never.

Two canoes of guards swept down the river ahead of them, then it was Alex's turn to guide the canoe into the current. In the prow, Daemyn kept the canoe straight, paddling to keep their speed faster than the current to maintain maneuverability.

Beside them, Rosanna gave a whoop as she and Isi dug in their paddles, swooping their birch bark canoe into the rush of the river.

Alex wanted to squeeze his eyes shut. Maybe even grip the side of the canoe and hold his breath as he used to when he started riding the river each morning.

Focus. Alex forced his grip on the paddle to loosen. His

heart pounding in his ears nearly drowned out the river's gushing roar.

A rock loomed ahead of them. Alex leaned into his paddle, fighting against the strength of the river to turn the canoe. But he had to be careful not to turn the canoe too much, otherwise they would turn broadside and capsize.

He cleared the rock and hurried to dig his paddle in on the other side to straighten the canoe out. They were doing a strange s-pattern across the current as Alex kept overcorrecting.

As they approached the next stretch, where they had to thread their way between two boulders, Daemyn leaned back and dug his paddle in, straightening the canoe out.

Alex winced. He'd already messed up.

No time for worrying about it. The canoe shot between the boulders with both Alex and Daemyn fending off. Immediately, the canoe dropped over a mini waterfall.

More rocks. More white, foaming water. By the time they shot from the last stretch of rapids onto the calm, broad stretch of water where the Gaulee River met the Kanawhee, Alex's hands were shaking. He let out a long breath and rested his elbows on his knees. He wasn't sure if he wanted to throw up or just curl up in the bottom of the canoe.

Rosanna and Isi's canoe flew onto the calm water. Both grinned at Alex. Rosanna slapped her paddle on the river, showering both her and Isi with droplets. "Well done, Your Majesty."

Isi grimaced and flicked water from her face. "Really? Couldn't you have celebrated in a way that was less wet?"

Rosanna smirked and splashed her paddle again.

Zeke and Captain Degotaga's canoe rushed onto the

Kanawhee and drifted next to Daemyn and Alex's on its momentum.

"We ain't dead. You done good, Your Highness." Daemyn rested his paddle across his knees, swiveling as much as he could in the canoe.

Alex clenched his hands tighter around the paddle. He tried out his best impression of the mountain accent Daemyn occasionally let slip through. "I ain't never doing that again."

Still, the praise felt rather good. For far too long, Alex had been the arrogant, helpless high king that Daemyn had to constantly rescue out of scrapes. He didn't want to be that person anymore, but instead become a person Daemyn respected.

Zeke shook his head. "You don't sound a'tall like one of the mountain folk. Your accent wouldn't fool a deaf hound dog."

Alex just shook his head at Zeke as they steered their canoes out of the rush of the converging rivers, making the turn to travel upstream on the Kanawhee River. At least Zeke was joking with him. That was an improvement from the glares Zeke had been giving him last year.

On the mountain above them, Castle Eyota's reddish stones glinted in the sunrise, its many turrets rising against the clear sky and the forested peaks of the mountains around them.

Next to them, the town of Eyota crowded the riverbank, slowly rebuilding after a century of neglect and ruin during Alex's curse. While the Kanawhee River wasn't filled with a multitude of canoes and keelboats the way it had been a hundred years ago, several long canoes were plying the river with the first shipments of fabric from Guyangahela, pottery from Neskahana, corn from

Pohatomie, furs from Mongadotte, and iron items from Buckhannock to sell at the newly rebuilt markets of Eyota.

It was the first step in rebuilding Tallahatchia to what it once was.

Now only the seventh kingdom, Tuckawassee, held out against Alex's rule as high king. Pohatomie wasn't firmly loyal like Buckhannock or Neskahana, but Alex's disastrous trip there had accomplished what he'd set out to do. For now, King Cassius of Pohatomie was willing to fall into line since it benefited him to do so.

Alex's fleet of canoes pulled up to the riverbank just below the castle in a sheltered spot between the town and castle.

Alex told himself he didn't breathe a sigh of relief when he climbed from the canoe and helped Daemyn heft it from the river onto Daemyn's shoulders. To participate in the friendship of this group, Alex needed to like adventure and like spending time wielding a canoe paddle.

And he did enjoy it. Some of it. He liked the slap on the back he got from Zeke for successfully navigating the Gaulee rapids. He liked the fact that he could hike the trail up the mountain to Castle Eyota without being as pathetically out of breath as he used to be. His shoulders were broader, his body muscled in a way he'd never been before.

But was all this change enough? Was he any better of a person on the inside?

He'd been arrogant. He'd been horribly ignorant of the needs of others. He'd been foolish to think he could change by his own strength.

Sometimes, all the work placed before him squeezed until he could barely breathe. He had been given these seven kingdoms to rule and the gift of intelligence at birth to help him do so wisely. If ever anyone had been placed in a position to do great things for the Highest King's glory, then surely Alex was.

And yet...he wasn't great. Every time he turned around, he ran into his own flaws and weaknesses. He didn't know how to be a friend. He didn't know how to be truly nice and giving to people. Most of the time, he made decisions for the kingdoms, never knowing if that decision would bring lasting peace or send them spiraling back into war.

At the castle, the guards waved in recognition and opened the gate to let them in. Alex gave a wave of acknowledgement back.

As the gate closed safely behind them, Fin Micco dashed up to them, his gangly legs and arms pumping, his shaggy black hair flying about his face. At fourteen, Fin was young to be a clerk for the high king.

But he was a descendant of Colonel Micco, who had loyally served Alex before Alex fell into his cursed sleep, and Daemyn had vouched that Fin was just as trustworthy as his ancestor had been. Fin acted as clerk and was taking over many of the manservant duties as Daemyn transitioned to the role of advisor.

Not that Alex needed a manservant as much as he had. Buckskin leggings and shirts didn't need the care the way the fancier styles of a hundred years ago had. And he didn't yet trust Fin to properly care for silk shirts without ruining them.

Fin skidded to a halt and rocked back on his heels. "Your Majesty, we received a message from Pohatomie."

"From King Cassius?" Alex straightened, motioning Daemyn over. Daemyn had been about to head out with Rosanna, off to finish the last details of the canoe they were building.

7

Daemyn joined Alex, then gave a nod to Fin as if to prompt him to keep talking.

"No, not King Cassius. Though he probably will be sending a message shortly. Our other sources in Pohatomie are faster." Fin was rocking back and forth with all his energy. The boy—Alex couldn't help but think about him as a boy—was forever moving.

Alex glanced at Daemyn. Other sources meant the message came from Daemyn's family in Pohatomie. "What's the message?"

"Oh, right." Fin cleared his throat. "Apparently King Cassius is betrothed. To Princess Uma, the second oldest Tuckawassee princess. They have yet to set a date, but rumor around Castle Fonthaven is that the wedding will be in the fall, probably at the Harvest Festival."

If this message had come from their contact in Castle Fonthaven, then it would be accurate. Stefan Vinzen was Daemyn's many times great grandnephew as well as King Cassius' seneschal, a man who would be entrusted with knowledge of the Pohatomie king's upcoming nuptials.

"Thank you for informing me right away." Alex gave Fin a smile and a nod. Remembering to thank those who worked for him when they did a job well was getting easier. "We'll need to act surprised when King Cassius sends his official announcement."

"Do you think he will?" Fin blinked, his entire body pausing for one whole second, before he went back to bouncing on his toes.

"Yes. He'll probably send me an invitation to the wedding." Alex gritted his teeth. An invitation he would refuse, no matter the political ramifications. He'd stepped into King Cassius's trap once and barely survived with his dignity intact. He wasn't about to do it again.

As Fin bowed and hurried back to his office to see if any more messages had arrived, Alex turned to Daemyn. Rosanna, Isi, and Zeke had quietly joined them. Alex forced himself to give a wry smile. "Well, it seems King Cassius took me up on my challenge to see to his own heirless state."

"A marriage between King Cassius and one of the princesses of Tuckawassee sounds like trouble." Rosanna was holding Daemyn's hand, the gesture so natural Alex wasn't sure if Daemyn and Rosanna were even aware they were doing it.

"Well, there are twelve princesses of Tuckawassee, and they are bound to want to marry eventually." Isi shrugged. "A king probably isn't a bad way to go, if you aren't concerned about love. Or the fact that he's probably a decade older than her."

A decade wasn't that much, all things considered. Daemyn was a hundred years older than Rosanna, sort of. While Alex had been cursed to sleep, Daemyn had been stuck not-aging for a hundred years.

If Alex ever found a girl who wasn't already in love with someone else, he would also be a hundred years older than her. Even if he'd spent those hundred years asleep, not dying over and over again the way Daemyn had.

"It will strengthen the alliance between Pohatomie and Tuckawassee." Alex grimaced. Not a pleasant thought. For a hundred years, those two kingdoms had been allies as they rebelled against the rule of the high king. If they were seeking a stronger alliance, then it was his rule they planned to rebel against this time.

War. Again. Alex would do a great deal to avoid another war.

CHAPTER 2

TAMYA

Princess Tamya of Tuckawassee stretched her leg toward the ceiling of the underground chamber, focusing on keeping her leg straight as she came close to touching her forehead to her knee. From there she swept into a spin before leaping into a spin. It was as if non-existent music had taken a hold of her fingers and toes, even if the glittering room around her remained silent except for the scuffing of her moccasins on the marble of the dancing pavilion.

Around her, her eleven sisters danced, following the strains of music only Tamya and her sisters could hear.

Tamya flourished her hand before bending at the waist. Would her sister, Queen Valinda, accept Tamya's idea of the new sewage system for the town of Greenbrier this time? Or would she reject the idea, as their father had also done before he'd died?

That was the frustrating thing about being the third daughter. Although she enjoyed all the benefits of being a princess, she had none of the power to actually accomplish anything to help her people. She was left to beg and plead with her father, then her sister.

If only she could stop dancing and go to bed, the better to wake up ready to tackle tasks first thing in the morning. There was the new sewage system Greenbrier desperately needed. The town market to organize. The disputes to settle between the merchants now setting up shop legally after having been smugglers during the war.

But, thanks to the curse, Tamya was stuck dancing from sunset to sunrise, night after night without respite, along with her eleven sisters.

That was the burden of nobility, after all. When a noble or royal child was eight days old, they were given one gift and one curse. The Fae distributing the curses and gifts to Tamya and her sisters must have been particularly unimaginative, as all twelve of them had the same gift and the same curse.

Supposedly dancing had also been their gift, but Tamya had yet to see evidence of that. It was hard to see something as a gift when they were forced to do it each and every night.

Around Tamya, the underground dancing hall glittered. A forest of gold and silver trees filled the edges of the room, their leaves shaped from precious gems, with paths pebbled with gemstones and semi-precious stones curving among them, providing glinting avenues to dance along.

Three of the walls had been draped with strands of gold and precious gems, tiled over with mosaics, or painted with scenes of the mountains in springtime while the fourth wall remained its original, roughhewn stone. Sections of it were damp with beads of water trickling down it while high in the wall near the front, a waterfall gushed from the single opening.

The waterfall poured into an underground river that curved around the edges of their underground sanctuary before it formed a small lake at the base of the stairs. Somewhere at the bottom of that lake, it must drain into another underground river that rejoined the Tuckawassee River far downstream.

This sanctuary had been their father's gift to them, crafted from all the gold, silver, and gems that had stockpiled in Tuckawassee during the years of war. A grand dancing hall to make their nightly curse more bearable and to keep them from prying eyes so that their curse remained a secret. Tuckawassee had too many enemies to let information like a curse leak to them. Who could tell how that knowledge could be used against them?

Tamya twisted, glancing to the single opening for the waterfall. It was their only peek into the outside world when they were down here, and even then, they couldn't see outside due to a bend in the crevice that allowed water from the Tuckawassee River on the other side of that wall to pour inside. Yet, the opening still allowed light inside, giving the first glimpse of hope each morning that their nightly curse was at an end.

Now, though, the opening was still black with night with hours left until dawn.

Tamya twirled across the marble floor of the dancing pavilion at the far end of the underground room. Her youngest three sisters, Moriah, Leigha, and Kira, played a game of follow the leader. The next oldest four Quinna, Panya, Octavia, and Nakeisha, played a round of cornhole, perfecting their aim with the sacks of dried corn even as they danced in place.

Ranielle had brought her spear along tonight, turning her dance into fighting moves while Shandra stood before the mirrored surface of one of the silver trees, braiding her hair into hundreds of tiny braids, adding in gold thread and gemstones as she worked.

Shandra's gaze flicked to the side where a table of refreshments had been set up. Five servants, three men and two women, stood beside it with vacant expressions clouding their eyes, a band of either gold or silver glinting around their wrists.

Tamya suppressed the ache in her chest, knowing Shandra's gaze wasn't lingering on the refreshments, but on one of the servants, a young man in a guard's leather vest, standing next to the wine decanters, vacantly waiting for one of the princesses to give him an order.

At the far side of the pavilion, Tamya's oldest sister Valinda, queen of Tuckawassee, balanced the leather-bound account book for Castle Greenbrier as the throne, going over the kingdom's expenses as she danced.

That left only Tamya's sister Uma, who wasn't dancing with the rest of them in the pavilion.

After glancing around, Tamya threaded her way between the trees to a quiet corner where Uma swayed as she stitched gems onto the bodice of the light purple fabric that would become her wedding dress. Uma had laid out the gems, needles, and thread on a bench beside her and used a tree to steady her hands while the rest of her danced.

The light purple dress with its accents of amethyst and jet would be stunning on Uma with her rich, brown skin and thick curls. Uma had inherited their late father's skin tone and hair texture while Tamya's hair was straight, taking after their mother's.

"Are you all right?" Tamya bounced on her toes in place, the movement enough to satisfy the curse for a while, at least.

Uma didn't glance up from the meticulous stitch she was lacing over a gemstone. "You are not my big sister, Mya. You don't have to check on me every night."

Yes, she did. Because the only sister older than Uma was Valinda, and Valinda was the one making Uma go through with this arranged marriage to King Cassius of Pohatomie. He was a decade older than Uma and someone she'd met only once fourteen years ago when then Prince Cassius had visited their father for a council of war. Uma had been ten and Tamya only eight, far too young to do more than curtsy properly when introduced, then scurry back to their rooms.

"You don't have to do this, Uma." Mya stretched her leg out behind her, the restless energy of the curse building against her best efforts. She couldn't imagine agreeing to an arranged marriage, ever.

"Yes, I do. This is what is good for Tuckawassee, and it is my queen's—and sister's—wish." Uma kept stitching away at her wedding gown, not even glancing up at Mya.

"But is it good for you?" Why wasn't Uma fighting this? Sure, Valinda was their queen. But she was also their sister.

Finally, Uma set aside her needle and looked up at Mya with something almost like desperation shining in her dark brown eyes. "I'm twenty-four years old. All I've ever wanted is to be a wife and a mother, and I'm not going to be that if I keep waiting around here for our curse to break."

That was the crux of the problem. Twelve princesses of Tuckawassee, yet none of them were married, not even twenty-six-year old Valinda. How could they marry anyone when they did their best to keep their nightly curse a secret?

And after what had happened with Neill...Mya tried to hide her wince.

Neill and Shandra had been growing close, before he'd taken it in his head to follow the sisters one night to discover what caused them to sleep so late each day. He had ended up snared by the curse, thanks to Valinda. Unless the curse was broken, he was as stuck as the rest of them. Perhaps even more so.

Had it been worth breaking Shandra's heart to preserve their secret? The rest of the castle knew the sisters always slept well into the afternoon each day and that the royal wing of the castle was off-limits during the night, the doors locked from the inside. The people probably assumed it had something to do with a curse, since everyone in all the kingdoms knew royalty received curses.

Father had always ruled with an iron hand, and no one had dared to indulge in something like curiosity when it came to the sleeping habits of his twelve daughters.

Now that Valinda was queen, preserving their secret was up to her. Perhaps it always had been. After all, they had snared five people into their curse, most of them in the years before Father had been killed. Neill and three Tuckawassee servants, along with a Tuckawassee man who had been caught spying, presumably for Kanawhee.

Would Valinda allow any of them to find love? Or would anyone they courted end up snared by the curse in the end?

Surely anything would be better than being married to King Cassius, a king rumored to thrive on manipulation of those around him.

"Then find someone around here. Someone safer. Someone who actually loves you." Mya didn't fault Uma for wanting to be a wife and mother. Uma would be wonderful at both.

It just wasn't a longing Mya understood. She'd never felt that deep-down, aching hurt for a husband and babies the way Uma had described it to her. Maybe, if the right man came along, maybe then she'd find herself actually longing for marriage.

But, right now, she simply didn't. It wasn't a truth she ever dared say out loud, especially not to Uma. A woman was supposed to want a husband and children. She didn't know what it said about her that she was actually happy to be unmarried and hoped to remain so.

"It's not that easy. If I could simply march out there and find a husband, I would've done so by now. Love doesn't work that way." Uma shook her head and adjusted her grip on her needle, even if she didn't return to her sewing. "If I am going to have a loveless marriage, then it might as well be one that benefits our kingdom. Besides, King Cassius is smart. He will see the benefit of keeping our dancing curse a secret. And, he's desperate enough for heirs that I'll have a means to bargain, if I need to."

That wasn't how marriage was supposed to work. It was all kinds of wrong. Mya wanted Uma to be happy and finally have the marriage and family she dreamed about. But not like this. Surely there was a better way than this.

Then again, what did any of them know of love and marriage? Mya thought her parents had loved each other, in their own way. Yet, their marriage had been filled with bargains and quarrels and her father always insisting on having one more child in an attempt for that ever-elusive son.

Instead, he'd gotten twelve daughters and a wife who

had succumbed to an illness only a few months after giving birth to Kira, the youngest sister.

What would Kira do without Uma? Uma was the only mother the younger girls remembered. They would be devastated when she left.

Dancing footsteps scuffed a clinking rhythm into the gemstones before Valinda's voice came from behind her. "It will be a good match, Tamya. King Cassius needs Tuckawassee too much to hurt Uma."

Yes, he did. But Tuckawassee needed Pohatomie too much to risk going to war over something as trivial as Uma's happiness. Pohatomie was Tuckawassee's only ally. Without them, Tuckawassee had no hope of standing alone.

But Mya didn't dare say that out loud to Valinda. Instead, she turned her stretch into a gliding pivot and faced her oldest sister with a smile.

Bangles of gold and emerald gleamed against Valinda's wrists and wove into her mound of curls tied into a poof on the top of her head. Her dark green dress swept around her legs gracefully, and even while she twirled and danced, the gemstone-studded crown of Tuckawassee never wobbled.

"Tamya, I would like a word with you." Valinda smiled as she dipped and swayed, but her words fell like ice, cold and sharp against Mya's skin.

Mya couldn't remember a time when she had ever been close with her oldest sister. Valinda had always been busy, training to be queen under their father.

Because of that, Mya couldn't blame Valinda for her hard edges. Their father had been a hard man, even if he'd loved them in his way. Valinda had carried the weight of always knowing that the moment the long-awaited little brother was born, she'd be replaced, as if all her hard work didn't matter.

But Valinda was still Mya's sister. And her queen.

With twirling steps, Valinda led the way down one of the twisting paths between the gold and silver trees until they danced in a secluded nook beside the stone-lined bank of the small lake with the river on one side, the painted wall on the other.

From there, Mya could barely see the rest of her sisters dancing in the pavilion. Trees obscured where Uma huddled over her wedding dress.

Mya faced Valinda and swayed in place, moving her arms back and forth to a song only the curse seemed to know. She braced herself for a lecture on duty and the good of Tuckawassee and to stop pestering Uma.

Valinda also swayed back and forth, moving her feet in a slow, steady rhythm. "Are you loyal to Tuckawassee?"

What kind of question was that? "Of course, I am. You know that."

"Uma is willing to do her duty for Tuckawassee." Valinda's dark brown eyes locked on Mya. "But I'm not sure you have the same courage or loyalty."

"You're asking Uma to marry a man she's never met. A man who is a decade older than her." Mya let her movements turn sharp, hard, following the angry music pummeling her chest. A sister should know better.

"A decade is not so unusual. But that's why I paired him with Uma, rather than you. She will make him the perfect, compliant bride, which is exactly what he is looking for." Valinda waved her arms, as if brushing away any concern for Uma's happiness with a man whose only criteria for a bride was *compliant*. "I have a different task for you. One that will make you the most powerful person in Tallahatchia, if you're brave enough."

If she was brave enough? What was Valinda planning? Mya's heart was building into a drumbeat at her temples. High King Alexander was the most powerful person in Tallahatchia.

High King Alexander. Who happened to be twenty-two years old.

The same age as Mya.

Surely, Valinda wouldn't...couldn't...

But she had already promised Uma away to King Cassius of Pohatomie. Was it really such a stretch to think Mya wouldn't be next? She faced her sister. "Surely, you don't mean..."

"I plan to arrange a marriage alliance for you with High King Alexander." Valinda's face remained smooth, as if she was discussing the weather rather than Mya's future. "A messenger has already been sent."

She'd sent the messenger before even mentioning this to Mya. Mya flourished her hands to keep herself from fisting them. "Why are you doing this? You know this isn't what I want."

"If you refuse, I could offer Shandra instead." Valinda's breezy moves swayed her skirt.

Shandra, who had already suffered a broken heart. Shandra, who of all of them, had already been hurt by Valinda's choices to do what was best for Tuckawassee even over her own sisters' happiness.

They were princesses. Tuckawassee was supposed to come first, no matter how much it hurt.

"But Shandra is too much of a dreamer. I need your steel and determination for this alliance, Tamya." Valinda's eyes speared into her. "I don't plan for you to simply rule as high queen at his side, not like Uma will rule as queen in Pohatomie. You are to become the power behind the throne."

With Valinda as the power behind her, of course.

"And, if that doesn't suit you, you can always dispose of him. After you have secured an heir, of course." Valinda waved her hand breezily, turning the move into a dancing step.

Secured an heir? Mya had to swallow hard. No way was that ever happening.

"For a hundred years, Tuckawassee has fought to secure rule over Tallahatchia. Father tried to conquer with armies and bloodshed." Valinda gestured down herself, then at Mya. "But we are women. This is how we conquer Tallahatchia. We will unite the kingdoms under Tuckawassee one marriage at a time. I have plenty of sisters, and the kingdoms have many unmarried princes. But your marriage to High King Alexander is the foundation. Without it, I can't build the kingdom generations of our ancestors fought and died for. The kingdom Father died for."

Mya's arms prickled with cold, something inside her shaken. This was Valinda's plan. She wouldn't stop at Uma or Mya. Each sister down the line would find herself bartered off to serve Valinda's vision for Tuckawassee.

This was their duty. A duty for which their father had died, killed by the mysterious Daemyn Rand who had caused such havoc for Tuckawassee.

Mya straightened her shoulders, letting the unheard music seep into her muscles at a simmer rather than a fury. Valinda was her sister and her queen. It was her duty to listen and consider. And, in the end, obey.

But, this future rested on more than Valinda's decision

and Mya's cooperation. Perhaps Mya still had a chance of escaping. "What makes you think High King Alexander would even agree to a marriage alliance?"

Valinda snorted. "He would do just about anything for the promise of peace. If he thinks a marriage alliance to you will permanently secure peace with Tuckawassee for all of Tallahatchia, he will do it."

There went that faint hope. Valinda was right. High King Alexander had gone to great lengths last year with Pohatomie. He had even bowed to King Cassius. A high king willing to bow to his enemy was exactly the type to marry for peace rather than love.

That sense of duty and love for his people was admirable, even if Mya didn't want to marry him.

Yet if she refused, Shandra would be traded in her place.

Even if duty to Tuckawassee might not be enough to compel Mya to do this, what about duty to her sisters? If Mya married High King Alexander and secured peace, she could see to it that her sisters met and got to know the princes Valinda intended them to marry. Maybe love could grow out of that, for them at least.

Besides, hadn't she just been lamenting her lack of power? As high queen, she could make a real difference in the lives of the people of Tuckawassee. The bridges connecting them to the other kingdoms could be rebuilt. Normal trade could resume and flourish. Tuckawassee gold, silver, and gems could once again flow into the rest of the kingdoms.

It was everything she had ever wanted and hardly dared dream of getting. If only she didn't have to marry a stranger to get it.

If Mya's arranged marriage was the foundation to

Valinda's plan, that meant she had leverage for one of the few times in her life. "I agree, but on a few conditions."

Valinda's eyebrows rose. "Such as?"

"I would like Shandra to be able to have time to heal and perhaps find love again. She's already been hurt enough."

"Very well. But if she gets over her broken heart, I will not hesitate to arrange a different marriage for her."

Fair enough. If anything about this plan was fair. "Fine. Secondly, let me help with arranging the marriages. As high queen, I will be able to bring together our sisters and all the available princes. After all, with Pohatomie, Kanawhee, and Tuckawassee secured, that leaves only four kingdoms. Only four of our sisters need to marry into those lines of succession. It doesn't matter which four, as long as they do. In the end, it might be better if at least some of the marriages appear to have happened because of love, not your direct arrangement. It will keep the rest of the kingdoms from becoming suspicious."

Mya didn't like that she was giving suggestions to help this plan succeed. But if she could secure happiness for her younger sisters instead of forced marriages, she would do it.

Valinda's smile curled onto her face. "Yes, I knew you were the right sister to make high queen. For all your resistance to the idea, you understand. You have the courage to make this work. I know I'm asking much of you. More even than Uma. But you will thrive as high queen. You have always been a leader among our sisters, and you will continue to lead them as high queen."

Valinda thought she would make a good leader? Mya couldn't help but straighten her movements, flexing her muscles to the straining point as she balanced on tiptoe. "You are assuming I will be able to control the high king."

"You will. That's why I have invited him to come here." Valinda's movements grew languid, the air around them thickening as if the curse itself was a physical presence there with them.

Beside Valinda, the branches of a gold tree began to sway and curl, almost like grasping fingers reaching for prey to snatch.

Mya's stomach dropped. Valinda didn't just intend to arrange a marriage with High King Alexander. She planned to snare him, just like Neill. Mya wouldn't be simply marrying a stranger. She would be marrying a man whose mind had been stolen and placed under Valinda's control.

Valinda's smile grew wider, like that of the great panthers that prowled the swamps to the south. "The Tuckawassee lured him into a curse once. We can do it again."

CHAPTER 3

DAEMYN

Daemyn inspected the canoe resting on trestles in the storage shed. The white birch bark was pristine, its white side facing inward with the pink-brown on the outside. The pieces had been precisely stitched together and onto the frame. Spruce gum kept every seam watertight. Painted designs and beadwork decorated the upper sections along the stern and prow.

It was almost too beautiful to actually set in the water, and Daemyn couldn't think of one more thing that needed to be done.

He should've been feeling excitement. Instead, the weight in his stomach felt more like panic.

"It's done." Rosanna wrapped her arms around his waist from behind, her head a soft weight as she leaned against his back.

Last fall, he'd resolved to stop holding back and truly live. And for the past eight months, he had.

But, increasingly, he'd been fighting this rising panic.

He'd died nine times in the past hundred years. He'd lost friends. Family members. He'd seen some of his relatives marry, only to lose their loved ones. Just because two people fell in love didn't mean both of them would survive long enough to enjoy that happily ever after. He had this nagging feeling, like he was constantly holding his breath, waiting for the next tragedy to come crashing into his life.

What if something happened to Rosanna? If her life ended up in danger, it would be because of him and his job as Alex's advisor and bodyguard. The Tuckawassee had no reason to wish her dead, now that Alex had awakened from his curse. She would have been safe, except that she had fallen in love with Daemyn.

What would he choose, if he had to choose between Rosanna and Alex? For a hundred years, he had been single-minded in his duty. His calling was to wake Alex. That was it.

But now he would be torn between his duties to Alex as his advisor and his new duties to Rosanna as her husband. How would he balance both duties?

He wasn't trusting the Highest King the way he ought. Even knowing this doubt was a lack of trust didn't make it go away.

"Daemyn?" Rosanna moved to in front of him and rested a hand on his cheek. "What's wrong?"

Nothing. His life was so unbelievably perfect that it itched at him. He didn't know what to do with a perfect life. He couldn't trust that it would last.

He had to trust. He knew it. He'd trusted the Highest King for a hundred years and nine deaths. He'd resolved to truly live with the time the Highest King had given him and no longer hold back.

Pushing the fears away, he smiled and rested his hands on her waist. This was where he wanted to be. If he voiced his fears, Rosanna would talk him through them, and maybe he would confide in her later.

For now, he didn't want to ruin this moment. They had worked on this canoe for nearly a year. This should be a moment for smiles and happiness. "Ain't nothing wrong. Our canoe is done, and we still like each other well enough."

"I reckon so. Does that mean there's a question you wanted to ask me?" Rosanna leaned closer, her hands resting on his chest. She could probably feel his heart as it pounded harder, faster.

There had been a time when he'd thought he'd never have a chance to ask this question as he'd watched generation after generation of his nieces and nephews grow up, marry, and have children of their own. He had been content for much of that time to simply be their uncle. He wouldn't trade those years or those bonds of family for anything.

But he wouldn't trade this moment for anything either. This lifetime was going to be so different from the life he'd experienced before, with Rosanna at his side and him at hers.

He reached up and tucked a strand of her black hair behind her ear. "Will you ride the river with me all the days the Highest King gives us?"

"Is that a marriage proposal?" Rosanna's mouth quirked, her eyes sparkling.

"Yes." He couldn't help but match her grin. She kept him from becoming too serious, too life-weary. She reminded him that life was an adventure, not a drudgery, as wild and mysterious as rapids stretching before them.

"That's my line." Rosanna tapped his chest with her fingers, flicking the fringe on his shirt to start it swaying.

"So your answer is yes?" For all his worry of losing her to death, he wasn't worried about this. Their intentions had been leading up to this point from the moment they'd started building that canoe, an ancient tradition for two people planning to marry. He'd known what her answer would be for months now.

"Of course, it's yes." Rosanna stood on her tiptoes and kissed his cheek. "We have the wedding half-planned already."

While building their canoe, they'd had plenty of time to talk, and somewhere around mid-winter, the logistics of their then hypothetical wedding had come up. After all, Rosanna's oldest brother Willem was cursed that he couldn't leave the borders of Neskahana, so the wedding would have to be there. They would need to give enough notice for all of Daemyn's far-flung relatives to make excuses and journey to Neskahana.

"It will be one interesting wedding, that's for sure." Daemyn was half-tempted to just elope with Rosanna. This wedding was going to be one of the biggest in the history of Tallahatchia, and not just because Rosanna was a princess.

He might not have parents or siblings any longer, but he had over a thousand relatives who had a list a hundred years' long of all the things that needed to be said and done at Uncle Daemyn's wedding, if he should ever get married.

Daemyn had done his best to be the model uncle during the many, many weddings he'd attended over the years. He'd avoided embarrassing the bride and groom. He'd given the most meaningful gifts he could think of. He'd been the helpful person who could be counted on to help set up and take down and clean up afterwards. He'd raised cabins and barns and participated in the traditional hunt the night before the wedding. There should be no reason whatsoever that the family would think they needed to embarrass him out of revenge.

Yet, there were a few of the wilder branches of the family who seemed to think it wasn't a proper wedding if the bride and groom weren't embarrassed enough.

Last time he'd visited Neskahana a few months ago, he'd sat down and had a long talk with Rosanna's father. Somewhere in between asking for her father's blessing and discussing where in Neskahana it would be best to have the wedding, he'd found himself apologizing in advance for his relatives' behavior.

Sometimes, it was really hard not to turn into the crotchety uncle they all joked he was.

Rosanna's grip on his hand shook him from his thoughts. She laughed, shaking her head. "Stop worrying about the wedding. Your relatives aren't going to be the only embarrassing ones. My brother is going to turn into a bear partway through the evening and you had better believe he will do his best to scare a few of your relatives and munch on the food in the most unmannerly way possible just because he can."

The thought brought a smile. Rosanna's younger brother Berend had been both cursed and gifted to turn into a bear at night. He had a thing for bear puns and reck- lessness, and yet, Daemyn couldn't help but be fond of him. Willem, Rosanna's older brother, was the steady, level- headed one of the family, even if he too went overboard with the bear puns. Daemyn couldn't ask for a better pair of brothers-in-law.

This time when Daemyn pulled Rosanna to him, he wrapped his arm all the way around her waist, holding her close. "I don't reckon I'll notice anyone but you."

She smiled, but he only caught a glimpse of it before he bent and kissed her.

CHAPTER 4

ALEXANDER

Alex held the nail with one hand and tapped it with the hammer until it would stay on its own. Then he swung harder, though without the practiced abandon of the workers around him. It took them only a few good whacks to drive a nail into place while he eased the nails in with twenty to thirty hits each.

But he got the nails in eventually, and his thumb no longer throbbed from being hit instead of the nail. Now, when Alex missed the nail, he hit the wood beside it instead of his thumb most of the time.

After enough swings to set his arm to aching, he drove the nail home and stepped back to give Daemyn room to place the next clapboard siding piece into place. Alex held the board while Daemyn positioned the first nail and drove it into the wood with a lot more ease than Alex had.

Then again, Daemyn had a hundred years to gain skills with a hammer and nail. Alex had just had plenty of sleep.

When that board was secured to the side of the house, Alex swiped his sleeve across his forehead, leaving a wet smear across the sturdy fabric. He plucked at the front of his shirt, trying to unstick it from the sweat coating his chest and back. Spring had already turned hot and muggy, banishing any thought of winter cold.

Zeke and Daemyn joined him, both dabbing at the rivulets of sweat that ran from their hairlines. Daemyn's black hair plastered to his tanned skin, his shirt almost as soaked as Alex's. "You did well today."

Alex flexed his fingers around the hammer. He had. And there was a certain satisfaction to aching muscles and thumbs when he looked at the house, knowing he'd helped with its construction.

Zeke smirked and clapped Alex on the back. "You can't hardly tell which boards are yours, Your Majesty."

Alex grimaced. There was the one board that wasn't perfectly lined up with the others. And the one where three of the nails were bent over instead of properly pounded in all the way. Not to mention the numerous dents in the wood where he'd missed. Even his best wasn't enough. Still flawed.

Daemyn shot Zeke a look before he gestured toward Castle Eyota rising high on the mountain above them. "We should head back. It will take a mighty good scrubbing to make us presentable."

Wasn't that the truth. A certain amount of sweat and stickiness was expected for a Tallahatchian summer, but Alex wasn't practiced in working up this kind of sweat. Nor had he expected to face the heat this soon in the year.

While Daemyn and Zeke passed the word along to Alex's guards and tracked down Rosanna and Isi, Alex approached the middle-aged woman and her daughter who were hauling buckets of clean water from the well for the workers to drink.

"Your Majesty." The woman dipped into the best curtsy she could manage while holding a bucket of water in one hand and a ladle in the other. "Would you like water?"

"Yes, thank you." Alex accepted the tin cup the daughter handed to him. She smiled, and he did his best to ignore her. She was maybe seventeen and pretty enough, but he wasn't about to flirt back with every single girl that flirted with him.

He would have, once. But not anymore. Now he was wiser, and he wasn't looking for a wife at the moment. He was doing his best to learn to be content as he was.

After Alex drained the cup, he handed it back, then gave a small nod to the mother, a widow whose husband died fighting for Alex. "I need to return to the castle now, but I believe your new home should be finished by nightfall."

"Thank you so much, Your Majesty, for arranging this and your hard work this morning. We are so very grateful." The woman gave another curtsy, as deep as she could manage.

But it was the way she looked at him that meant the most. As if she actually respected him. He, the once arrogant high king, was somehow, slowly, gaining the respect of his people. Not by parading around in fancy silks and making demands, but by working hard and serving. He found himself giving her a genuine smile. "It was my pleasure."

His guards gathered around him, and Alex fell into step with them on the main street of Eyota headed for the castle. All around him, new buildings rose along the street or the fixed up old buildings glowed with new life. Shops were open. People bustled between the buildings. After a hundred years of neglect, Eyota was rising from the crumbling rot and decay to once again be the center of trade instead of the center of war.

As they left the town, Daemyn and Rosanna were behind him, holding hands and talking quietly with an occasional soft laugh. Zeke and Isi strolled together behind them.

Moments like this, Alex's aloneness ached with the empty space beside him. His friends were all paired up, happy and laughing. And Alex wasn't.

Still, he could barely manage to make and keep friends. A serious relationship was probably too much to ask.

Sure, he had that one relationship with Mirabelle a hundred years ago. But that had been shallow, mostly consisting of kissing.

Was that the only romantic relationship he could manage? The curse he'd fallen into in Pohatomie only proved he wasn't ready for a deep relationship.

Alex's shoulders relaxed as he stepped through the gates of Castle Eyota. Home.

The courtyard bustled with activity, from the guards training on one side to the servants hauling water from the well across the other. There weren't as many guards and servants as there had been a hundred years ago. Alex couldn't afford to hire the numbers that had worked at Castle Eyota back then, but he had hired enough to make the castle function.

Each of the dignitaries from the other kingdoms were in charge of cleaning their own rooms and bringing some of their own servants. As most of the royalty had grown more self-sufficient in the hundred years Alex had slept, none of them seemed to mind.

As he crossed the grand entrance headed for the stairs and his room, his mother fell into step with him. In her early forties, High Queen Mother Verena was still beautiful. Her long blond hair hung in a braid down her back, not even a hint of gray yet showing. Her dress was one from a hundred years ago that she'd remade to be simpler to fit the current, rugged style.

His mother was still young, and probably felt her own loneliness even more keenly than he did. For the rest of Tallahatchia, High King Atohi's death was a distant event that happened a hundred years ago. But to Alex and his mother, it had only been a little over a year. Alex still expected to step into the study and find his father there. He still turned to look for his father during meetings, only to realize the decisions now rested on Alex's shoulders.

"How is work in Eyota progressing?" His mother reached as if to pat his arm but stopped, probably after seeing the grime and sweat covering him.

"Very well. It feels alive again." Not like it had when he'd first woken up. Then, it had been overgrown with vines and filled with abandoned structures. Infested with rats and cockroaches and various rodents. Only a few hardy people remained, struggling to make ends meet in what once had been a thriving town.

The town existed to serve Castle Eyota. It flourished because of the trade the high king encouraged and protected between the kingdoms. Without that, the town had collapsed within years after Alex's cursed sleep began.

As they reached the top of the stairs and turned the corner into the wing that housed his study and his room, his mother paused, facing him. "It is good to see you working so hard. It makes me think that perhaps the mistakes your father and I made will not have the consequences I feared."

"What do you mean?" Alex shook his head, then

glanced around at the cluster of guards, the servants carrying buckets of hot water down the hallway, Daemyn, Zeke, Rosanna, and Isi all trying to surreptitiously sneak by. "Let's step into the study."

He held the door for her, then took the seat behind his father's desk.

No, his desk. His study.

Would he ever look around this room and feel like he belonged here, like he was as worthy to occupy this desk and this space as his father had been?

A few account books and historical tomes filled the shelves, along with a few knick-knacks the high kings had collected over the centuries. In one of the bottom shelves, the gem-studded branch that served as the high king's scepter rested on its stand.

In the seat across from him, his mother folded her hands in her lap. "Don't you blame us for the way we raised you?"

"You loved me." Alex leaned his elbows on the desk, the posture making him feel more like a boy facing his mother than a high king giving orders.

"Perhaps we loved you too much." His mother stared past him to the window beaming sun onto his back. "Back then, we thought you would only have twenty-one years to actually live life. And that made it hard to ever reprimand you or say no. We showered you with every-thing you ever desired. At the time, I didn't think it would harm anyone. My heart already hurt too much thinking about your coming curse to worry that I was spoiling you."

"I was still the one who became proud and arrogant and selfish." Even when he'd realized that about himself, he'd never blamed his parents. Would he have turned out differently if his parents had disciplined him more and let him indulge his own pleasures less?

Perhaps. But perhaps not. The way he had been, Alex probably would have rebelled against their discipline and done whatever he wanted anyway. "I don't blame you."

"I blame myself. It's a guilt I carry before the Highest King each and every day." His mother's gaze dropped back to her lap, her hands clenching and twisting together as if she wasn't sure what to do with them. "Because your father and I should have known better. The Highest King promised a cursebreaker. We should have trusted in that promise. Instead, you had to journey all the way to the threshold of Beyond to be told what we should have been telling you all your life. That there was hope. That a cursebreaker would come, even if we couldn't have specified it would be a princess."

After the wonders he had seen at the threshold, he would never regret it, no matter the doubt that had spurred him into that journey.

His mother sat with her back poker-straight, even if her head sagged. "After your grandfather, we should have seen the direction you were headed."

"My grandfather?" Alex had few memories of his paternal grandfather. He had died when Alex was ten, and Alex only remembered seeing him on the throne or scowling as he strolled down the halls. He'd been scary to a child, and Alex had mostly avoided him.

"He was a cruel man. He made great demands on the seven kingdoms, and it was under him that the first seeds of rebellion started. Not just in Pohatomie and Tuckawassee, but in all the kingdoms. When you were born, he still ruled, and I think it was because of him that Tuckawassee and several of the other kingdoms made their plan to bide their time and free themselves from the high king's rule when your curse struck on your twenty-first birthday."

Alex's breath caught. He'd been sheltered from this truth for most of his life. He'd known rebellion simmered in the kingdoms back then, but he'd never been entirely sure why. His father had been a good king. Not perfect, but still good. Of that Alex was certain.

The memories of that time were hazy for those living now. In Tuckawassee and Pohatomie, the disdain and distrust of the high kings had been passed down for generations, even while the reasons had been forgotten.

He'd assumed it must have started with mistakes his father made, unintentionally. Or it had started when the kingdoms had seen the arrogant person he'd become and feared what would happen when it was his turn to rule.

Perhaps that had been part of it. But if they had seen the path he'd been walking, they would have assumed he'd be a high king like his grandfather.

"When your father became high king, he did his best to pacify the kingdoms. But the root of rebellion had grown deep, especially in Tuckawassee. None of his efforts were enough to pull it out." Finally, Alex's mother lifted her gaze to meet his. "Your father wasn't a perfect high king. Perhaps, if he had gone to the lengths you have to restore peace, maybe he would have succeeded. But he had been raised by a hard man, and he was struggling to hold the kingdoms together. He did the best he could, and I'm not sure anyone in his situation could have done better."

"I know Father was a good high king." No number of failures or mistakes could shake Alex's faith in that. After all, Alex knew from experience that it wasn't the failures that defined a person, but how they learned and changed because of those mistakes.

At least, that was what he hoped. He desperately hoped he'd be remembered for far more than simply being the prince who'd failed and fallen asleep.

He'd rather be remembered as the high king whom the Highest King had rescued from his failures.

"Yes, he was." A sheen covered his mother's eyes, even if the tears didn't fall.

CHAPTER 5

ALEXANDER

Dressed in a simple, silk shirt and buckskin leggings, Alex sat tall in his ornate chair at the end of the long table set up in the great hall. His crown perched on his dark brown hair, etched with symbols for each of the seven kingdoms.

Daemyn sat to his right, also dressed in a silk shirt and buckskin, in his role as Alex's chief advisor. Princess Rosanna had the seat next to Daemyn's, though there was no trace of their handholding or courting whispers now. They were all professional business when at this table.

Prince Josiah of Buckhannock, one of Daemyn's great-great-grandnephews, was loudly telling a story about the time he jumped off a waterfall that was clearly too high and too dangerous. His audience across the table, Prince Tyrell of Monongadotte, leaned forward, though he didn't nod along. Doing so would have shaken the branching elk antler crown from his head.

Next to Prince Tyrell, though with plenty of space left

between them to avoid the antlers, sat Prince Mekhi from Guyangahela, the twenty-four-year-old younger brother of King Zaydon.

Besides Daemyn, the only non-royalty at the table was Lord Admetus of Pohatomie, since King Cassius had neither children nor siblings or even close cousins to send as his representative. Lord Admetus was also the only representative married and over thirty. The other kingdoms seemed to think sending their younger generation to mingle and meet each other would foster friendships that would aid with the political alliances they were forming.

At the foot of the table, Alex's mother sat regally, acting more like a mother overseeing a bunch of squabbling children than a queen. She helped give the needed wisdom and experience that Alex suspected all of them, except perhaps Daemyn, lacked at that table. The perils of having a bunch of young people between the ages of eighteen and twenty-five in charge of running the united kingdoms.

Now if only Tuckawassee would deign to send a representative, this Council would be complete.

Lord Admetus cleared his throat and tapped a small rock painted with the corn cob symbol of Pohatomie on the table, the signal that he wished to speak. When Alex pointed to him with the foot-long staff he used at these meetings, Lord Admetus stood. "I have an announcement to make on behalf of my king, King Cassius of Pohatomie."

Considering he already knew this announcement, Alex worked to appear suitably attentive. "Please, go on."

"King Cassius is pleased to announce his betrothal to Princess Uma of Tuckawassee, the second daughter of the late King Rachan and the sister to Queen Valinda. The wedding is expected to take place at the first of the three Harvest Festival Balls later this year. Invitations will, of course, be extended to all of the royal families of Tallahatchia so that King Cassius may share the joy of his nuptials with all the seven kingdoms."

More like rub this marriage alliance in Alex's face. Alex kept his pleasant smile plastered in place. "You may extend my heartfelt congratulations to your king. While I will be unable to attend, my mother High Queen Mother Verena will attend in my place. She is eager to re-acquaint herself with the kingdom of her birth."

A subtle reminder to King Cassius that Mother was originally from Pohatomie. She should be seen as one of their own and treated as such.

Across the table, Mother gave him a small nod. They had discussed this shortly after word arrived about the betrothal. Mother did want to return to Pohatomie to see the castle of her childhood once again, and after the problems Alex had run into last time, it made more sense to send her. Hopefully the fact that she was from Pohatomie would keep King Cassius from deciding to use her against Alex in some way.

As Lord Admetus regained his seat, the door to the council room opened, and Captain Taum, the head of Alex's personal guards, hurried inside. He leaned down and whispered for only Alex to hear, "A messenger from Tuckawassee has arrived and asked to speak before this Council."

A messenger from Tuckawassee? Now? What prompted them to finally respond to his overtures?

He'd find out soon enough. There was no reason to bar them from entering. Not when he had spent the past year trying to invite them in. "Send in the messenger. I will hear them out."

He said his response loudly enough for the whole table to hear. The few whispered conversations fell quiet as all eyes turned to the door.

Captain Taum positioned himself behind Alex's chair before he motioned toward the guard he'd left at the door. The guard opened the door and held it as a woman dressed in leather armor over her buckskin strode inside, her expression hard. Gems and strands of silver wove through her tight black curls.

Something about her seemed familiar, but Alex couldn't place her until both Rosanna and Daemyn stiffened.

Alex had seen her on the day he'd been woken from his curse. She was the Tuckawassee major who had tried to stop his waking, then tried to kill him shortly afterwards.

Forcing a smile onto his face, Alex stood. "Major Beshko. Allow me to welcome you to Castle Eyota properly this time."

She halted a few paces away, flanked by two other Tuckawassee soldiers. Behind her, Captain Degotaga, Isi, Zeke, Josiah's bodyguard Asa, and several of the guard captains for the other dignitaries filed into the room, arranging themselves along the wall where they could spring into action if necessary.

Major Beshko smiled, though her eyes hardened as her gaze flicked to Daemyn before settling back on Alex. "It's Colonel Beshko now."

Apparently treason to the high king was well rewarded in Tuckawassee. Alex returned to his seat, but he didn't offer Colonel Beshko one. "Please proceed with your message."

Colonel Beshko planted her feet and clasped her hands behind her back. "Her Royal Majesty Queen Valinda of Tuckawassee wishes to announce the betrothal of her sister Princess Uma to King Cassius of Pohatomie."

The colonel paused and swept a glance around the table as if expecting surprise. When none came, she fixed her gaze on Lord Admetus. "Ah, I see King Cassius has already seen fit to announce his joyous news himself."

Lord Admetus nodded, even though her statement hadn't needed his agreement. Alex couldn't spot any glances or gestures that would indicate there was a hidden Pohatomie-Tuckawassee plot at work here.

"In light of her sister's betrothal to King Cassius, Queen Valinda has graciously decided to offer her sister Princess Tamya in a marriage alliance to you, High King Alexander."

Alex froze, breath catching, mind whirling. Shortly after waking he had considered, then rejected, the thought of a marriage alliance with Tuckawassee. He wasn't sure how he felt about having one sprung on him now.

"If this marriage alliance is agreeable to you, Her Majesty Queen Valinda invites you to visit Tuckawassee to meet her sister in person and celebrate the betrothal there."

Alex felt more than saw the sharp looks Daemyn, Rosanna, Josiah, and his mother were all sending him. Stepping foot in Tuckawassee would be beyond foolish. He gestured for them to stay silent, even as his gaze remained fixed on Colonel Beshko. "I appreciate this generous offer of a marriage alliance. Such an alliance would secure a lasting peace that would benefit both Tuckawassee and all of Tallahatchia. I do wonder, however, if it would be possible for Princess Tamya to journey here.

My duties as high king keep me very much tied to Castle Eyota."

"Yet you have found time to visit all the other kingdoms." Colonel Beshko's gaze was sharp.

Alex didn't bother to point out that he had, in fact, not visited Monongadotte or Guyangahela. And cutting through the corner of Buckhannock on the way home from Pohatomie didn't count as a proper visit there either.

Colonel Beshko's stance remained poised. "Is not Tuckawassee worthy of the same courtesy as the rest of the kingdoms? Or are we always to be treated as second class citizens because of the actions of those in the past?"

How she managed to say that with a straight face, Alex didn't know. Queen Valinda might be able to claim innocence of her father's war, but Colonel Beshko had been very much involved.

To Alex's right, Daemyn's hand clenched across his stomach. Alex had heard how then Major Beshko had ordered Daemyn killed. The scars Daemyn had from that encounter marked his chest, back, and stomach.

Just like last year in Pohatomie, the Tuckawassee were backing him into a corner. If he refused, they would use it to fuel their complaints that he was treating them unjustly. If he went, he would walk into a trap.

Unless this marriage alliance was genuine? Was it possible Queen Valinda was as tired of war as the rest of Tallahatchia and was willing to bargain for peace?

That didn't explain the year of silence on the part of Tuckawassee. Or why Tuckawassee would choose now to suddenly start cooperating. Nor why they would be so insistent that he visit them instead of their princess coming to him.

This would need careful consideration. Alex faced

Colonel Beshko, trying to look as regal as possible. "Thank you for delivering your message. My captain will see to it that you and your companions are provided rooms and refreshments after your journey. Please let him know if there is anything else you require. I will give you my answer in the morning."

"Very well, Your Majesty." Colonel Beshko bowed and followed Captain Taum from the room.

Leaving Alex to figure out just how far he was willing to go to secure peace for Tallahatchia.

Alex faced the Council, holding his hands up for silence before anyone decided to spew their opinion on this new development. "This Council meeting is adjourned. I will, of course, be speaking with all of you to gain your advice and your kingdom's opinion on this after I have spoken to my advisors."

He stared down Lord Admetus, daring him to stop and attempt to start a discussion. Lord Admetus must have sensed that Alex had no wish to hear his opinion, especially not then, for he scurried past Alex and out the door without a word.

Perhaps Lord Admetus needed time to decide what Pohatomie's stance would be. Pohatomie, after all, liked the fact that they were Tuckawassee's only ally. It gave King Cassius power, not only over his own kingdom, but over Tuckawassee as well. If Tuckawassee managed to put one of their own on the throne as high queen, they would reverse the diplomatic power and Pohatomie would instead depend on their good will.

Prince Tyrell rose, the elk antler crown remaining steady on his head. He and Prince Mekhi struck up a conversation as they strode from the room. Prince Josiah followed them out, though he glanced over his shoulder at Daemyn as if hoping to gain permission to stay.

That left Alex's close advisors remaining in the room, with Daemyn and Rosanna on his right and his mother at the far end of the room. Zeke and Isi still waited by the door.

He probably could just start the discussion right here. But the great hall was cold and large. The meetings here were all official business between the representatives of the kingdoms.

Alex didn't want the official opinions of Neskahana or Buckhannock. He wanted advice from his friends. "Why don't we head for the study?"

The smaller and cozier room would provide a better place for planning, even if the study still felt like it belonged to his father.

As the others filed out, Alex's mother halted beside him, glancing at the others, then back at him. Clearly waiting for everyone else to leave.

As soon as the door closed behind Daemyn, the last to leave, Alex sank bank into his chair and tried to smile, though the expression felt tight, as if his mouth wasn't sure what way it was supposed to curve. "I would appreciate some advice."

His mother sank into the chair to his right that Daemyn had vacated. "I'm not sure if the story I have to tell you will clarify things or add to your burden."

Something else Alex hadn't heard. "What story?"

His mother shifted, staring past Alex toward the banners covering the wall behind him. "I'm not sure your father ever could have gained the loyalty of Tuckawassee. Not after how your grandfather had broken his promises to Tuckawassee."

Broken promises? This was the first time Alex had heard this. "What happened?"

His mother's gaze flicked to him before going back to the wall. "Your grandfather promised the Tuckawassee a marriage alliance, and Tuckawassee probably would have been pacified if they'd gained one of their own as high queen. But, in the end, your grandfather decided he wanted an alliance with Pohatomie more. Your father didn't argue, since he and I had been attracted to each other. It seemed like a dream come true at the time, since neither of us would have cast aside duty on our own to break his marriage alliance with Tuckawassee."

"Perhaps I should accept this marriage alliance with them now. Offer to fix the past." Alex couldn't help the resigned monotone to his voice. A marriage alliance with an enemy wasn't what he wanted.

He wanted what Daemyn had found with Rosanna. What Zeke had with Isi.

But he was the high king. With that position came many advantages, but also many duties and burdens. Perhaps this was one of them. Maybe a marriage alliance was the best he could expect.

"Alex..." His mother reached across the table and rested a hand on his clenched fist. "I know the joy of having loved and been loved. That's what I want for you, if the Highest King wills it. A marriage alliance can work. Love can be a choice, and two people forced together like that can fall in love. But I have also seen it end in miserable marriages more times than I have seen it lead to happiness. Both of you need to be willing to choose love. Both of you need to be committed. You will be a better high king with the right woman at your side, not simply some random princess you were forced to marry."

There was wisdom to his mother's words. Then again, she had ruled as high queen at his father's side for over a decade. She knew more about what it took to rule Tallahatchia than Alex did.

Was there a way to do both? To arrange a marriage alliance, but condition it on time for them to get to know each other before the marriage happened?

It still sounded so cold. A mere political arrangement. A marriage was supposed to be warm. Loving. Tender. Not simply a random man and woman thrown together because they had no choice.

But that was what the Tuckawassee were proposing. Was he willing, if this was the cost of peace? "I will think about it."

"I know you will consider this carefully." His mother reached out to pat his hand. "I thought you should know the full history, though it may not have bearing in this situation. It has been a long time. The Tuckawassee may not even remember the reason the tension started."

"Thank you." Time to change the subject. Alex rested his free hand on top of hers. "I know it has only been a year. But if you ever meet someone who makes you feel like you are ready to move on, don't hold back on my account, all right? I will be happy for you and will understand. I know it isn't a betrayal of Father's memory. Not that you need my permission or anything. I just want you to be happy too."

He understood loneliness too well to wish it on his mother. She could have many years yet ahead of her, and she didn't have to spend it alone. And he certainly didn't want her to think she needed to for his sake.

She squeezed his hands. "Thank you. I'm not ready yet,

but it does ease my mind to know you won't be opposed when I am."

He strolled around the table and kissed her cheek. The past year and a half had been difficult on both of them. Even if happiness wasn't in his future, he hoped it was in hers.

Chapter 6

Daemyn

Daemyn leaned against the wall in Alex's study, letting the conversation flow around him. By the desk, Captain Taum was arguing against going to Tuckawassee while Rosanna was speculating on ways Alex could try to convince the Tuckawassee princess to come to Kanawhee, even as she argued against the marriage alliance.

Somehow Josiah had joined this private meeting uninvited, and he seemed to think Alex should go, as long as they used the same strategy they had in Pohatomie and had royalty from all of the other kingdoms go along too. Tuckawassee wouldn't dare kill all of them.

Zeke and Isi were talking among themselves quietly in the far corner while Asa, Josiah's bodyguard and Zeke's older brother, had taken station by the door, observing as Daemyn was.

Alex too was observing, standing next to the window and looking out at the nighttime mountains, his back to them. As the volume rose, Alex turned, holding up his palms. "Silence, please."

Even though he hadn't raised his voice, everyone trailed off, a hush blanketing the room. Good. Alex had come a long way in the past year, enough that when he spoke, the others respected him enough to listen.

Alex's gaze settled on Daemyn. "What is your opinion?"

Honestly, Daemyn would rather keep Alex far away from Tuckawassee. It was simply too dangerous.

But, Alex had a duty as the high king. He couldn't shirk dangers like this when it was necessary.

And that meant Daemyn couldn't set aside his duty to walk into those dangers alongside Alex.

"You should at least appear that you are considering this marriage alliance, even if you decide against it." Even if that meant venturing into Tuckawassee, much as Daemyn didn't like it. But rather than say that, Daemyn asked the one question no one else had. "What do you wish to do, Your Majesty?"

Alex's gaze dropped to the desk. "A hundred and twenty-five years ago, my grandfather broke a marriage alliance between my father and a princess of Tuckawassee. While it wasn't the only reason Tuckawassee rebelled, it was the spark that ignited their rebellion. If a broken marriage alliance started this, then maybe a fulfilled marriage alliance is the only thing that can end it. If that is the case, then regardless of the danger, I have to go."

Exactly what Daemyn feared. But if this was what Alex wanted, it would be Daemyn's job to make it happen. "This will not be like Pohatomie. King Cassius has always preferred manipulation to outright rebellion. The Tuckawassee will not hesitate to kill you. If you step foot in

Castle Greenbrier, there is a good chance you will never get out alive."

"Believe me, I know. I know this is a trap. If it's a trap to lure me into Tuckawassee to kill me or if the marriage alliance itself is a trap, I don't know. Maybe the Tuckawassee princess plans to marry me, then stab me on our wedding night." Alex leaned both palms on his desk, his head bowed. "The truth is, if the Tuckawassee want me dead, they will find a way to get to me eventually."

Daemyn felt the weight that burdened Alex's shoulders. He'd felt it himself for a hundred years, knowing his connection to Alex's waking put a target on his back. It was not easy to go through life knowing death could be lurking around every corner, in any bite of food brought to one's mouth, behind every shadow.

"You don't have to make it easy on them." Captain Taum crossed his arms, his face hard. "Water hemlock grows as a weed in the ditches of Tuckawassee. If you march in there, any food or drink you consume could be laced with that poison."

Daemyn grimaced. The Tuckawassee favored killing their enemies using the poisonous water hemlock, since that plant grew so prolifically in their kingdom.

Alex fisted his hands as he leaned on the desk. "As long as Tuckawassee remains in rebellion, I will never be safe no matter where I am. My father was murdered right here in Castle Eyota. All they have to do is play at peace, bide their time, and slip poison into my food just like they did with my father."

"We will remain vigilant, Your Majesty. You don't have to take this risk." Captain Taum planted his feet as if he personally planned to be an immovable wall between Alex and danger.

"I know you will do your best. But my father's guards were doing their best, and he still died." Alex sighed and shook his head. "Tuckawassee has made this gesture. If there is even a slim chance their offer of a marriage alliance is genuine, then I have to try, no matter the risk."

"Unless you mobilize Kanawhee's army, I cannot send enough guards with you to guarantee your safety." Captain Taum's face remained hard, his scowl deepening.

"I know. Besides, this is ostensibly a gesture for peace. I can't reply by marching an army into Tuckawassee." Alex finally raised his head and glanced at Daemyn again. "That's why I plan to go with only Daemyn to guard me."

Captain Taum started, glaring first at Alex, then at Daemyn. "You can't possibly intend to enter Tuckawassee with a single bodyguard. That's suicidal."

"As you pointed out, it won't matter if I have one guard or twenty. I will be vulnerable no matter what. In this case, I believe guards would just be a liability. They are more people I have to worry about the Tuckawassee poisoning or imprisoning or using against me." Alex shook his head. "No, I trust that if anyone can get me in and out of Castle Greenbrier alive, it's Daemyn."

That trust settled on Daemyn's shoulders. He didn't want to be solely responsible for Alex's safety in Tuckawassee.

But, Alex's reasoning was sound, and Daemyn found himself nodding. "With only two of us, we can bring our own food and drink with us. We will eat or drink nothing they give us. Zeke, I'd like you to hide in the forest outside of Castle Greenbrier. We'll check in with you every day, and you can pass us fresh food and water."

Zeke nodded, but he studied Daemyn with something almost like worry.

A smile quirked the corner of Alex's mouth. "I knew you would know how to make this plan work. It's risky, but the political statement will be worth it. It will show I am committed to peace by only arriving with a single guard. And, in some ways, it may turn out to be a show of strength that I would dare enter Tuckawassee so unguarded. I'm hoping it will rattle them."

Alex had a point. If he couldn't march in with an army, then perhaps acting confident enough to need only one guard would be even better.

"Daemyn..." Rosanna's fists clenched as she faced him. Captain Taum apparently wasn't the only one unhappy with this plan. "Don't think I'm going to sit safely in Castle Eyota while you take on this risk."

He didn't want Rosanna anywhere near this danger. His heart tore at the thought of having to choose between his duty to Alex and his love for Rosanna. If they went through with this plan, Daemyn would go with Alex, leaving Rosanna without his protection.

But he also wasn't going to become the type of person to tyrannically forbid her when she was a strong, capable person in her own right. Yes, he should protect her. But he also needed to trust her to support him and fight at his side when necessary. Even if that trust didn't come easily.

"I'd like you and Isi to stay at the cabin on the Nanahootchie Creek. We'll need someone stationed there to relay messages in case we need to signal for help." Over the past hundred years, Daemyn had developed a relay system of flashing lights that could send messages across Tallahatchia quickly. Rosanna had learned the code he used during the two months they had been separated shortly after they had started courting.

Rosanna held his gaze and nodded, letting him know

she understood. While this was a safer job than going into Castle Greenbrier, it was still important. If things went wrong—as they probably would—it would be up to Rosanna to organize their rescue.

Daemyn turned to Captain Taum. "I'd like you and your men along with Captain Degotaga and Rosanna's guards to be also stationed there. While there will be only sixteen of you there, you will be within striking distance if we need to leave Castle Greenbrier in a hurry."

"Very well." Captain Taum's scowl eased a fraction, as if he were somewhat mollified that he wouldn't be letting Alex stray too far from his protection.

"Sounds like a workable plan." Alex straightened, appearing less burdened than before. "Tomorrow, I will inform Colonel Beshko that I intend to accept the offer to visit Tuckawassee, but will reserve judgment on the marriage alliance. I will also inform her that I can't leave for another two weeks and that she is to return ahead of me to carry my message back to her queen. That will buy us time to put our plans into place."

Daemyn nodded. Another wise move.

Alex's voice strengthened, as if in growing confidence that this might actually succeed. "I'd rather enter Tuckawassee alone than under her escort to keep the presence of those in this cabin a secret. Captain Taum, in this time, I'd like you to start mobilizing Kanawhee's army and send them to the border in as small, inconspicuous groups as you can manage. If something does go wrong, I want the army ready and close by."

"Very good, Your Majesty." Captain Taum bowed, finally appearing at ease with this plan.

"If we don't leave for two weeks, then I'll send a message to my father. He can also quietly assemble

Neskahana's army along Tuckawassee's northern border."
Rosanna gestured from herself to Josiah. "Perhaps it would
be wise to inform all of the kingdoms that you intend to
visit Tuckawassee."

"Good suggestion." Alex tapped his fingers on his desk.
"I would hesitate to have anyone else enter Tuckawassee as
Josiah suggested, since there is a good chance Tuckawassee
will merely see it as an opportunity to kill everyone. But
knowing the rest of the kingdoms are ready to launch
attacks if I'm harmed might stay Tuckawassee's hand. As
much as they don't necessarily want peace, I don't believe
they want war either."

A valid point. While Alex slept, the war had been
fought with Tuckawassee and Pohatomie on one side and
Neskahana, Buckhannock, and Kanawhee on the other,
with Monongadotte and Guyangahela remaining mostly
neutral.

But now if war broke out again, Monongadotte surely
would join their side, and Guyangahela could probably be
persuaded to do so. With such odds, King Cassius would
be unlikely to commit to open hostilities and would opt for
neutrality, leaving Tuckawassee fighting alone against the
might of five kingdoms.

If it came down to it, would Tuckawassee dare kill
Alex, knowing that four, perhaps five, kingdoms would
likely retaliate?

Would the kingdoms fight if Alex were killed? Even
Daemyn couldn't be sure. Alex, as high king, was the
person who tied Tallahatchia together. If he died, the line
of the high kings would be ended. At least while he slept,
Daemyn could rally Neskahana, Buckhannock, and
Kanawhee under the hope that the high king would return.

Without Alex, there might not be a Tallahatchia.

Daemyn would just have to do his best to keep Alex alive, even inside Tuckawassee.

When Alex dismissed them to start sending messages and alerting the army, Daemyn halted outside the door to the study. Zeke, Josiah, and Asa halted with him, facing him with arms crossed.

"Are you sure about this?" Zeke glanced around the corridor, then lowered his voice. "You killed the late king of Tuckawassee. If his daughters know, then they have as much or more of a reason to kill you than they do the high king. I can go into Castle Greenbrier with Alex instead of you."

Daemyn shook his head even before Zeke finished speaking. He trusted Zeke, but he couldn't bring himself to give this task to anyone else. "You know the forest outside of Castle Greenbrier well, but you have never explored the castle itself like I have. I have a better chance of getting the high king in and out safely. But I'm depending on your judgment to know what to do if something seems wrong. I'll check in every morning and evening, but a lot can happen between then. Your quick thinking may be the difference between life and death for us."

"All right." Zeke nodded and clapped Daemyn on the back. "You ain't got nothing to worry about."

"What about us?" Josiah grinned, full of a nineteen-year-old's enthusiasm for danger. "What do you want us to do? Don't tell us you want us to sit this one out."

"I'll send out a message tonight, letting the family know I'm going to Tuckawassee with the high king." Daemyn faced them, his muscles tense. In the last hundred years, he'd never given this order. "I'd like everyone who can to hightail it to Tuckawassee. Asa, I'm putting you in charge of rallying the relatives. Josiah, listen to him and do whatever he tells you."

Asa rested a hand on his long knife at his waist. "The family ain't never let you down in a hundred years, Uncle Daemyn. We ain't about to start now. If the Tuckawassee want to play rough, we'll tear their castle apart to get to you, mark my words."

Daemyn might not have his parents or his siblings any longer, but he had this fierce, incredibly loyal family backing him up. It gave him hope that maybe, just maybe, he and Alex would come out of Tuckawassee alive.

CHAPTER 7

TAMYA

Tamya strolled down the hall from her bedroom, the early afternoon sunlight streaming through the windows.

One of the doors along the hallway flew open, and Kira trotted out of her room, holding a pair of her moccasins. "My moccasins have holes in them again."

Another pair of moccasins worn through during their nights of dancing. Dancing all night on the marble stones or gemstone paths was hard on the buckskin. Mya took the ruined moccasins. "We'll get you another pair."

"But I really liked these." Kira's lower lip stuck out in a pout. "I wish we didn't have to dance every night."

"I know." It would be nice to sleep through the night like a normal person. But Mya never had. Not even as a baby. None of her sisters had either. They had always lived under this curse, dancing from dusk until dawn. Mya had been old enough to take care of her sisters when they had been babies kicking and wiggling all through the night instead of sleeping.

From the next room, Moriah and Leigha tottered out, rubbing their eyes. They still wore their cotton nightdresses and their nightcaps to protect their hair at night. "We don't want to dance all night either."

What was Mya supposed to say? It wasn't like any of them had a choice. Moriah, Leigha, and Kira were only ten, nine, and eight. They had so many years yet to live under this curse.

Long ago, Mya's mother had held them in her arms and told them stories of cursebreakers ending the curses plaguing long ago princes and princesses.

But that had been long before Moriah, Leigha, and Kira had been born. Their mother had grown weary. Her stories of hope and cursebreakers had tapered off, then ended long before her death.

Their father never told such stories. He'd told them stories of power and riches and the future glory of Tuckawassee.

Perhaps it was time Mya shared with her youngest sisters the stories their mother had never had the opportunity to tell.

"Come on. I want to tell you story." Mya led her three youngest sisters into Kira's room and sat on the bed. Even though Kira was too old, Mya pulled her onto her lap anyway while Moriah and Leigha tucked onto either side of her.

To give her hands something to do, Mya tugged off Kira's nightcap. Kira's hair was more like hers, thinner and in waves rather than curls. Mya divided Kira's hair in half, then started braiding it. "Long ago when the curses fell on the original seven kings, they were told that the curses could be broken. Every curse would have a curse-breaker."

"Does that mean our curse can be broken? We won't have to dance forever?" Moriah's face lit.

Perhaps Mya shouldn't have given them this hope. "Maybe. High King Alexander was cursed to a sleep like unto death. He slept for a hundred years before his curse-breaker came and broke his curse."

Leigha hugged Mya's arm. "I don't want to dance for a hundred years."

She had been trying to give her sisters hope, but she'd just made them more miserable.

"You won't." They'd all be long dead before a hundred years was up. Mya forced herself to smile as she finished one of Kira's braids. "Let me do your hair, then we can eat, all right?"

Distracting them with food always worked. Mya made quick work of Kira's braids, then she carefully eased Leigha's hair into two puffs on either side of her head, taking care not to break the brittle strands by rubbing in a nourishing oil. For Moriah, she helped her scrunch the kinks into bouncy strands around her head.

By the time she finished, laughter was filling the hallway from their other sisters. Kira wiggled from Mya's lap and dashed from the room with Moriah and Leigha on her heels. Mya followed at a slower pace, heading for the dining room.

Yet, she paused outside of Shandra's door. Shandra sat on her bed, staring down at a string of silver studded with a few pieces of quartz.

Mya stepped inside, then shut the door behind her. "Do you want to talk about it?"

Shandra started, then swiped at her face. "No."

"Did Neill give you that?" Mya sat beside her sister. There was so little she could do for Shandra. Neill was stuck in their curse, robbed of his mind. Unless their curse broke, there was no hope of saving him.

And Valinda was in no hurry to see their curse broken.

Shandra nodded, then wrapped it into her hair. "Are you going to do it?"

"Do what?" Mya helped Shandra tuck the last strands of her hair into a knot at the top of her head.

"Marry High King Alexander just because Valinda said so. And let her steal his mind the way she did Neill's." Shandra's fingers balled into fists.

"I don't know." Mya shrugged, stood, and tugged Shandra to her feet. "We don't even know if High King Alexander will agree to come here, much less agree to the marriage alliance. But, if he does, I bargained with Valinda. You won't be forced into a marriage alliance."

Shandra huffed and rolled her eyes. "As if that makes it better. You bargained for me, but what about for the rest of our sisters?"

Mya opened her mouth, but she couldn't come up with a good answer. Was there a good answer?

Her silence must have been answer enough for Shandra. Her eyes had a glint to them as she yanked the door open with more force than necessary. "That's what I thought."

"Shandra..." Mya trailed off. What was she supposed to say? They were princesses. They had a duty to do what was best for Tuckawassee, and, as queen, Valinda decided what was best.

Shandra turned in the doorway and glanced over her shoulder at Mya. "You could stop her, you know. I think you might be the only one of us who can."

With that, Shandra swept from the room.

Mya swallowed. What did Shandra mean by that? Why

would Mya want to stop Valinda? It was her job to support her queen. Nor did she have the power to do anything. She didn't even have the power to help the town of Greenbrier upgrade their sewage system. It was the only capital town in Tallahatchia that still dumped sewage in the river.

Shaking her head, Mya strode from Shandra's room. As frustrating as it was, she was stuck. Valinda was the queen and their sister. They owed her their loyalty.

Ranielle skidded to a halt in the hallway in front of Mya, carrying her spear. Her hair was currently in many tiny braids, with those braids tied back. "Valinda was looking for you. Colonel Beshko returned from Castle Eyota this morning."

Mya's stomach clenched. Colonel Beshko would have High King Alexander's reply. Within a few minutes, Mya would find out if she was going to be married off to a stranger.

Shandra had been wrong. Mya had no power to stop any of this.

Still, talking about cursebreakers with the girls had sparked something inside her. High King Alexander had survived his curse, and he no longer lived under its shadow. What must that be like, being free?

She might not want to marry him, but it would be interesting to meet him. To find out what life could be like after a curse.

At least, until Valinda managed to drag him into their curse. Something sour filled Mya's stomach at that.

But this is what would be best for Tuckawassee. After a hundred years of war and rebellion, the other kingdoms would never trust Tuckawassee enough to let them regain an equal footing. Not unless they married into the high king's throne.

He might not come. If he was wise, he wouldn't. He had to know entering Tuckawassee would end very badly for him, no matter what kind of trap her sister set.

Mya followed Ranielle from their family wing to the throne room, where Valinda conducted more private meetings that didn't need the vastness and grandeur of the great hall. Mya took a deep breath and stepped through the ornate doors guilt with gold and studded with jet and amethyst and diamonds. When Ranielle didn't follow her, Mya's stomach twisted tighter.

Inside, Valinda sat on her throne with Colonel Beshko waiting off to one side at the base of the dais.

Mya held her head high and crossed the room. "You sent for me?"

Valinda gestured at Colonel Beshko. "High King Alexander has accepted our invitation to visit Tuckawassee and has agreed to consider the marriage alliance if both of you find it agreeable after you've met."

Mya clasped her hands behind her back and refused to let that pierce her. Valinda wouldn't give her a choice about accepting. For the good of her sisters, Mya had to marry High King Alexander. No matter how she felt about him.

Maybe he would be the one man who could actually make her want to get married and have children. Wasn't that what people always told her? That once she met the right man, her thoughts about marriage and children would miraculously change. As if her current thoughts and opinions didn't matter. They could be washed away at any moment by finding that mysterious "right man."

If that was the case, she didn't want to find him. Because she liked herself as she was. It was uncomfortable to think that falling in love could change the core of who she was as a person.

It wasn't that she despised children. She loved her little sisters. She looked forward to being an aunt more than anything. That didn't mean she wanted it for herself.

Instead, her dreams had always been for healing for Tuckawassee. While Uma had been playing with dolls and Valinda played being queen, Mya had always been the loyal advisor, chattering to anyone who would listen about ways to improve Tuckawassee's trade or travel.

There was so much work to be done in Tuckawassee. Sewage systems that could be updated. Bridges that could be built. Trade that could be established with the other kingdoms once peace was achieved. Her days could be filled with work, if Valinda had given her that chance.

Instead, she would marry High King Alexander and have to help Tuckawassee from afar.

She glanced at Colonel Beshko before facing Valinda. "When is he expected to arrive?"

Mya had expected he would travel back with Colonel Beshko, but as there had not been an elaborate welcome party, she assumed he wasn't here.

Valinda's mouth curled, though Mya couldn't tell if it was a frown or a smile. Whatever the expression, it was something slick and calculating. "He chose to send Colonel Beshko ahead. Probably to buy himself time to prepare countermeasures to whatever trap he believes we have planned. Not unexpected. As he intended to leave two weeks after Colonel Beshko did, he has probably just left Castle Eyota."

Then it would be roughly another two weeks until he arrived. Two weeks to wrap her mind around the thought of this arranged marriage.

"Colonel Beshko," Valinda's gaze sharpened. "Please gather ten of your most trusted men and station them along the border. I would like to observe High King Alexander as he enters Tuckawassee before he knows we are watching. I'd like you to meet him with another ten of your men at the convergence of the Nanahootchie Creek and Tuckawassee River and escort him and his retinue the rest of the way to Castle Greenbrier."

"It will be done, Your Majesty." Colonel Beshko bowed and exited the room. She and her men would need to hurry if they planned to arrive at the border before High King Alexander did.

When they were alone, Valinda stood and strolled down the stairs until she faced Mya. Her gaze searched Mya's face, her features softening. "You still aren't happy with this plan."

"I'm not exactly thrilled about an arranged marriage." It was the safer of her misgivings to admit.

"I know. But I wouldn't do this if I didn't think you would be happy in the end." Valinda's expression eased into a smile. A soft smile the likes of which Mya hadn't seen since their father died. "You will be the one in control, Mya. He won't be able to force you to do anything you don't want to do. Instead, you can make him be your dream husband. He will be exactly what you want him to be."

Something about that seemed very wrong. And yet, was it also wrong that a part of Mya found it comforting? She might be marrying a stranger, but she wouldn't be at his mercy.

Instead, he would be at hers.

Valinda glided closer, her steps graceful even though they weren't dancing right now.

"Besides, I know how much you want to help people. As high queen, you will be able to build towns and villages and improve life for everyone in Tallahatchia. Isn't that what you want?"

It was tantalizing. Mya would have the power to encourage the rebuilding of bridges all across Tallahatchia. She would especially oversee rebuilding efforts in Kanawhee, a kingdom even more devastated than Tuckawassee. Surely, as high queen, her proposals would no longer be ignored. She would no longer be helpless.

"Yes, it is." Mya couldn't meet Valinda's gaze. For her kingdom, for her sisters, for her dream, she had to go through with this.

Valinda stepped forward and hugged her tightly. "I will take care of all my sisters. We will never be overlooked again."

Mya leaned into her sister, hugging her back just as tightly. This was the bond she'd hold on to, no matter what. They were sisters, and together, sisters could take on the world.

CHAPTER 8

DAEMYN

Daemyn held Rosanna close, her head on his shoulder, her breath warm against his neck. They had retreated behind the shelter of the little cabin hidden up a side creek from the Nanahootchie Creek while the others unpacked and Alex saw to it that his and Daemyn's gear was stowed in their canoe.

This was the first time Daemyn and Rosanna would be apart for more than a couple of days since she moved to Castle Eyota to represent Neskahana at the Council. And, it was the first time since he'd met her that he would face danger without her with him.

As much as he didn't want to put her into danger, it shook him knowing how much he drew strength from her. After his hundred years alone, he wouldn't have guessed he would end up a part of one of those clingy couples who couldn't function apart from each other. It was different, experiencing a relationship instead of always observing from the outside, and it made him feel somewhat guilty for the times he hadn't understood his nieces and nephews when they'd struggled to be apart from their husbands and wives.

"Rosanna..."

She leaned back and pressed her finger over his mouth. "If you say *stay safe* one more time, I'm going to ask Alex to hurry up and finish packing. I'm the one who will have Isi and fourteen other guards looking after me. The only thing I'll have to worry about is boredom. You're the one actually going into danger."

He clasped her hand, changing what he had been about to say to, "I know. Just...if you run into trouble, head for Frennie's. That's where the relatives are congregating."

Frennie, one of Daemyn's great grandnieces, lived near the border of Tuckawassee and Kanawhee. Ever since her husband Ted had disappeared and presumably died during a scouting mission inside Castle Greenbrier, she had supported herself and her children by making moonshine and trading it to the passing travelers and Tuckawassee soldiers, picking up news that she passed along to Daemyn.

"I'll be fine." Beneath his hands, Rosanna's back stiffened as she straightened her spine, meeting and holding his gaze without wavering.

Of course she would. He had fallen in love with her because of who she was. A capable woman with a good measure of her own abilities. If she said she could handle something, then she could.

Instead of offering yet more unneeded advice, he leaned down and kissed her, pulling her tight against him. "I love you."

It had been here at this cabin where he'd told her the truth about himself. That he had lived a hundred years and worn many names and identities while waiting for Alex's promised cursebreaker.

What he hadn't told her had been the confusing mix of attraction and weariness he'd been feeling then. How much she'd made him think of the life he could have had if he hadn't volunteered to be the one to find Alex's curse-breaker. Back then, he'd thought what he had now with Rosanna had been impossible.

Instead, the Highest King had gifted him with this second life he hadn't even known to want.

"I loved you first." Rosanna whispered between kisses. Her fingers were warm against the back of his neck. "And don't you forget it."

"Ain't about to." He murmured against her hair.

A throat cleared, turning into a coughing fit. Daemyn pulled back from Rosanna just enough to glance at Isi over Rosanna's head.

Isi leaned a hand against the cabin's wall. "Sorry. Choked on my own spit. Carry on. Actually, don't carry on. I was sent to fetch you. High King Alexander is ready to leave."

Alex might be ready, but Daemyn wasn't.

Rosanna sighed. "You just want to kick us out of here so that you and Zeke can have some privacy to say goodbye before he leaves."

Zeke planned to give Daemyn and Alex a head start in case the Tuckawassee were watching for them. While they stuck to the rivers, Zeke would cross the Tuckawassee River, then follow the river on land before camping out in the mountains above Castle Greenbrier.

"That too." Isi smirked, crossing her arms.

Rosanna pulled away from Daemyn, her fingers sliding down his arm to clasp his hand. "I guess this is goodbye."

If things went wrong, this could be the last time he ever saw her. Still, he didn't want to say goodbye. Goodbye was too final, even knowing the danger. Daemyn forced his legs to move, heading around the cabin. "I'll see you in a little over two weeks. It ain't that long."

"I'll keep us busy, don't worry." Isi nudged Rosanna with an elbow as she fell into step with them. "We have a wedding to plan, after all. I even brought along the materials so I can start on the beadwork on your dress. You won't have time to miss him."

"And I'll keep you so busy you won't miss Zeke." Rosanna's smile wasn't as bright as it normally was, but at least she was smiling. The expression lit her dark brown eyes, her movements swaying her black braid across her back.

At the creek's edge, Alex stood in the shallows, holding their canoe. "You ready?"

No.

"Yes." Daemyn turned to Rosanna and gave her one last, quick kiss.

"Stay safe." She squeezed his hand as if she didn't intend to let go.

"You done stole my line." He traced the backs of his fingers over her cheek, then forced himself to step away. He was in the hands of the Highest King, as was she. As he well knew, all the powers in Tallahatchia couldn't cut their lives any shorter than the Highest King had already decreed.

If only that made it easier to trust that she would stay safe. That he wouldn't lose her because he had chosen to follow Alex into danger.

It took a lot of strength, but he forced himself to let go of her hand, turn, and walk to the creek's bank.

There, Zeke waited, his own pack already slung over his shoulders with his bow and quiver.

Daemyn paused next to him. "If I miss checking in..."

"I'll rally the relatives. I reckon you been telling that to my family since my grandfather was a baby." Zeke clapped him on the shoulder. "I got your back."

As did Josiah and Asa and Frennie and all of the various, scattered branches of the family. "Thanks."

Daemyn stepped into the creek, then held the canoe steady while Alex climbed into the prow. Daemyn folded his legs into the seat at the stern, grabbed his paddle, and shoved off. He didn't let himself glance over his shoulder. He needed to focus on what they would face ahead.

He navigated them down the side creek and into the flow of the Nanahootchie. At the first sheltered spot, he swung the canoe into the bank.

Alex glanced over his shoulder. "Why are we stopping?"

"We're switching places." Daemyn stowed his paddle next to his hardwood staff along the inside of the canoe. "Unless I miss my guess, the Tuckawassee are waiting for us ahead, and if you want to make a proper entrance, you need to be the one steering this canoe. From here on out, the Nanahootchie and the Tuckawassee are smooth. You can handle them."

Not to mention, if Daemyn were in the prow, he could better shield Alex from the oncoming Tuckawassee.

"If you insist. But if I accidentally broach the canoe, dump us in the river, and humiliate both of us in front of the Tuckawassee, I'm blaming you." Alex shipped his paddle and hopped out of the canoe much more easily than he would have a year ago.

They swapped places and sent the canoe downriver once again. As they neared the convergence with the Tuckawassee River, Daemyn glanced over his shoulder. "Stick to the center. The current is going to be strong and shove us a around for a minute or two before spitting us into main river."

"Got it." Alex's jaw tightened as he dug in his paddle.

"Last chance to turn around." Daemyn added his strength to keeping their canoe steady in the river.

Alex's paddlestroke faltered for a moment before he regained the rhythm. "As much as that sounds tempting, I don't think I have a choice. But if you don't want to go with me, we can go back, and I'll ask for someone else to volunteer. I know you have a lot to live for, and I don't want you to feel forced into this."

"I ain't being forced." His heart might ache leaving Rosanna behind, but it felt right to be here with Alex. "I'll do my level best to get you in and out of there alive."

"I know." Alex went quiet, his paddlestrokes splashing rhythmically, the river gurgling against the birch bark of the canoe. "And, Daemyn? I know last time we went into danger like this, it didn't end well for you."

Daemyn had been beaten and locked up in a tiny hole of a dungeon cell in Pohatomie. On Alex's order. Sure, he had been under a curse at the time. But it had still rankled that a curse had been able to toy with his mind so completely. In the end, Daemyn had escaped because Rosanna, Zeke, and Josiah rescued him. Not because of anything Alex had done to correct his mistake.

"This time will be different. I promise I will trust your instincts and listen when you voice concerns." Alex's voice lowered. "And, I promise, I'm going to do my best to make sure you get out of this alive as well."

Daemyn dug his paddle into the river, not willing to glance at Alex. He'd never reckoned on hearing such sentiment from Alex.

Yet, he didn't quite trust it. He wanted to believe Alex

would try. Alex had changed a lot in the months since that trip to Pohatomie. He was wiser. More capable.

But he hadn't faced any real challenges since then. Would Alex keep his promises this time around? If he didn't, Daemyn might never see Rosanna again.

As they neared the Tuckawassee River, the water gripped their canoe, hurtling it along. Daemyn worked to keep the prow centered and moving faster than the current to give Alex maneuverability.

After all the practice on the Gaulee, Alex managed a decent enough job. There were a couple of times they careened closer to the boulders along the banks than Daemyn would have liked, and they entered the Tuckawassee off kilter and came far too close to sweeping into the bank instead of shooting into the main river.

But they didn't capsize, and Alex straightened them out just as five canoes shot into the main river from a hiding spot behind a cluster of boulders at the convergence. It was a sheltered cove Daemyn and Zeke had used many times to observe this river junction.

Colonel Beshko steered the lead canoe, gems glinting in her black hair.

Daemyn gripped his paddle and faced the Tuckawassee, his stomach knotting.

If they'd had any doubts, it was too late to turn back now.

CHAPTER 9

ALEXANDER

As Castle Greenbrier came into sight around a bend, looming over the river, Alex's chest tightened, his heart thumping harder in his ears. He'd talked over this plan so many times, he hadn't thought he'd be scared.

But, staring at that castle, it punched into him that he might not step foot outside those walls again if things ended badly.

What other choice did he have? He could have remained at Castle Eyota and tried to negotiate for a marriage alliance from there. He could have continued to slowly work toward peace with Tuckawassee.

But those plans would leave the seeds for rebellion still here. Maybe in ten, twenty, a hundred years, Tuckawassee would rebel again.

No, to bring about true peace, he needed to cut off the rebellion at its source here in Tuckawassee.

Either that, or die trying.

Alex let himself be directed toward the bank next to the

castle and managed to even look competent as he steered the canoe straight into the sandy shallows, avoiding the scattered rocks. Daemyn hopped from the canoe first, holding it steady as Alex swung himself from the canoe, his feet splashing into the cool river water.

The cold water steadied him, calming his racing heart. He could do this. He had to trust the Highest King and face whatever came.

Castle Greenbrier's gray stone was damp from the river splashing against the outer wall. The castle's keep rose along with the mountainside, the final wing topped with a tower that overlooked the river in all directions.

After he and Daemyn carried their canoe onto the bank, Daemyn untied their packs, handing over Alex's. The Tuckawassee didn't protest when Alex strapped his dagger to his waist, nor when Daemyn gripped his staff and strapped on his long knife.

Then again, why would they? There were just the two of them. The Tuckawassee could take them down in minutes if they wanted to.

"Please, follow me. My men will see to your canoe." Colonel Beshko gestured toward the castle, then strode up the path without glancing back to see if they were following.

Not that she needed to. Her men could prod them along with the spears they had pulled from their canoes if Alex and Daemyn balked.

Alex raised his chin and marched after Colonel Beshko, his shoulder blades crawling with the knowledge that the guards were moving his canoe—his one means of quick escape—to a mystery location. Daemyn's footsteps were a mere whisper on the sandy path behind him, but it was still reassuring to have him at his back.

The path zigzagged up the side of the mountain in a steep slope. Alex's calves burned, his breathing growing hard and fast, by the time the path changed from sand to gravel as they leveled off higher up the bank and joined the main road stretching from the castle to the town of Greenbrier downriver.

Unlike in Pohatomie, where the road between the castle and the village bustled with people, here only a few people were on the trail at this time of the early afternoon. They stepped aside as Colonel Beshko led the way down the path, staring silently as Alex strode by. He smiled but didn't wave.

Ahead, the gravel changed to cobblestones as short, knee-high walls rose on either side of the road leading up to the main gate. A single large gate set into a round tower. Due to the height they'd climbed, the entrance to the castle was higher than its own courtyard. The outer wall ran in layers and from here, Alex could catch glimpses into the courtyard ahead of and below him.

As he stepped through the gate, the cool interior air washed over him, shivering against his spine as if he were entering a dungeon. He forced himself to keep walking forward as if confident he wasn't going to die in that castle.

The gate opened into a round tower room with minimal decorations, unless racks of spears counted as decoration. From there, the tower opened into a great hall with stairs leading into the rest of the castle. A row of tall, arched windows overlooked the courtyard and the river, filling the space with light and illuminating the tapestries hanging across the opposite wall.

Alex's gaze focused on the twelve ladies, from girls to young women, arranged in a line waiting at the far end of the room. All of them wore silk dresses in various bold hues that set off well against their dark skin. Gems and strands of gold glittered in their hair, sparkling in the beams of sunshine.

Only one wore a crown—a large gold thing with spikes and gemstones—with her curls piled on top of her head and woven with gold and diamonds.

This must be Queen Valinda. She stood just in front of her eleven younger sisters in a regal, deep purple dress. When he halted in front of her, she gave a curtsy so small she barely dipped two inches. "Welcome, High King Alexander. We appreciate that you have condescended to visit us, your most disloyal subjects."

As if she had given him much of a choice. Either he risked his life or he risked war by refusing.

Alex gave her the most genuine smile that he could manage. She was already trying to anger him, and he refused to rise to such obvious bait.

He was not here to flaunt power but to humbly seek peace. Alex bowed at the waist, deeper than was necessary but not enough that he would look like he was groveling. "I am but a servant to the Highest King and therefore, your servant."

Queen Valinda's dark eyes studied him, her mouth twisting into a smile. "I see the rumors coming from Pohatomie are true. You are the High King who Bowed."

That was far better than being known as the high king who slept. Alex let his smile turn wry. "I'm not sure what you might have heard. But I have learned it is best not to think of myself too highly. I am here now to ask how I can best serve the people of Tuckawassee."

She studied him, still as a statue. Had his words surprised her? Had she been expecting a high king like his grandfather had been years and years ago?

Finally, she blinked and gestured behind him. "I see you have brought your loyal guard dog."

Alex gritted his teeth. Once again, he and Daemyn had agreed on the pretense that Daemyn wasn't anything besides a manservant and bodyguard. "He is rather loyal." He waved his hand, as if Daemyn wasn't worth introducing. Hopefully, they wouldn't think to ask. "Are you going to introduce me to your sisters?"

Queen Valinda's mouth twisted, like she was suppressing a grimace, but she pointed at the youngest of the girls. "Kira."

The girl couldn't have been more than seven or eight with her hair done in two braids whipping around her head as she threw herself into a bouncy curtsy.

"Leigha, Moriah, Nakeisha, Octavia."

These four girls bobbed curtsies in quick succession. Alex wasn't exactly sure on their ages, but Octavia, the oldest of these four, couldn't have been more than fifteen.

"Panya, Quinna, Ranielle, and Shandra."

These four girls were older teenagers. They curtsied with less enthusiasm than the younger girls. Shandra's gaze was strangely hard while Panya and Quinna kept their gazes focused on the floor as if shy. Ranielle's gaze swept over him, studying, though not in a flirtatious way. More like she was searching for weaknesses in his stance that she could exploit if they ever fought against each other.

Queen Valinda skipped the next sister and jumped to the first one in line. "This is Uma. She's betrothed to King Cassius of Pohatomie."

Alex smiled. "My congratulations again on your upcoming marriage. I wish you happiness." Strange how he found he meant those words. King Cassius was a manipulative man, and not one Alex would wish even on his enemy.

Princess Uma smiled and curtsied in return, though her gaze darted from him to the floor.

"And this," Queen Valinda pushed the last sister forward, "is Princess Tamya."

The sister she'd bargained to him for a marriage alliance.

Princess Tamya wore a light pink dress, her dark brown hair falling down past her shoulders, straight and shining. Her stance was poised, and when he met her gaze, she stared right back at him without looking away, her gaze just as assessing as his had been.

Alex held his breath, waiting for his heart to give a lurch or his brain to freeze or his palms to start sweating. Some hint of attraction. Any attraction.

But...nothing.

She was lovely. He registered that much, but it was a cold noting of a fact. When he looked at her, he didn't feel anything of the instant attraction he'd felt for Mirabelle a hundred years ago. Not even a lesser form of the heady warmth he'd felt when under the curse of infatuation for the servant girl Elara in Pohatomie.

But, maybe that all right? Both of those relationships—if the cursed love he'd had for Elara could be called a relationship—had ended badly.

He didn't need attraction. Love wasn't merely attraction, after all. It was more than that.

He would just choose to like her, and that would be that. If the Tuckawassee wanted him to marry Princess Tamya, then he would have to make it work.

Besides, he didn't know her yet. Attraction didn't have to be instant. He needed to give her a chance. With enough time, surely he would feel something for her. It wasn't like being attracted to beautiful women had ever been difficult for him. He just needed to get to know her.

Then why did he feel like he was trying to talk himself into this?

He forced himself to smile and bow, the movements as smooth and charming as a lifetime of training could make them. "It is a pleasure to meet you, Princess Tamya. I look forward to getting to know you over the next week."

"One week?" Queen Valinda fluttered her hand by her chest. "That is hardly enough time. Surely a month would be better."

"I spent less than a week in Pohatomie and Neskahana. You would not wish for the other kingdoms to accuse me of favoritism, would you?" Alex's smile felt sharp, even to himself. "I have already taken the liberty of informing the other kingdoms that I plan to visit Castle Greenbrier for one week. If I don't leave on schedule, then I fear they might get the wrong idea and take drastic measures."

Queen Valinda's returning smile also shone razor sharp. "We wouldn't want that, would we?"

Good. Queen Valinda now knew what she would risk if she harmed him in any way or tried to prevent him from leaving.

Hopefully it would be enough of a deterrent. Alex's and Daemyn's lives depended on it.

Mya picked at her food, sneaking glances at High King Alexander sitting in the chair between her and Queen Valinda's throne at the head of the table. Mya needed to give him a chance. Perhaps she would be attracted to him if she spent enough time with him.

Maybe attraction was something that grew with time. She knew love wasn't instant, but she hadn't expected attraction to take this much work as well. Why did anyone ever get married if trying to fall in love was this cold and boring?

Though, attraction, love, and respect didn't matter to Valinda's plan. They would snare High King Alexander and control him by their dance.

But it would be easier—for her—if they were attracted to each other. He would be mindless and under her sister's control, but some of that attraction might remain. Neill seemed to recognize Shandra, even if he didn't seem to understand what was going on besides the need to follow orders.

Mya forced a smile onto her face. If she didn't at least try to make conversation, he would grow suspicious. Or assume she was overly shy. "So, Your Majesty, I hear you have been a big proponent of the rebuilding efforts in Kanawhee."

"Yes." High King Alexander returned his filled fork to his plate. "I have mostly concentrated on rebuilding Eyota and establishing trade on the rivers. But I've also encouraged the building of bridges along the Cheyandoah Trace between Kanawhee, Neskahana, and Buckhannock."

The Cheyandoah Trace was an ancient trail that ran along the spine of the mountains that formed the backbone of Tallahatchia. Side trails branched from it into each of the kingdoms along the mountain ridges. If the rivers were the lifeblood of Tallahatchia, then the Cheyandoah Trace was its backbone.

Should she share about her own passion for rebuilding Tuckawassee? Then again, why not? Mya didn't reckon it was a secret. "I've been overseeing rebuilding here. I've mostly focused on some of the sewage systems in the towns that were a health hazard."

She resisted the urge to grimace. Talking about sewage systems was probably on the list of topics not to talk about when trying to appear attractive. She cleared her throat. "And, well, anyway, I'd also like to start rebuilding the bridges in Tuckawassee as well."

"Which is something you'll be able to do, once this marriage alliance brings peace." Valinda was all beatific smiles and regal posture. "Don't you agree, Your Majesty?"

The high king studied Valinda like he was searching for the trap in her words. "Rebuilding the bridges in all the kingdoms is something that I hope will happen once peace is achieved, yes."

They had a mutual passion for building infrastructure. So why didn't that make her heart pound or her stomach flutter? Sure, she'd like to talk with him more. But on a professional level to swap ideas. Nothing more.

She glanced at the high king again, catching sight of his bodyguard out of the corner of her eye. The bodyguard— or was he a manservant—was standing straight as the hardwood staff he carried, eyes alert as he surveyed the room.

When they'd sat for dinner, Valinda had offered him a meal in the kitchen, but the high king had airily announced that his bodyguard couldn't possibly leave him and would eat later. It almost made Mya sorry for the man, and she had the urge to start feeding him scraps under the table like the guard dog Valinda had accused him of being.

She tried to think of another question to ask. Any question. What did she want to know about the high king?

Nothing, apparently.

The silence lengthened to the point of discomfort.

High King Alexander cleared his throat, stirring the food left on his half empty plate without bringing any of it to his mouth. It seemed the tension was playing havoc with his appetite. "What do you like to do to relax?"

"I like to dance." Mya ignored Valinda's glare. It wasn't like it would give away their secret to say she liked dancing. She jabbed at the venison on her plate. High King Alexander wasn't the only one who had lost an appetite. "Do you like to dance?"

"I enjoy the dancing at balls." Alex tapped his plate with his fork. "But I reckon it's the interaction with people that I enjoy the most."

In other words, he didn't enjoy dancing simply for the joy of dancing.

Not that Mya had that much joy of dancing left after so many years of being forced to dance through the night.

Finally, Valinda pushed her plate away and stood, ending the meal.

High King Alexander shot to his feet, then paused to bow. "Thank you for the meal. It has been a long day of travel, and I would like to retire."

"Very well. Ranielle can escort you to your room. I assume your bodyguard will be sleeping on a pallet on the floor?" Valinda quirked an eyebrow.

"Yes, he will." High King Alexander nodded to Valinda, glanced at Mya, then followed Ranielle with his bodyguard trailing at his heels.

Valinda caught Mya's arm and tugged her aside as their sisters pushed to their feet, heading to their rooms to catch a quick nap before sunset sent them to the underground dancing pavilion.

Mya sighed. She really needed that nap. "Please don't yell at me. I didn't tell him anything he can use to figure out our plan."

"I know. You are doing an admirable job of acting like you think this marriage alliance will be real." Valinda waved her hand, as if brushing any pique away. "Did you recognize his bodyguard?"

"No. Should I?" Mya glanced over her shoulder, but High King Alexander and his bodyguard had disappeared out the door.

"Colonel Beshko told me he is Daemyn Rand."

"*The* Daemyn Rand? The one Colonel Beshko killed and he didn't stay dead?" Mya stared at the door. The man hadn't looked like anything that special. His black hair, brown eyes, and tanned skin were nondescript.

"Colonel Beshko suspects he killed Father."

Mya's chest tightened, but she couldn't name the emotion aching in her throat. Pain and sorrow, yes. But she mourned the lack of a true relationship with her father as much as she mourned his death. "What do you plan to do?"

"Nothing much, yet." Valinda's teeth flashed as she smiled. "But you and I are going to pay a visit to the high king and his bodyguard tonight."

CHAPTER 11

ALEXANDER

Carrying a spear, Princess Ranielle led the way from the dining room on the main floor of the castle and through the great hall past the windows that overlooked the tiered courtyards and gardens inside Castle Greenbrier's outer walls. Below, the Tuckawassee River rippled under the late afternoon sunlight.

Alex expected her to lead the way up the grand staircase to a guest suite there. Instead, she continued past the grand staircase and turned toward a set of double doors with a squad of six guards stationed in front of it.

Six guards? That was rather unusual for inside a palace. Unless...but Queen Valinda wouldn't give him a room in the family wing, would she? Why would she want Alex nearby?

The guards opened the double doors, and Princess Ranielle strode inside without even checking if Alex and Daemyn were still following. Inside, a single hallway with doors on either side stretched until it ended in a wall with a window.

Princess Ranielle halted only a few feet inside and gestured to the first door on the left. "This is your room. For security, the doors to this wing are locked at night. Don't attempt to wander the castle. I doubt the guards would be understanding. The garderobe is across the hall."

Their room was across the hall from the latrine. Not the usual room given to guests due to the smell drifting from the room.

"My sisters and I have rooms down the hallway. Don't get any ideas or *I* won't be understanding." Princess Ranielle twirled her spear, gave Alex a glare, then positioned herself next to the door as the rest of her sisters filed past, sneaking glances at Alex and occasionally giggling.

With one last glance over his shoulder, Alex hurried inside the room. Any second now, his stomach was going to rumble and give away the fact that he hadn't eaten a bite at that fancy dinner they'd served.

As Daemyn shut the door behind them, Alex waited in the center of the room, the wad of food he'd rolled in a napkin and stuffed into his shirt squishing warm and damp against his stomach. His very empty, growling stomach. Food was supposed to be on the inside, not pressed against his skin on the outside.

Daemyn leaned against the door, muscles tense. After several long minutes, he finally relaxed and stepped away from the door. "We're safe for the moment."

"Good." Alex extracted the wadded-up food from his shirt, trying to touch it as little as possible. The smell of roast venison and cornbread filled his nose, sending a rush of saliva into his mouth. "It's a shame we can't eat this."

"I reckon it's likely safe, but we ain't taking any chances." Daemyn shoved the lock on the door into place.

"How should I dispose of this?" Alex pinched the napkin between two fingers as he held it up. If there was any poison in this food, he didn't want to get any residue on his fingers.

He glanced around the room. It was comprised of only a single room that served as the sitting room and bedchamber. A few chairs clustered by the fire while the bed took up most of the space along the far wall. The floor lacked rugs while the walls were bare except for the wooden wainscoting and plaster covering the stones. A single window let in the fading light of early evening.

Daemyn crossed to the window and peered out. "Good. We have forest below us. I reckon we can get food from Zeke this way."

Alex joined him, peering out. From here, the tower wall dropped straight down for a good fifty feet to the mountainside. While a swathe of about ten feet had been cleared around the base of the tower, the forest grew thick beyond that until broken by a cliff level with the tower. "Reckon Zeke will know to bury this if I throw it out the window? I'd hate to poison some innocent coyote."

"We can't leave it rotting in a corner. You did a mighty fine job of pretending to eat at supper, but they'll figure out what you did if they find the food here." Daemyn stepped aside, giving Alex room. "Zeke is mighty sharp. He ain't about to let this set around where a body could find it."

Alex tied the corners of the cloth napkin and tossed it out the window. It fluttered in an arc before splatting onto a rock far below. The castle staff would notice a bunch of napkins missing by the end of their visit, but missing napkins were better than dying of poison.

Besides, from what he observed, Tuckawassee hadn't been as cut off from Guyangahela and its fabric as the rest of the kingdoms. It seemed, despite their neutrality, Guyangahela had been willing to continue trade with Tuckawassee. Or perhaps smugglers had found the smaller mountain range that divided Tuckawassee and Guyangahela an easy trade route during the war.

When Alex turned, he spotted the thin mattress left on the floor in the corner with their packs set on top of it, left by a servant. Alex gestured. "We probably can't eat the food we brought with us now, can we?"

His stomach gave another loud gurgle. He didn't want to complain. He didn't want to be that helpless prince who couldn't stand something as simple as missing a single meal.

But he wasn't used to skipping meals and toughing it out. He just wasn't.

Daemyn reached into his shirt and pulled out a canteen and a bulging pouch. "I kept our food with me."

And that's why Alex had brought Daemyn along. Who else could be this wisely paranoid? "Wise choice."

Daemyn uncapped the canteen. "Stick your hands out the window."

Alex did so, and Daemyn trickled some of their water over his fingers. Alex scrubbed the residue of the food from his hands, then dried them on the spare napkin Daemyn had somehow managed to swipe. The spare napkin went out the window as well.

Then, they sat at the small table and divided up the meal. Two pieces of dried venison. Four slices of dried apple. And a wedge of cheese wrapped in waxed cloth to keep it moist.

Everything was still dry and boring and hardly enough after the feast Alex had just sat through without eating a single bite. But this food was safe.

After all, even if the food during the meal the Tuckawassee queen had served him had been safe, since it had been served to everyone at the table, they could have rubbed the poisonous water hemlock on his cup or his fork.

He'd have to be careful about putting his hands near his face while he was here. Anything he touched could be poisoned. He glanced at the bed. The pillow. The blankets. The furniture in the room around them. Something in him shrank away from touching any of it.

One week. He just had to survive one week. Then, surely, the Tuckawassee would have no choice but to let him go. They didn't want another war anymore than he did, right?

Alex washed down a bite of the dried meat with a sip from the canteen, then passed it back to Daemyn. "How soon will Zeke get here?"

"Likely during the night. We're due to check with him just before dawn." Daemyn drank from the canteen, then capped it.

This was going to be one long week. Alex forced himself to take another bite of the slightly too dry cheese, his mind remembering the smell of the warm, juicy roast he'd slipped into a napkin rather than his mouth.

This wasn't that bad. After all, he'd choked down worse, like that stew made from meat that might or might not have been possum or raccoon or some other rodent that he'd eaten with Daemyn's family over a hundred years ago. Then again, at least that stew had been warm and filling and savory. This meal was just dry.

Daemyn chewed the venison as if its stringy texture didn't bother him. "It's suspicious they put us in the family wing. This is the one section of Castle Greenbrier I haven't explored in several decades. Last time I tried, the Tuckawassee chased me all the way to Neskahana."

"That was when you met Rosanna, wasn't it?" Alex forced himself to finish his piece of cheese. He'd been mentally complaining about his hunger. He couldn't now complain if he didn't like the food that was available.

"Yes." Daemyn nodded, but he cocked his head as if listening to something Alex couldn't hear. After a moment, Daemyn stiffened.

Alex froze, holding his breath. What had Daemyn heard? What was wrong?

Daemyn sprang into action, stuffing his canteen into his shirt and sweeping the last of their meal into the pouch.

A knock sounded on the door. Alex quickly brushed any crumbs from the table, then off himself as he stood.

"Stay behind me." Daemyn stalked to the door, right hand on his long knife as he cracked the door open with his left.

Through the narrow crack, Alex caught a glimpse of Queen Valinda and Princess Tamya standing there.

Queen Valinda peered past Daemyn as if he wasn't there, her gaze focusing on Alex. "Your Majesty, we come with a gift."

Highly suspicious, but what could Alex do? Have Daemyn slam the door in their faces? That would defeat the purpose of trying to foster peace and bonding with Princess Tamya before a possible marriage alliance.

Alex let his regal façade settle over him and waved at Daemyn. "Let them in."

Daemyn stepped aside, opening the door wider. Still, he positioned himself partially behind the door, as if prepared to slam it closed if necessary.

Queen Valinda held up a bottle with a deep, purple-red liquid inside of it. "You mentioned you were tired after your long journey, so I thought a glass of wine would help you sleep. This wine is Castle Greenbrier's specialty. We grow the riverbank grapes right in our castle courtyard."

"I don't—" Alex started, but Queen Valinda was already pouring some of the wine into a glass.

She held it out to him. "For a restful night."

He didn't take it. This whole situation stank to the tallest mountain it was so suspicious. What kind of fool did they think he was that he would drink that? Even if the wine wasn't poisoned, he didn't dare even touch his lips to the glass because the glass might be rubbed with water hemlock.

Princess Tamya took the glass and drank about half of what Queen Valinda had poured before she held it out to Alex. "It isn't poisoned, if that's what you're worried about."

Hesitantly, he took the glass. She had at least confirmed it wasn't poisoned with water hemlock. It was so deadly it was impossible to build an immunity to it. Nor would anyone risk holding wine poisoned with water hemlock in their mouth or touching a poisoned glass to their lips.

But that didn't mean the wine couldn't be poisoned with something else. It was possible to develop an immunity to snake venom or something like that.

"Perhaps you don't wish to drink alone." Queen

Valinda poured three more glasses, handing one to Daemyn before claiming glasses for herself and Princess Tamya.

He could bobble the glass. Spill the wine or drop the glass entirely, though it would be a shame to shatter a goblet that had probably been blown in Neskahana over a hundred years ago. But either of those options would make his refusal to drink the wine obvious, and they might try more drastic measures after that.

Daemyn sniffed his wine, then sipped it. Taking Alex's glass, he repeated the sniffing and sipping before he handed it back. "It is safe enough."

What was that supposed to mean? Did that mean Daemyn thought he should drink it? Or just pretend to drink it? Or that whatever was in his glass was only mildly deadly?

Placing his mouth exactly over the spot where Princess Tamya had, Alex cautiously took a sip into his mouth, though he didn't swallow.

Queen Valinda and Princess Tamya were staring at him like a pair of vultures waiting for the wolves to finish eating. He forced himself to dry swallow to make it look like he'd actually swallowed.

They still stared at him. How was he going to sip more wine or bid them goodnight with his mouth already full?

Strangely enough, Daemyn tossed back his glass of wine, gulping it down and visibly swallowing. He wiped his sleeve over his mouth, then handed the glass back, grinning like the most backwards of mountain folk. "That there is mighty good."

If Daemyn had drunk it, then it must be all right. Alex swallowed his mouthful, then gulped down the rest. It wasn't dignified, and he got the immediate urge to cough. The wine held a rich, grape flavor, the liquor part not as strong as he had been expecting. For being the castle's specialty, Alex had tasted much finer wines than this.

He handed the glass back to Princess Tamya. "Thank you for your thoughtfulness. Now, I would like to rest after my journey. Goodnight to both of you."

He was probably a little too abrupt in the way he swung the door closed. He drove the locking bolt into place, then leaned against the door, listening to the sounds of footsteps outside.

When they faded, he turned to the room to find Daemyn peeling off his shirt. Alex caught sight of the large, wine colored stain across the back before Daemyn balled it up. "I reckon I got to ask Zeke to soak this to try and get that stain out."

A weight dropped into Alex's stomach. Daemyn hadn't actually drunk it. Had Alex just made a mistake? Had he just messed up all their careful paranoia and poisoned himself? "I drank it."

"Far as I could tell, yours was fine." Daemyn tossed his shirt out the window, then knelt and dug around in his pack. "Still, it wouldn't hurt to practice dumping it down your back for next time just to be safe. Just because yours was safe this time don't mean it will be safe next time."

"What do you mean, mine was safe?" Alex pushed off the door, crossing his arms. "What was in yours?"

"Valerian. It's pretty pungently bitter, which is why they tried hiding it in wine. Still smelled it." Daemyn shrugged as he yanked his spare shirt free of his pack. "It ain't a poison. It makes a body sleepy."

"But mine didn't have valerian in it? Why would they want you to be sleeping and not me?" Alex rubbed at his stomach. Was it his nerves and imagination twisting his stomach into knots? Or had there been something in the wine? "If they wanted to stab us in our sleep, then wouldn't they want both of us sleeping soundly?"

"They must want me out of the way for some reason." Daemyn pulled the shirt over his head. He tied the front laces at his throat. "Reckon there's only one way to find out."

CHAPTER 12

ALEXANDER

Alex lay tense and still in the bed as the last of the light faded outside of the window. Daemyn had assured him the pillow and sheets were safe. Apparently, water hemlock had a carrot kind of smell to it that would be recognizable on something like a pillow.

In the corner, Daemyn stretched out on the pallet, his breathing deep and even. Had he accidentally drunk some of that drugged wine and fallen asleep?

Alex shifted, trying to keep his own breathing even. The Tuckawassee queen was planning something tonight, and odds were, his bride-to-be was in on it.

If he married her, would he have to spend the rest of his life living like this? Always on edge, terrified that one day she'd slip poison in his food?

An arranged, loveless marriage was one thing. An arranged, loveless marriage to someone actively trying to kill him was something else entirely.

"For a body with as much practice sleeping as you have,

you're mighty awful at pretending it." Daemyn's voice was low, his breathing still even.

How did he manage to still look asleep even while talking? Alex huffed out a breath. "I'm not the one who supposedly downed a glass of drugged wine. If the Tuckawassee find me tossing and turning, they won't think anything of it."

"Someone's coming." Daemyn's voice dropped to a whisper, his body relaxed as if in sleep.

Alex flopped onto his back. He was glad they were finally coming. Waiting was worse than facing whatever they had planned.

As the last rays of sun faded in the brilliant pink and purple of the sunset, scuffing feet and voices filled the hallway. And was that, giggling?

A knock sounded on his door. Alex forced himself to wait, groaning and rolling over as if he'd been awakened from a doze.

"Your Majesty?" The knock came again.

"Coming." Alex rolled off the bed. At the door, he paused and glanced over his shoulder at where Daemyn lay doing a very good imitation of sleep. With a deep breath, Alex unlocked the door and opened it a crack as Daemyn had instructed, keeping the door between him and whatever awaited.

What awaited was a gaggle of princesses in swirling dresses. Two of the younger ones approached him, one bouncing and smiling while the other peeked at him shyly. The bolder one was the youngest princesses. Kira, wasn't it? She smiled up at him. "Come with us."

Queen Valinda was downright nasty to use her adorable little sisters in her dastardly plot. If this was a dastardly plot. Alex wasn't sure. This certainly didn't look like any attempt to kill him he'd ever seen. People usually didn't bring eight-year-olds to assassination attempts.

"Where are we going?" Alex cautiously opened the door wider. What kind of trap was this?

"Dancing, off course." Kira grabbed his arm and dragged him from the room.

He found himself surrounded by princesses. Kira was telling him something, as if he was her new best friend. Moriah and Leigha, the next two youngest, were eying him warily. But the next princess older than them, Nakeisha, gave him a tentative smile when he looked her way.

What was going on? This was not at all what Alex had expected. He didn't dare glance over his shoulder to see if Daemyn was trying to follow them.

Queen Valinda led the way down the hallway away from the double doors to the rest of the castle. As far as Alex could tell, this corridor ended in a blank wall with a window set in its center.

Princesses Shandra and Tamya pulled aside a rug, revealing a trap door. It appeared to be made of a thin slab of granite etched with a flower pattern filled with gold. Even with the hinges providing leverage, it took four of the sisters to lift the granite. A set of stairs disappeared into the darkness.

Princesses Ranielle, Quinna, and Uma produced lamps, lighting them from one of the candles in the sconces and distributing the lamps among the sisters.

Queen Valinda led the way down the stairs. Alex found himself shuffled along with the princesses. Were they leading him to the dungeons? But why would Queen Valinda take along her little sisters, dressed in silk ballgowns and gems styled in their hair, for an excursion to lock him in a dungeon cell? Unless she thought he'd be more cooperative being herded by a pack of little girls than he would by guards?

Which was probably true. He didn't dare resist with children around.

As they rounded a corner in the stairs, a glow became visible from somewhere below. The farther Alex trudged down the curving stairway, the brighter the glow became until they rounded the final bend and stepped into a blaze of glittering light.

Alex blinked several times as his eyes adjusted to the unexpected glare.

He stood on a small square of stone blocks with a vast underground room spread before him. Water from a small lake lapped at the edge of the blocks where he stood while a river wound its way from the lake to the far wall, where a waterfall gushed from up high, its water glistening in the light from the six mirrored lanterns filled with candles arranged three to either side of the room, beaming so much light into the space that it glowed as if in warm sunlight rather than the darkness of underground.

On the other side of the lake, a forest of trees spread before him, their trunks wrought in silver and gold. Some of their leaves were also made of the precious metals while others flashed with leaves fashioned from diamonds, emeralds, rubies, and other precious stones. The entire ground was graveled with sparkling, semi-precious stones with paths paved in gems winding between the trees.

For a moment, he caught his breath, lost in the glinting wonder of this place. Had he ever seen a place with such wealth of beauty before?

He let out a long exhale. Yes, he had. A place of even more wonderous beauty that didn't need candles to banish the darkness.

Alex had stepped foot on the very threshold of Beyond. He had followed the Highest Prince himself through a forest of gemstone trees grander than the spindly things before him now. He had knelt before the throne of the Highest King and been overwhelmed with the sheer weight of that light.

No, compared to that, this was a paltry imitation.

An imitation. That's exactly what this was. Alex sensed that now. Sensed the heaviness in the air, the *wrongness* that curled in his stomach. This was an attempt to create Beyond on earth. Where the threshold had been rest and peace, this underground room before Alex held nothing but danger.

"Come on!" Kira waved toward the lake, where three small pole barges were tied to iron rings set in this stone platform. Her sisters were already climbing on board and grabbing poles.

Should he turn around and run back up the stairs while he had a chance? After those cursed glass slippers in Pohatomie, he'd learned to be far more wary of things that didn't seem right.

And there was something off about this place. So much glittering beauty, just like those glass slippers.

In Pohatomie, he'd learned his own weakness. He wasn't strong in resisting temptation. He would willingly choose his own downfall.

What would it take to be snared this time? Would it happen the moment he stepped foot on those gemstone paths? Or when he touched one of those trees?

A wisp of a draft caressed his skin, bringing with it the scent of a fresh, green forest, open sky, and that almost remembered song he'd heard at the threshold of Beyond. He was not alone, and he would not be facing this by his own weakness, but in the Highest King's strength.

"Why don't you join us, Your Majesty?" Queen Valinda's voice yanked away the memories and the feel of the remembered breeze.

All of the princesses had climbed onto the barges, four to a barge, with two of the older sisters paired with two of the younger sisters.

Queen Valinda, Princess Uma, and Princess Tamya each stood at the front of their barge, poles in hand. When he focused on her barge, Princess Tamya glanced away, her lips pinched tight. She had yet to say a word to him all evening. Her shoulders hunched, her arms pressed tightly to her sides even as she gripped her pole.

Had he offended her in some way? Said something wrong?

No, her stance didn't seem angry and offended. More... guilty. Was she uncomfortable with what Queen Valinda planned for him tonight?

While he didn't have any brothers or sisters of his own, he'd observed how deeply the bonds of family ran with Daemyn's family, and he couldn't blame Princess Tamya for not standing up to her sister. Why would she choose a high king she barely knew over her sister and kingdom?

But that didn't mean Alex wouldn't work on that guilt. If she felt guilt, then she had a conscience and a heart. He would reach her the same way Daemyn had reached him all those years ago. By returning cruelty with kindness.

Alex smiled and stepped onto Princess Tamya's barge, which also held Princesses Quinna, Nakeisha, and Kira. He took the pole from Kira. "Allow me, my lady."

Kira giggled and willingly handed over the pole. "It's too short for you because I'm little."

The pole was far too short. He had to stoop to touch the bottom of the shallow lake with it and help shove off. He fumbled and nearly dropped it as he struggled to match Princess Tamya's rhythm standing in the barge ahead of him. "As I am inexperienced at poling a barge, it is probably just as well I don't have a longer pole. I would probably knock someone overboard."

"I'm not very good either." Kira announced solemnly. She then launched into an explanation on how to properly pole a barge.

Alex struggled to keep a straight face as her instructions were given in such a serious, proper manner. She was probably reciting the instructions she'd received from one of her older sisters.

Princesses Tamya, Quinna, and Nakeisha ignored him as they poled the barge across. Their barge lagged behind, and Alex wasn't sure if it was because of his bad poling or his added weight. He wasn't a large man, but he still weighed more than any of the princesses.

As soon the barges scraped bottom at the far side of the lake, the princesses hopped off over the front, and Alex followed. He helped Kira, Tamya, Quinna, and Nakeisha pull the barge partway onto the embankment of gemstone gravel that served as a shoreline.

As he straightened, he caught sight of ripples at the edge of the lake farther down the shoreline from where the princesses had banked the barges. The ripples spread across the lake before vanishing in the larger waves the barges had made during their crossing.

What was it? Was there some freakish monster fish or muskrat or some other creepy critter living in this underground lake?

Then he spotted the faint wet mark in the pebbles in the shape of a moccasin print.

Nope, not some creepy critter. Daemyn.

Alex let out a breath and turned toward Kira. "Where are we going now?"

It was easiest to focus on this youngest princess. She felt safe in a way her older sisters weren't. Maybe she was in on Queen Valinda's plot against him. Maybe the Tuckawassee were sinister enough to use a child to lure him in.

But he could pretend to be oblivious a lot easier with Kira's broad grins, bobbing braids, and giggles than he could with the uncomfortable silences with Princess Tamya, the edgy feeling with Queen Valinda, and the downright shy glances of most of the princesses.

Around him, all of the princesses stiffened, then launched into dancing at the exact same time.

What in Tallahatchia was going on? Alex halted and stared as eleven princesses and one queen twirled and leapt and waved their arms in a flurry of dancing.

"Come on." Kira twirled on the path ahead of him, pointing even as she stood on tiptoes and swayed. She danced along the path, even as her sisters branched out into various paths.

Alex followed, gazing around at the gold, silver, and diamond-studded trees. He'd never seen a wonder quite like this on earth. It didn't compare to Beyond, but he could still appreciate the craftsmanship that had gone into creating this place.

Perhaps that was the wrongness he was feeling. A beautiful place like this shouldn't have a feeling of menace to it. It shouldn't be striving to be an earthly Beyond but instead should be pointing toward that

Beyond, using its shimmer of glory to reflect that glory.

He found himself reaching for one the branches of the trees but stopped himself. Even if he wanted to just trail his fingers over the golden branch to appreciate the handiwork, he didn't dare touch anything down here.

The trees cleared up ahead, opening into a large circle paved in marble with columns holding up a roof formed of trailing gold and emerald ivy.

Off to one side, a table draped with a pristine white tablecloth offered a bounty of desserts and decanters of various drinks. Two men and three women stood sentry behind it, their gazes hazy and distant as they stared straight ahead. Where had these people come from? Was there another entrance that connected to the servants' quarters of Castle Greenbrier?

All of the servants wore a bracelet around their wrist made of twining branches and leaves in silver, gold, or diamond. Perhaps those bracelets identified these servants as the ones allowed to come down here?

Maybe Daemyn would be able to talk to them tomorrow in the servants' quarters. Servants talked to other servants, and Daemyn especially had a way of appearing invisible and servant-like that made others either overlook him or trust him, depending on their station in life.

Either way, Alex wasn't about to eat anything offered on that table. It was probably safe, considering the sisters wouldn't be able to tell in advance which items he'd eat. But something strange was going on down here. He needed to be wary. Far more wary than he'd been in Pohatomie.

Several of the princesses twirled into the dancing pavilion from some of the side paths. Queen Valinda moved in swooping leaps across the pavilion to stand swaying before a golden throne at the far side of the pavilion from where Alex stood. She beckoned, smiling. "Join us, Your Majesty. Tonight we celebrate renewed peace between Tuckawassee and the high king."

Was that all this was? A celebration of peace? Or a trap? Alex strode forward, his footsteps crunching first on the gemstones, then scuffing on the smooth marble. What would happen if he joined the dance? Was this the thing that would trap him into this curse?

For this was a curse. He could recognize the signs. The way they had burst into dancing at the exact same time. The fact that none of them stopped moving, as if they couldn't. The stilted movements of one of the sisters, Nakeisha, as she tried to knit while dancing.

To dance or not to dance? That was the question.

What would Queen Valinda do if he didn't play along? Would she skip trying to curse him and head straight to putting poison in the wine next time?

Alex strolled farther into the dancing pavilion. When Kira twirled past, he bowed. "May I have this dance, my lady?"

She grinned and took his offered hand. He spun her around, causing her to break into a peel of giggles. As Moriah twirled past, she joined them. Moments later, they gathered Leigha into their circle as well.

Alex didn't feel any different. Would he notice if a curse was setting in? He hadn't noticed last time.

The three youngest princesses were smiling, giggling. He spun each of them in turn. This was more fun than a formal ball. He'd never had younger siblings. Was this what it was like to have little sisters?

Queen Valinda might want to kill him, but Kira, Moriah, and Leigha were young. They most likely didn't know their sister's plan. He could at least give them an evening that didn't feel like a curse.

After a few more spins, he asked Nakeisha to dance. Then Panya and Quinna and Ranielle. Even Uma.

Then, finally, he had no one left besides Queen Valinda and Princess Tamya. Since Queen Valinda looked perfectly content to dance regally by her throne and dancing with her wasn't on his list of things he wanted to do, he held his hand out to Princess Tamya.

When she took his hand, he should've felt some kind of connection. Instead, all he felt was how awkward her hand felt in his, and the reaction deep in his gut was that he wanted to pull away rather than tug her close.

They were strangers. He just needed to give it time. Once he talked to her more, attraction would come.

Wouldn't it?

CHAPTER 13

DAEMYN

Daemyn crouched in the shadows next to the wall of the underground room, peering between the trunks of the gold and silver trees. In all his exploring of Castle Greenbrier, he'd never found this place, hidden as it was at the end of the family wing. The late Tuckawassee king had always kept tight security around his daughters. Probably because he'd had a lot to hide.

How long would the princesses be forced to dance? By Daemyn's reckoning, they had started dancing as soon as the sun had set. Logically, that would mean they would dance either until midnight or until dawn.

Interesting that they all had the same curse. He'd never seen that before, and he'd seen a lot of gifts and curses over the past hundred years.

Could Alex become snared in this dancing curse? Daemyn eyed the way Alex was interacting with the princesses, searching for any sign of the unfocused look Alex had gotten when under that infatuation curse in Pohatomie.

Alex stopped dancing with Princess Uma, halting completely as he glanced around. Surely that was a good sign he wasn't caught in the curse yet if he could stop dancing even for a moment.

As Alex took Princess Tamya's hand, Daemyn inched closer still, scanning the trees and the dancing pavilion. On the far side from Daemyn, a table held delicacies and drinks. Several servants stood behind it wearing the unfocused eyes and stilted movements Daemyn had expected to see from Alex.

Princess Quinna beckoned as she twirled, and one of the male servants picked up a decanter and glass. He marched forward, stepping into the brighter light surrounding the pavilion, and poured something that was either wine or grape juice into the glass, still with that blank expression on his face.

Daemyn froze, his muscles stiffening. He knew that servant. But that was impossible. Because he'd thought him dead.

Ted Chauncey had married Frennie, one of Daemyn's great grandnieces. He'd joined the family cause and went missing on a scouting mission at Castle Greenbrier three years ago. Everyone, including Daemyn, had assumed him long dead, probably poisoned and dumped in some lonely, mountain grave.

But Ted was right here in Castle Greenbrier.

How had Daemyn missing seeing him on his last scouting mission? Daemyn had scouted so thoroughly that he'd ended up with then Major Beshko on his tail all the way into Neskahana until Rosanna and her guards had rescued him. Even if he hadn't found this underground room, he had spent time in the servants' quarters. He should have seen Ted there.

Something was truly wrong if Ted had stayed here without escaping or contacting the family for three years. Ted truly loved Frennie. He would never leave her and their young children like this unless he was forced.

What sort of curse was this? Could Daemyn rescue Ted and those servants?

And how did he prevent Alex from falling into it as well?

Daemyn settled into a more comfortable position to watch and wait. The princesses didn't show any signs of stopping as midnight came and went. Alex, thankfully, didn't take any of the offered food or drink. Daemyn hardly dared hope Alex would actually get through this without getting cursed. He seemed to attract curses worse than a hound dog attracted ticks.

The night dragged on. Partway through the evening, Alex bowed out of dancing and started a board game with five of the younger sisters. After a few hours of that, he moved on to talking with some of the older princesses, including Princess Tamya.

Daemyn kept himself awake by studying every detail of the room. From what he could tell, this underground room was under the large, main courtyard of the castle. The far wall had a culvert near the ceiling with a waterfall gushing through and cascading into the underground river and lake. Since the culvert must be level with the surface of the Tuckawassee River, the outer wall of this room held back the river, extending deep underwater.

Finally, the culvert in the wall above the waterfall lightened to the soft gray of coming dawn.

The princesses danced their way down the gemstone paths, herding Alex along with them. Alex's gaze remained clear and alert. No signs of any curses.

As soon as the princesses vacated the dancing pavilion, the servants began packing up the refreshments, piling them onto a tea cart one of the women pulled from underneath the cloth-draped table. Without a word spoken between them, Ted and the servants headed off in the opposite direction as the princesses. The other male servant broke off from the others and headed toward the nearest mirrored lantern and began snuffing the candles.

Daemyn glanced from the retreating princesses to the servants. Should he follow Alex to make sure he stayed safe? Or the servants to find out where they were going?

As much as Daemyn wanted to save Ted, keeping Alex safe was the priority. The servants most likely had a separate door connected to the kitchens. Perhaps they even had their own secret rooms. If he dared leave Alex for a few minutes during the day, he would scout the kitchens again to find the entrance from that side.

But, for now, he had to follow Alex and make sure he wasn't snared in a curse during the last few minutes of the night. Besides, he if lingered here any longer, that servant might stumble across him, though the servant might be too far gone under the curse to notice or say anything.

Daemyn hurried after Alex and the princesses as quickly as he dared, sticking to the shadows by the wall.

A shaft of morning light brightened the culvert, turning the crest of the waterfall pink. At that instant, all twelve of the Tuckawassee sisters stopped dancing. With barely a pause, they climbed onto the barges and poled themselves across, taking Alex along with them.

Daemyn watched from the far side until all of the barges docked, the princesses disembarked, and they headed up the stairs with Alex in their midst.

Nothing had happened. That was probably the

strangest part of the whole night. Even more strange than the hidden forest of gold and silver trees and all twelve sisters dancing through the night. There was clearly a curse at work, and there must be a way for them to curse others, like Ted.

And yet, Alex hadn't been caught in it. There hadn't even been a moment that looked like they had tried to curse him.

Still mulling it over, Daemyn slipped into the water of the underground lake and swam across. He took a deep breath and climbed the stairs. He refused to give in to the tightness in his chest caused by the dark, narrow space. It was just a short climb, then he would be out in the open again.

But stairs only grew darker until he was feeling his way up. His head bumped into something hard, and he felt above his head.

The granite slab was back in place.

He put his back to the slab but froze. How long should he wait before trying to leave? He had no way of knowing if someone was standing right outside in the hallway. If he even lifted the slab an inch to peer out, that much movement would be noticeable to anyone in the hallway.

Daemyn sat on the steps and forced his breathing to remain steady. He could afford to wait a few minutes. Sure, it was dark. Enclosed.

He wasn't trapped. He could always go back down the stairs and try to find where the servants had gone. But Alex would notice Daemyn wasn't in the room. He would assume Daemyn had followed. Surely he would come back for Daemyn when it was safe.

If Alex was that observant.

No, this was fine. It wasn't like being locked in that dungeon in Pohatomie.

The slab of granite made a scraping sound. Daemyn pressed his back to the wall. If that wasn't Alex, he didn't want to be caught by whoever it was.

But the slab only raised an inch. "Daemyn?" Alex's voice hissed. "If you're down there, then you'd better help. I'm stronger than I was, but I'm not that strong."

That was definitely Alex. In his own mind and not cursed or coerced.

Daemyn put his back to the slab and pushed. Between him and Alex, they lifted it, and Daemyn slipped out while Alex held the slab balanced on its hinges. Together, they eased the slab back into place, covered it with the rug, and retreated back to Alex's room.

"Sorry it took me so long to go back for you. I waited until all the princesses were asleep." Alex shrugged and yawned. "At least, I think they're asleep. They've been quiet for a while and Valinda stopped poking her head into the hallway to squint at our door suspiciously."

"You did well." Daemyn nudged him. "And you didn't get cursed."

Alex scowled and sank onto the bed. "I don't think they even tried. Do you think they can draw me into their curse? I know I nearly got drawn into a curse in Pohatomie, but that's not common."

"I recognized one of those servants. He's a relative who disappeared three years ago while scouting Castle Greenbrier." Daemyn shook his head and strode toward the window. "I don't think he stayed all this time willingly."

"I see. Guess we'll have to keep our guard up." Alex scrubbed a hand over his face. "Now, unless there's anything else, I'd like to get some sleep. That was a long night."

"I need to check in with Zeke. Try to stay awake until I get back." It should be safe enough, with the door locked. But Daemyn didn't like leaving Alex alone, even for a few minutes.

Alex groaned and flopped back on the bed. "Fine. Don't take long."

His own weariness pressed against his shoulders, but Daemyn forced himself to remain alert. After crossing the room, he opened the window. Down below, an owl was hooting in a particular, recognizable pattern. If Daemyn had taken any longer, he would've missed Zeke.

He leaned out the window and softly gave a mourning dove's coo. Then he ducked below the window's opening.

In the faint, dawn light, Zeke should be able to see the outline of the window well enough. Hopefully.

Something zipped over Daemyn's head and clattered against the wall next to the door. He found the thin line the arrow had trailed and hauled on it hand over hand. As the thin line pooled at Daemyn's feet, he reached a thicker rope. He tied this to the leg of the bed.

Alex watched the proceedings with the blinking, squinting look of someone barely staying awake.

After glancing around to make sure no Tuckawassee guards were patrolling the area, Daemyn climbed down the rope hand over hand, reaching the bottom within minutes.

"I was about to go to fretting." Zeke's voice came from the darkness next to the castle wall.

Daemyn leaned against the wall beside him, face to the forest to watch for any guard patrols. "It turned out to be an eventful night."

He quickly summarized what had happened, from the

drugged wine to the underground dancing pavilion. "Your uncle Ted is alive. He's somehow gotten cornered into that dancing curse, far as I can reckon."

Zeke froze, staring off into the forest. "Poor Aunt Frennie. And the young'uns. Do you reckon I ought to pass the word along he's alive?"

Daemyn paused, then nodded. "Yes. They have grieved him long enough. But don't let her go and tear Castle Greenbrier apart just yet. We need to be mighty careful."

Zeke nodded, the movement visible in the growing light. "Will do. Rosanna sent a message about the date for the wedding."

Daemyn waited, but Zeke didn't continue. "And?"

Zeke grinned. "How does in two weeks sound?"

"Two weeks?" Sounded good to him but he'd thought planning and putting together the wedding would take longer than that.

"You gave the order for the family to assemble. Rosanna figures if they're all here already, there ain't no reason to make them all trek out this direction again in a month or two." Zeke leaned against the wall, still grinning. "Makes sense to me. After we're done here, assuming we don't all die, we can head into Neskahana and get you hitched."

Two weeks until he married Rosanna. A good motivation to survive this trip into Tuckawassee. "Tell Rosanna it sounds like a good plan to me. And pass the word along to the family. Perhaps with only two weeks' notice, Frennie won't go too wild on the planning."

"Reckon you ain't got a chance there. She's been planning the shindig to celebrate your wedding from the moment she done saw you and Rosanna together that first time." Zeke slapped Daemyn's shoulder, but his grin faded a moment later. "Rosanna also said to tell you to stay safe."

"I'd tell her the same thing, but she banned me from saying it anymore." Daemyn glanced at the mountain looming over Castle Greenbrier, wishing he could climb up there and send the message to Rosanna himself.

It had only been a day, but he already missed her so much it ached. He missed holding her hand. Her smile. Her laugh.

And he missed having her watching his back. She would have had good insight into Valinda and her sisters, and probably would have figured out their plan by now.

Daemyn gestured to the mountain. "Can you tell Rosanna and Isi what happened last night? With the dancing curse and the underground room?"

"It ain't going to be easy putting all that into the code, but I'll do my best." Zeke held out a leather satchel. "Here's more supplies. Reckon I'd best get under cover for the day."

Daemyn took it, glancing up the way he came. "I'll pull in the rope and hide it in our room. I'd like to have a way to hightail it out of here in a hurry if we need it."

And they might need it. The Tuckawassee princesses might not have tried anything that night but that didn't mean Alex was safe. Not by a long shot. And Daemyn wasn't about to get himself killed off only a few weeks before his wedding.

CHAPTER 14

TAMYA

A knock sounded on Mya's door far too early in the day. Was it even noon yet? She would have rolled out of bed and stumbled to the door as she was, but with High King Alexander camped out in their wing, she didn't want to embarrass herself by just opening the door.

"Coming." She pushed herself out of bed, threw a blanket over her shoulders to cover her nightgown, and glanced at the mirror. Her hair frizzed out of the braids she'd put it in to keep it from becoming tangled during the night, but she didn't look too horrendous.

When she unlocked and opened the door, Valinda stood there, not High King Alexander. Valinda's gaze swept up and down Tamya, her lip curling as if in disgust that Mya hadn't managed to look presentable after rolling out of bed with only five hours of sleep. Valinda, of course, was fully dressed in a light purple dress. A tiara with jet and amethyst glittered against her black curls. "I wish to speak with you in my study in a few minutes."

"Give me a few minutes to dress." Mya waited until Valinda nodded and swept away before she shut the door. It wouldn't do to slam her door in her queen's face.

Mya quickly dressed, pinned her braids into a swirl at the top of her head, then peeked into the hallway again. No one else seemed to be stirring yet.

She hurried from her room, down the hallway, past the guards at the doors, and across the great hall to the study.

Valinda already reclined in the padded chair behind the desk. With High King Alexander in their midst during the night, she hadn't gotten caught up on paperwork as she usually did. "Thank you for coming promptly, Mya. I wished to speak, and I didn't want to risk the high king or his manservant overhearing."

Of course this had to do with Valinda's plot. It seemed to be all they talked about right now. Mya clasped her hands behind her back and planted her feet. "I noticed you didn't attempt to draw him into our curse last night."

"All a part of the plan." Valinda's smile slicked across her face. "He was wary last night. He's waiting for us to spring a trap. But for this to work, he needs to let his guard down long enough for the curse to lure him in."

Mya tried to force away the sick taste in her mouth. This was all so...cold. But what else had she expected out of Valinda? She had stolen Neill's mind and Shandra's happiness to preserve their secret.

High King Alexander was their enemy. His manservant Daemyn Rand had killed Mya's father. Why would she feel any discomfort at drawing him into their curse?

Besides, if she was forced to marry him, wouldn't it be easier if he was controlled by their curse? Instead of a husband, she would be gaining a very obedient pet.

Why did her stomach churn even worse at that thought?

"I see." It was all Mya could manage, and Valinda was waiting, as if for an answer.

"Invite him to spend the day with you. Take him to visit Greenbrier or whatever you would do if you were genuinely interested in him. Get him to start thinking our only plan is a real marriage alliance." Valinda waved her hand, as if brushing away any concerns about how devious that sounded. "We'll strike tonight. Once the high king is under our control, we'll dispose of that manservant of his. Maybe we'll have High King Alexander poison him. Or Colonel Beshko has expressed interest in being the one to eliminate him. She's still miffed that he didn't stay dead the last time she killed him."

Mya shouldn't feel so uncomfortable. Not over the death of the man who had killed her father.

But how could Valinda so coldly plan a man's death? Not with an arrest, trial, and execution, if found guilty in the proper manner of justice. But with poison or Colonel Beshko's revenge.

Perhaps that was a part of being queen. Valinda had the burden of Tuckawassee resting on her shoulders. She didn't have the luxury of squirming over cursing others to protect their secret or disposing of a man like Daemyn Rand who had been Tuckawassee's enemy for generations.

For all Mya longed for more power to do more for the people of Tuckawassee, she didn't want to be like Valinda. Cold. Calculating.

Mya wasn't in command. It was her duty as a princess and sister to follow Valinda's orders. "Very well. I'll take him into Greenbrier today. If I wake him up now, we can eat in town."

"Good plan. A shared meal is a classic bonding technique." Valinda gave a sharp nod, then reached for a stack of her paperwork. "Dismissed."

Mya hurried from the study. Why did every interaction with her sister lately leave her skin crawling and itching? It was like talking to their father all over again.

Their father had always had Tuckawassee's greatness as his goal. Valinda was no different. That was a goal Mya should support.

Back in the royal wing, her sisters were stirring for the day. Shandra brushed past Mya, giving her a sharp look on her way out the door. Ranielle eyed the two of them as she hefted her spear and left for a practice session with the guards.

Giggles came from Kira's room, and when Mya peeked in, she spotted most of the younger girls playing with their dolls and doll castle. It all looked pretty normal, except that Mya was pretty sure the evil queen in the story was threatening to kill everybody.

Mya was stalling. She'd already walked past High King Alexander's door three times now.

With a deep breath, Mya marched to the door and knocked. She could do this. It was merely a walk to Greenbrier. She wouldn't think about trying to make him relax and let his guard down. She definitely wouldn't think about pretending this was an actual courtship for a real marriage alliance.

The door was opened by the high king's manservant Daemyn Rand. He was dressed in a tan, linen shirt and buckskin leggings that looked identical to what he had been wearing the day before. The outfit was about as nondescript as it got, and with his downcast eyes and hunched stance, he didn't look like someone threatening.

Was this really the same man that her family had fought for a hundred years? He didn't look like much, to be honest.

Mya drew herself straight. "I wish to speak with the high king."

It was rather obvious. After all, she wasn't there to talk to Daemyn Rand. But it was the expected thing to say.

Daemyn nodded, then stepped aside, standing against the wall as if he was trying to disappear against the stones.

High King Alexander strode through the doorway, dressed in a red silk shirt, buckskin leggings, and moccasins that laced up to his knees. "Good morning, Princess Tamya. Did you rest well?"

How did he manage to sound so sincerely gracious when he knew none of them had slept for long? Mya forced a practiced smile. "Yes, I did. Thanks for asking. I was wondering if you would like to walk into the town of Greenbrier with me today? We could grab a bite to eat, then I can show you the town. It has been a long time since a high king has walked the streets of Greenbrier."

High King Alexander glanced over his shoulder at Daemyn Rand, as if asking his manservant for permission.

Then again, Daemyn Rand was also doubling as the high king's bodyguard, so he probably had a say in what the high king did. Mya studied the manservant-bodyguard again. He was tall and muscular enough, and he must be skilled for High King Alexander to trust him as his only bodyguard here in Tuckawassee.

Yet, with the way he was standing with his eyes down, shoulders slumped, he didn't look like the person she'd want guarding her back in enemy territory.

Daemyn's gaze lifted long enough to meet High King Alexander's, then he nodded. "It should be safe enough, Your Highness."

Wouldn't that be *Your Majesty*, not *Your Highness*? Why was the high king putting up with such disrespect from his manservant? She would suspect it was an inside joke, except that the manservant had said it in such a monotone manner that it didn't have a trace of humor.

"Yes, Greenbrier is very safe. We'll be taking a squad of guards, of course." Mya was supposed to be making the high king relax, not make him suspicious that she was taking him out of the castle to have him killed in a back alley of Greenbrier. "Your bodyguard can come as well."

"Actually, I think my manservant has duties here to take care off." High King Alexander glanced at Daemyn Rand again.

This time, something flickered in Daemyn's gaze for a moment before he nodded.

High King Alexander turned back to Mya and held out his arm. "Very well, Princess Tamya. I would be honored to have you show me Greenbrier."

By the time Mya and High King Alexander walked into the great hall, heading for the castle's outer doors, a squad of guards was waiting for them on Valinda's orders.

Soon, Mya found herself strolling arm and arm down the winding road toward Greenbrier. She kept shifting her grip on High King Alexander's elbow, all too aware of his muscle beneath her fingers. But not in a swoony, his-muscles-felt-so-strong kind of way. More like her back was stiffening with how much she didn't want to touch him.

When they were partway down the mountain, the trail narrowed, and they had to move to the side to let a man pulling a handcart pass them. High King Alexander dropped his arm so that they could walk in a line instead of side-by-side. When the cart was past them, he thankfully didn't offer his arm again. Perhaps he'd found it as awkward as she had.

"So..." High King Alexander cleared his throat. "Do you have a favorite place to eat?"

"There's a tavern on the main street that makes a great succotash. And their brisket and biscuits are good as well." Mya's tension faded as they passed the first few buildings of Greenbrier.

Wooden buildings lined either side of the cobblestone main street. With the guards marching around them, the townsfolk cleared the street to give them room. Mya waved at them as she passed, calling out greetings to a few of them.

The distant roar of the Rantahala Falls grew louder, a boardwalk leading off the far end of the town to a trail beside the dark rock of the falls. She probably should lead High King Alexander over there once they finished their lunch. A hike by a waterfall would be romantic, right? Maybe then she would feel something for him besides how much she wanted the day to be over.

"You must visit Greenbrier often." High King Alexander tipped his head in the direction of the baker's wife, who had waved and called a greeting.

"I visit several times a week." Mya shrugged. She couldn't do much for the rest of Tuckawassee, but she could help this town.

At least until Valinda married her off and she went to live in Castle Eyota in Kanawhee.

"Your people clearly love you. And you love them." The high king smiled, though the smile faded quickly. "That is admirable."

She probably should find that compliment endearing.

But, for some reason, it just made her want to put even more distance between them.

Courting felt so...forced. The longer she was with High King Alexander, the more she wanted to run as fast as she could the other way.

Mya attempted a smile. "Thank you. But I'm not doing it to be admirable or anything. It's the right thing to do."

"And that's what makes it admirable." High King Alexander glanced at her, grimaced, then sighed. "Look, I'm not just saying that because we're trying to court each other. I'm saying it as one leader who cares about his people to another."

Why did those words warm her more than his compliment had?

When she smiled, the expression felt more genuine than her previous smiles. "You've been doing a lot of rebuilding in Eyota. Do you have any ideas that I could implement here in Greenbrier?"

High King Alexander scanned the street as they headed for the tavern. "This town is already very well laid out. The sewage in the street ditches could use some work."

"Exactly! That's what I've been telling my father and sister for years." Mya led him into the tavern, where they each ordered brisket and a side of succotash, a dish of corn, beans, tomatoes, and whatever other random vegetables happened to be in season.

Somehow, the conversation about sewage systems continued through their meal. He had many intelligent ideas on how to implement the system. Strange that the topic didn't seem awkward or gross. Just the two of them exchanging ideas for how to make life better for the kingdoms they cared about.

Once they finished, Mya pushed to her feet. "Would you like to see what we have dug so far for the new sewage system? It isn't much, since Valinda hasn't authorized more yet."

"Yes, I would like to see it." High King Alexander jumped to his feet, then strolled at her side from the tavern.

The digging site was at the very far end of town, tucked into the edge of the forest. It was downstream of the town, away from the wells where the townfolk drew their drinking water.

A few workers were in the pit, digging it deeper. They glanced up, waved, and called greetings as Mya approached.

"The work is coming along nicely." Mya halted at the edge and waved at the high king. "This is High King Alexander. I'm showing him around Greenbrier."

"It is a pleasure to be here." High King Alexander gave the workers a smile and a nod before he paced around the pit. "Will there be drainage field spreading from this main holding pit?"

"Yes." Mya pointed to the stakes pounded into the ground. "We currently have three tunnels planned for the drain field, branching off downhill."

"A good plan." High King Alexander strolled along one of the drainage lines marked by the stakes. "Have you thought about putting additional, smaller pits along these, and then branching out into an even broader drainage field? It would give your sewage system more capacity and help disperse the liquids faster."

"That is the plan, eventually. For now, we're starting with this." Mya shrugged. "But I hadn't thought to broaden it out. That's a good suggestion."

"More digging." One of the workers grumbled.

"Digging isn't so bad." High King Alexander dropped

down into the pit and held out a hand. "I'll take a turn, if you'd like."

The worker eyed him for a moment, as if doubting a high king would deign to get his hands dirty digging. But then he shrugged and handed over the shovel.

High King Alexander thrust the shovel into the ground, stomped on it, and levered a small shovel-full from the ground. Far less impressive than the amount of dirt the worker was shifting, but at least the high king was pitching in. It wasn't something Mya had been expecting.

Then again, High King Alexander was nothing like what she'd been expecting. If she'd been spending time with him merely as a friend, without the pressure of a marriage alliance and his impending cursed state hanging over her head, the day would have been pleasant. His thoughts on integrating the new sewage system into the town of Greenbrier had been helpful.

Too bad he would be cursed and mindless before the night was out.

CHAPTER 15

DAEMYN

Daemyn strolled into the kitchens of Castle Greenbrier. As much as he didn't like watching Alex wander off alone with any of the princesses, especially all the way into Greenbrier, he had needed this chance to explore the castle. Again. He'd obviously missed a few things the last time he'd scouted the place.

The scullery maids glanced up as he entered but continued scrubbing pots and chopping vegetables.

The rotund cook blocked Daemyn's way and crossed his brawny arms. "You aren't welcome here."

"Pardon. I ain't had a meal yet today. Mind if I grab a bite?" Daemyn tried to keep his posture submissive, his gaze downcast. It usually made others underestimate him.

"Fine. But don't go snooping around. Don't think I don't remember you from a year ago." The cook jabbed his ladle at Daemyn. "I got my eye on you."

This was why Daemyn usually let a few decades go by between scouting missions. It was a lot easier when enough time had passed that people had either forgotten about him or died.

With the cook glaring at him, he couldn't do as much poking around as he would have liked. He found a bowl and one of the maids ladled a stew into it.

The stew was probably safe, but after all the lectures he'd given Alex, Daemyn wasn't about to be the one to break first.

As he pretended to eat, he glanced around the room. He didn't see Ted or the other servants from the underground room.

A maid piled several trays with baked goods and meat pies before loading them onto a tea cart. After a few minutes, while Daemyn did his best to appear engrossed in the stew, the cook took the tea cart and pushed it down a hallway lined with doors, most likely to storage rooms.

Daemyn had explored most of those rooms last time he was there, though he hadn't been able to search all of them. He'd placed a priority on getting close to the princesses and searching the king's study. In that, he had succeeded, both in ruling out all the princesses as Alex's cursebreaker and in learning about a planned Tuckawassee raid on Neskahana.

The brawny cook halted in front of a door at the end of the hall and took out a set of keys. After unlocking the door, the cook disappeared inside, closing the door behind him.

Daemyn slurped at another spoonful of soup without actually eating any of it. When he flicked his gaze around the room, a number of the maids were watching him as they worked. He probably wasn't going to get a chance to sneak off and explore what lay behind that door anytime soon.

The door to the kitchens swung open, and two

Tuckawassee soldiers marched inside, both carrying spears and dressed in thick leather vests. The female guard had gems glittering in her black curls while the male guard's dark black curls puffed around his head.

Someone must have tipped off the guards that he was here. Daemyn wouldn't be scouting any more of the castle that afternoon.

Daemyn held up a spoonful of soup. "Just getting lunch. Want some? This stew is rather good."

Both the guards stared back at him with identical blank expressions.

Very well-trained guards. Still, the set of their jaws and the way they gripped their spears stated that they were watching him and he shouldn't even think about scouting the castle.

DAEMYN TOOK his bowl and spoon and added them to the pile of dirty dishes by one of the scullery maids, fumbling the bowl to dump most of the stew over the stack of plates to obscure the fact that he hadn't eaten anything.

Normally, he would have offered to help and gained the trust of the entire kitchen staff by taking on the task of scrubbing the pots and pans. But it seemed they had already made up their minds about him. He was the enemy, and he wasn't welcome.

As he strode out of the kitchens, the two guards fell into step behind him. Were they assigned to watching him?

Daemyn wandered from the servant wing into the great hall, pausing beside the long bank of windows. A line of grape arbors filled the space directly below the windows, with cobbled paths winding beside the arbors and into flower gardens.

He wasn't accomplishing much, but he might as well wander the castle. At least the parts that the Tuckawassee would allow him to enter.

Stepping through the door next to the windows, Daemyn took the stairs into the flower gardens, strolling the paths. If only Rosanna were there. It would have been a lot nicer to walk hand-in-hand with her rather than stroll by himself.

He glanced over his shoulder. Not totally by himself. The two guards still trailed behind him no matter where he went.

Daemyn halted at the top of another set of stairs. Down below, the large, main courtyard spread out, ringed on three sides by the outer walls of the castle with the Tuckawassee River rippling against the wall. From his vantage point, he could just make out the drop off and rising mist of Rantahala Falls.

The underground room lay beneath that large courtyard. It must have been built when the castle was. Perhaps as a defensive measure. A way to collapse the courtyard if enemies ever breached the walls.

He wasn't sure how that information could help him. Still, he liked to know the layout of the castle he was in. Just in case.

After several more minutes, Daemyn wandered back through the gardens and into the castle. He saw a few of the princesses at a distance, but he didn't try to approach them.

The guards followed him all the way back to the great hall, past the wall of windows, and into the royal wing. They halted next to the other guards by the doors, though facing inward, watching him.

It seemed Daemyn should have gone with Alex after all.

He would have accomplished more by watching Alex's back than he had trying to explore the castle.

Still, he'd wandered around the castle without Colonel Beshko making an appearance. Daemyn would have thought she would be the first to volunteer to keep an eye on him.

Where was she? She'd been there yesterday when she had escorted them to Castle Greenbrier. But he hadn't seen her since.

And, somehow, Daemyn didn't reckon that was a good thing.

CHAPTER 16

ALEXANDER

Alex stepped into his room and locked the door behind him. That had been a better day than he had expected. Princess Tamya seemed nice, and she had good ideas. Queen Valinda would be wise to listen to her.

Too bad Alex couldn't feel anything remotely like sparks or warmth or attraction when he was with her. She was nice. Smart. Passionate about rebuilding projects. Everything that Alex should be attracted to.

Inside the room, Daemyn lay on his cot. He cracked an eye open. "I see you didn't get killed while you were out of my sight."

"Shocking, I know." Alex sank into one of the chairs by the table and held up a sack. "I brought leftovers for you. I figured the tavern's food was probably safe, though I made sure I ordered the same thing as the princess and swapped food with her in case the tavern keeper took it into his head to poison me."

It probably hadn't been wise, but the food had smelled

far too tempting. It had been the best meal Alex had eaten since he'd left Castle Eyota.

Daemyn must have thought the risk worth it as well, for he rolled off the pallet, sank into the chair across from Alex, and dug into the brisket and biscuits. "Did you learn anything from Princess Tamya?"

"Nothing much besides she's strangely passionate about sewage systems. If we survive this, I might hire her to take on rebuilding Eyota." Alex relaxed against the back of the chair. "How was scouting?"

Daemyn grimaced. "I didn't get very far. The cook remembered me from last time, and a pair of guards followed me everywhere."

"I don't think they bought your whole manservant act this time." Alex frowned. Daemyn's invisibility as a servant had been an asset, one Alex had been counting on.

But the Tuckawassee had been hunting Daemyn for too long and knew too many of his secrets.

"But at least no one tried to kill me and at least pretended to be polite." Daemyn shrugged and polished off the last biscuit.

Was that a good thing? Did it mean that the Tuckawassee truly wanted peace?

Or were they just biding their time, putting on a good mask, until the time was right to strike?

THAT NIGHT, Alex found himself once again in the underground dancing hall. He held Princess Tamya's hand as he twirled her through a few steps of the dance. It was strange, dancing without any music besides the scuffing of their feet on the marble floor of the dancing pavilion.

Even without music, all the princesses flowed through dancing steps as if they followed some rhythm he couldn't sense.

Princess Tamya leaned away from him, as if wanting to put as much space between them as possible. "Um..." Her eyes focused on the floor, the ceiling, the walls, anywhere but him.

They had spent all day together, and it seemed, now that they had discussed sewage systems, they didn't have anything left to talk about.

Alex cleared his throat. "The Rantahala Falls were impressive."

Princess Tamya gave him a smile so fake and strained that Alex nearly winced. "You said that already. Several times today."

"Sorry." So much for his intelligence. It apparently failed him whenever princesses were involved. What else was he supposed to talk to her about? Was there a government policy they had yet to discuss? While they didn't seem to have anything personal to talk about, policies and politics seemed to bring out the best discussions. "What are your thoughts on promoting the use of currency over the barter system?"

Princess Tamya's smile lifted higher, genuine this time. "I'm from Tuckawassee. Of course, we're in favor of currency. It makes our gold and silver more valuable."

"Probably why most of the other kingdoms are resistant to the idea." Alex spun her toward the edge of the pavilion and stopped dancing. "Though, for a currency to work, it would still be the market in Eyota that would determine values of products. In that sense, the power would still rest in the trading center, not Tuckawassee."

"True. But we would become more valuable to the high

king and the market. Too often, our gold and gems are considered unessential, since they aren't as necessary to basic survival like Pohatomie's corn or Buckhannock's iron." Princess Tamya planted her hands on her hips as she continued to sway in front of him.

After a few more minutes of discussing economics, Princess Kira dance-dashed up to them, followed by Princesses Leigha, Moriah, and Nakeisha. Princess Kira grinned up at them. "Mya, will you play hide and seek with us?"

Princess Tamya glanced from her sister to Alex. "I'll play if High King Alexander will."

It would help pass the time. And Alex had wanted to chance to talk to Daemyn, assuming Daemyn was lurking around that underground room keeping an eye on him.

"Sounds like fun. I've never played before." Alex had observed the servant children in Castle Eyota playing, so he knew how.

"You've *never* played before?" Princess Kira stared at him as if she couldn't imagine never playing hide and seek.

Actually, all of the princesses were staring at him. Alex shrugged. "I didn't have any siblings. I had no one to play with."

"Then I'll go first!" Kira jumped up and down, and her sisters rolled their eyes.

"Just make sure you give us enough time to hide." Princess Tamya grinned and tensed, poised to run to hide, though she kept moving her feet and hands with a dance.

Kira put her hands over her eyes, spinning in place as she counted. "One. Two."

Alex bolted down a path headed for the deeper shadows along the inside wall, keeping an eye out for the other princesses. He passed Uma, tucked in a corner by a tree as she stitched away, adding gems to a dress. Princess Moriah dove underneath a tree shaped like a mini willow tree with gold branches draped all the way to the ground.

Alex halted in the farthest corner of the wall beside the lake and crouched behind a tree. Was Daemyn even down here? Would he be able to slip in close enough to talk?

"Your Highness."

Alex jumped, bumping his head on a branch. He glanced behind him. "You are very good at being invisible."

Daemyn leaned against the wall in the shadows. "Lots of practice."

"I was thinking you should leave early tonight." Alex gestured toward the lake and the stairs out of the underground room. "If you sneak out of the castle when it's still dark, you can send a message to Rosanna yourself. I'm sure wedding planning would be easier if you don't have to pass notes through Zeke."

Daemyn glanced from Alex to the door. The fact that he was actually thinking about leaving Alex there alone showed how much Daemyn missed Rosanna. "I ain't about to leave you here."

"Nothing happened last night." Alex nodded toward the rest of the room. Princess Kira was racing between the trees. She'd found Leigha and was headed toward the waterfall side of the room. "They've been very genial so far."

"That don't make it less suspicious." Daemyn crossed his arms.

"I know. I'll be cautious." Alex checked on Kira's progress. She'd found Princess Tamya and they were on their way back in his direction.

Daemyn raised his eyebrows.

"Look, I'm not about to get cursed the moment your

back is turned. I'll be careful." Alex huffed a breath. "Besides, what could you actually do to stop me from falling into a curse? By the time you hurry across the room, it would probably be too late."

"All right." Daemyn pushed off the wall. "But if you fall into another curse, I ain't waiting around another hundred years to break it."

"Wouldn't expect you to. Just send along a great-grandson to rescue me eventually." Alex glanced around the tree. "Better hurry. I think Kira will find me in a minute or two."

"Don't get cursed." Daemyn gave him one last look before slipping into the water of the lake with barely a ripple to mar the surface.

Alex shook his head and crouched behind the tree again. It was going to be so much fun to be an adoptive uncle to Daemyn and Rosanna's children and watch Daemyn give that stern look to someone else for a change.

Kira dashed along the path, then skidded to a halt next to him. "Found you! You aren't very good at hide and seek, High King Alexander."

Alex pushed away from the wall, smiling. "Like I said, I never had any brothers or sisters to play with when I was growing up. I haven't had a lot of practice at this. At least I wasn't found first."

"We still need to find Moriah and Nakeisha, then it will be Leigha's turn." Kira skipped off down the path.

Alex shrugged. If he was going to be stuck down here all night, playing hide and seek was a lot more fun than dancing with Princess Tamya.

CHAPTER 17

DAEMYN

The cool night air wrapped around Daemyn as he hiked up the mountain behind Castle Greenbrier. He drew in a deep breath, his tense muscles relaxing for the first time in the past two days.

Near the top of the mountain, a large outcropping cut across the path. He worked his way to the far side where the rock would block the light from Castle Greenbrier below. There, Zeke sat with his back to a tree near a drop off, a lantern in his hand.

In the distance, a light flashed in the code: *...elk or buffalo.*

"More wedding details?" Daemyn sank onto the ledge next to Zeke.

"Oh, good. You're here. You can answer all the questions." Zeke handed over the lantern. "Rosanna wants to know who you want standing with you, and the family wants to know if we're going to be hunting buffalo or elk for the traditional hunt. I'm assuming we aren't hunting bear."

"Definitely not bear. And we're going to have to hunt during the day. Her brother is going to want to go along, and I ain't about to risk one of the family deciding to hunt him by mistake." Daemyn worked the lantern's shutter to flash a light to let Rosanna know he was there. "Oh, and I'd better make sure the family knows to hold off on bear hunting while we're in Neskahana."

"Might be a good idea. Some of the relatives are mighty fond of bear." Zeke put his hands behind his head and leaned back against a tree.

The last thing Daemyn needed at his wedding was for Rosanna's brother Berend to accidentally get eaten.

The light on the distant mountain flashed again. *I love you.*

"I reckon that was for you." Zeke jabbed a thumb at him.

"Could have been Isi talking to you." But Daemyn still sent *I love you too* back.

This mission to Tuckawassee already felt far too long. He just had to get Alex through the next couple of days, then they could head north into Neskahana. Just a few more days to keep Alex from getting poisoned, cursed, or otherwise killed.

It was going to be a long few days.

Chapter 18

Alexander

Would this night ever end? Alex rubbed at his eyes, trying to stay awake. A fog filled his brain, and all he could think about was the soft bed he'd left behind in the room he'd been given. Two nights in a row without sleep were catching up with him. How did the princesses manage to dance through the night every night? They must get used to it, training themselves to stay awake at night and sleep during the mornings.

All he wanted was sleep. He glanced at the shadows under the nearest silver tree. Would any of the princesses notice if he curled up under the tree and slept?

Alex sank onto a bench to the side of the dancing pavilion. Sometime in the past few minutes, all twelve of the sisters had gathered there, twirling and spinning until Alex's head whirled.

A servant approached, holding out a glass of water.

Water. He was so thirsty. He'd danced and played hide and seek and talked and danced. All night long.

Just a sip. Surely a sip wouldn't hurt.

He found the glass in his hand, raising it to his mouth.

No. He dumped the water on the ground and set the glass on the bench beside him with trembling fingers. No. He might be tired, but he wasn't going to make the same mistakes as last time. No food. No water. Stick to Daemyn's plan. He'd already broken it enough by eating food at the tavern with Princess Tamya.

"You can't rest now, Your Majesty. It's almost dawn." Queen Valinda blurred in front of him, his eyes too tired to focus.

Alex pushed to his feet, swaying. A soft mattress. A pillow. Closing his eyes.

"You don't want to be left behind." Princess Tamya grabbed his arm, alternating between pulling and pushing him along the path back to the barges and the lake.

He was surrounded by the princesses on the path as they danced their way toward the lake.

Was the air growing thicker or were his arms growing heavier? Alex shook his head, trying to stay alert and awake.

The trees on either side of the path seemed to be reaching for him, trailing gold, metallic fingers over his hand and arm.

He could almost hear the faint strains of some kind of music, beckoning to him. Calling him. Strains of a haunting lullaby soothing his mind, his heart.

His fingers were reaching for a gold branch, tracing its delicate golden leaves.

Take me. It whispered in the building music. *You will never have burdens again.*

He would never have to struggle under the weight of being the high king. He wouldn't toss and turn at night wondering if he would do or say something that would spark another war. He wouldn't ache with the weariness of holding the seven kingdoms together with such a tenuous grip. Nor would he have to worry about poisons or assassinations.

No more burdens. No more weight resting on his shoulders.

The faintest hint of a draft whispered against his cheek before the heaviness in the air brushed it away.

Had he ever been truly carefree? Even as a high prince, when his every need was met, his every wish granted, he'd still had the weight of his curse pressing on him.

All he'd have to do is reach out and snap off a branch. Just a quick tug, and he'd never have to worry again. He would finally have peace and happiness. A life without burdens.

The princesses were a whirl of flashing silk around him. Everything glittered and spun, the air hard to breathe.

His hand reached out. The gold snapped easily in his hand, giving him a nine-inch-long branch with delicate, gold leaves.

The branch in his hand moved, snaking down his hand toward his wrist, the metal cold against his skin. He held still, letting it, the music murmuring in his ear, *No burdens. Peace.*

A breeze shivered down his back, prickling against his skin. For an instant, his head cleared. The lilting music vanished.

But it was enough. His hand snapped into focus, even if the rest of the world still tumbled in a blurry haze. What was he doing? He gaped at the gold branch, twisting itself around his wrist.

No, no, no. Not again. He'd walked right into a curse yet again. He shook his hand, tugged on the gold, but the soft metal wouldn't budge. It was only inches from completely encircling his wrist, and when it did, he'd be lost.

Strength. He needed strength.

He grasped for the memories the breeze had brought, his lungs filling with the scent of turquoise waterfalls and deep forests, and heard the faint echo of the Highest Prince telling him, *Ask.*

Not again. Please. I can't get it off.

The heaviness in the air swept away on the breeze, as the twirling solidified into twelve sisters dancing.

Around his wrist, the gold stopped moving. It was just a branch made of gold, and this time when he tugged, it bent easily in his fingers.

Queen Valinda's gaze narrowed on him as she twirled past, her mouth set in a hard line. Princess Tamya's eyes were wide as she studied him.

He had to pretend he was oblivious. That he didn't know what had almost happened to him.

He looped the branch into a circlet, faced Kira, and settled the makeshift crown on her hair as she twirled past. "A crown for the liveliest princess here. I enjoyed seeing what it is like to have a little sister for an evening."

Kira grinned and touched the crown. Such an innocent gesture. Did she know what had almost happened to him? Did she know that the dance could catch others in the curse?

Princess Tamya had known. Alex could read that much in her expression, though she wouldn't meet his gaze.

The marriage alliance was just a trick. He'd known Queen Valinda probably hadn't been sincere, but apparently Princess Tamya wasn't either. All those attempts at conversation had all been a waste of time. She didn't intend to get to know him or make a marriage alliance work. She just wanted to help her sister trap him.

Glad to know the only girl currently offering to marry him wanted to turn him into a mindless servant controlled by a cursed dance.

Over Kira's shoulder, the culvert over the waterfall brightened with a shaft of light. Around Alex, all of the princesses stopped dancing.

The cursed dance must be over for the night. Finally. All Alex wanted to do was collapse into bed and sleep the morning away.

The princesses dropped into a weary silence as they walked the rest of the way to the barges and climbed on.

Alex helped pole them across the lake. As they neared the far side, he could just make out damp splotches on the stone platform. Great. As if this night couldn't get any better. Daemyn's footprints hadn't had enough time to finish drying.

As their barge nudged against the stone, Alex faked tripping over his pole and tumbled into the cold water. He came up sputtering. At least he was awake now.

"Are you all right?" Princess Tamya peered down at him, holding out her pole. Princesses Quinna, Nakeisha, and Kira leaned over, staring at him.

There went any chance of recovering his dignity.

Instead of reaching for Princess Tamya's pole, he swam to the stone platform and heaved himself out of the water in the exact same spot Daemyn had. Alex made sure he rolled, shook, and got water all over the place. That should hide any signs that someone else had also climbed out of the water there.

He grabbed one of the lanterns and headed up the stairs without waiting for the princesses. It wasn't chivalrous, but he needed to hide Daemyn's drying footprints. It wasn't like he had anything to say to any of the people tromping up the stairs behind him.

At the top, he paused by the door to his room. He didn't have a whole lot of energy left to spare on being polite.

But, he had to pretend he was the oblivious high king. He was already in enough danger without them realizing he suspected their plot.

He forced himself to turn and smile at Queen Valinda, Princess Tamya, and the gaggle of their sisters crowding the hallway. "Thank you for a wonderful evening."

Then, he stumbled into his room, shut the door behind him, and leaned against it, his clothes still dripping onto the floor.

Daemyn sat up from where he had been stretched out on the pallet, pretending to be asleep. He raised an eyebrow.

"I don't think we packed enough clothes for this trip." Alex wrung out his sleeve, adding to the puddle on the floor. "But, on the bright side, I didn't get cursed tonight. Even though they tried."

Daemyn pushed to his feet. He wore dry clothes, probably his last set of dry and clean ones, considering he'd managed to go through two sets of clothes in a single evening since he'd poured wine down the back of his shirt earlier.

Crouching, Daemyn dug through Alex's pack, yanked out Alex's last set of spare clothes, and tossed it to him. "What happened?"

Alex peeled his wet shirt over his head. "Something with their dance. Next thing I knew, I was hearing music and reaching for a branch on one of the gold trees. When I broke it off, it started twining around my wrist. I knew if it finished, I would be stuck." Alex tugged the dry shirt over his head and rubbed his wrist. "The Highest King saved me."

He would have fallen right into the curse, just as he always did, except for the strength of the Highest King filling him, clearing his head, stopping that cursed dance from dragging him in.

They had tried, but he hadn't been cursed. For the first time in his life, he'd avoided a curse instead of plunging headlong into it. Even though it had confirmed that Tuckawassee's gesture of peace had been nothing but a trick, he had much to be thankful for.

CHAPTER 19

TAMYA

He hadn't been taken by the curse last night.

Princess Tamya found herself oddly grateful for that. All last night, her stomach had churned, her chest tight. She had struggled to pretend to happily chat with High King Alexander as if nothing was wrong. As if she didn't plan to lure him into a curse that would put him under their control.

"How was he able to stop it?" Valinda paced across her study, her shadow marching in time across the wall as she blocked the early afternoon light streaming through the windows. "We've never had anyone avoid being cursed like that."

He had almost been cursed. Mya had seen the way the branch had started twining around his wrist. It should have been inevitable.

Except that it wasn't. What was so special about High King Alexander that he could avoid being lured in by their dance?

It reminded Mya of the stories of hope and curse-breakers that her mother used to tell. If High King Alexander could avoid being trapped in their curse with them, then could the curse be broken? Was it not as powerful as it seemed to be?

Perhaps there was hope for Shandra and Neill after all. Maybe Mya wouldn't have to keep dancing every night for the rest of her life.

"Do you think he suspects?" Mya leaned against the wall in a pool of sunlight, soaking in the warmth. "Surely he noticed something was wrong last night. It would be hard not to figure out what had nearly happened."

"Maybe. He has certainly given no indication that he is suspicious." Valinda shook her head, sending her cascade of braids swinging over her shoulders, the gold and gems twined into her hair glinting in the sunlight. "He was cheerful enough at lunch."

Mya frowned. At the late lunch they'd hosted once everyone woke up, High King Alexander had been nothing but smiles and charming conversation. But his actions seemed almost too innocently clueless.

After spending the day with him in Greenbrier the day before, Mya knew just how sharp he could be. His discourse on sewage systems, economics, and politics had been insightful. Someone that astute wouldn't be oblivious to nearly being cursed.

If he realized they had tried to trap him in a curse last night, wouldn't he have tried to leave Castle Greenbrier today? Or stop the talks of a marriage alliance? Yet here he remained, still spending the lunch acting as if he was trying to get to know her. As if he still thought the marriage alliance would be a genuine marriage. It didn't make sense.

Valinda halted, staring unfocused at the wall. "Unless he has his own trap in the works. Maybe his talk of peace and alliances is just a cover for overthrowing Tuckawassee."

"Do you really think he'd show up with a single servant if he planned to overthrow us? He'd need his whole army to do that." Mya tapped her fingers on the windowsill.

"Unless he intends to poison us. He may see it as vengeance for our ancestor who poisoned his father."

"We searched everything they'd brought with them. Nothing but clothes." It had been the first thing their guards had done when bringing the high king's packs to his assigned room the day he arrived. Mya shrugged. "Maybe he is just desperate enough for peace that he intends to stick it out even knowing we tried to drag him into our curse."

"That doesn't change the fact that he avoided it, making him the first person besides Father to know how secretly powerful we are but not be under our control." Valinda's hands tightened into fists as she faced Tamya. "We will try again tonight, and this time we can't let him escape. He can't be allowed to remain out of our control now that he knows about our curse."

"Of course." Mya bowed, the words tasting like ash in her mouth. Why was she feeling so guilty about this? It wasn't like she cared about High King Alexander. Sure, it had been pleasant to talk about town infrastructure with him, but that didn't change anything.

A slight breeze curled through the window and brushed against Mya's hair.

This was wrong. So very, very wrong. And yet, Valinda was her sister. Tuckawassee was her kingdom. To go against Valinda would mean turning traitor against her queen, her kingdom, and most importantly, her sister. Sisters didn't betray each other. They stood by each other no matter what.

That was the power of their gift and their curse, after all. Their curse wielded power in that underground dancing pavilion because they stuck together as sisters.

"In the meantime, stick close to the high king." Valinda gripped Mya's shoulders. "Keep an eye on him. I know you can do this."

Mya nodded and drew a deep breath. "All right."

She stepped from the study. Where would she find High King Alexander at this time of day?

As she crossed through the great hall, she found High King Alexander pacing by the windows. At her footsteps, he turned, a broad smile on his face. "I was just thinking it looks beautiful outside. Would you like to go for a walk with me? I believe you mentioned the gardens at Castle Greenbrier are extensive."

As much as she wanted to say no, she couldn't. Valinda had asked her to keep an eye on the high king. Besides, she was supposedly planning to form a marriage alliance with him. It would look odd if she avoided a chance to talk with him.

She forced a smile. "They are."

He stood there, still staring at her.

Oh, right. She hadn't actually said that she'd walk with him. She drew in a deep breath, keeping her brittle smile in place. "I can show them to you." She gestured to the double doors next to the windows.

He held the door open for her, but he didn't offer her an arm. They fell into step side by side, strolling the brick walk that meandered through the garden.

The garden folded in terraces up the side of the hill

toward the main castle keep while below the garden, the castle's large courtyard sprawled at river level, guarded by the outer wall.

High King Alexander studied the courtyard for a moment. He was probably thinking about the underground dancing pavilion that lay beneath that ordinary-looking courtyard where Tuckawassee soldiers marched in formation and practiced with their spears.

Mya needed to stop him from thinking about last night in case he hadn't put the pieces together yet. She waved toward the grape arbors lining the garden path. "These are the riverbank grapes the castle staff uses to make wine."

Probably not the best distraction. He was probably thinking about Mya and Valinda suspiciously giving him wine the past two nights.

High King Alexander strolled along the arbors. "These are impressive."

Mya inhaled the green, sweet smell of the grape leaves. It was too early in the spring for the grapes to start growing, but Mya could picture the bunches filling the arbors in the fall. "These grapevines have been tended here since Castle Greenbrier was built."

"That is a lot of time and care." High King Alexander traced a hand over one of the broad leaves. "It is that kind of history I want to preserve for all of Tallahatchia."

Mya swallowed down the pain in her chest. Why was she feeling this weight in her stomach?

High King Alexander turned to face her, crossing his arms. "I came here in good faith to foster peace. I don't have any agenda other than that."

He knew. Mya's breath caught in her throat. He knew they'd tried to curse him. And yet, he was still here. As if he still held out hope that he could bring about peace.

How could she possibly go through with cursing him tonight? He was a good high king. The type of high king who could bring Tallahatchia together, if Valinda were to give him a chance. Mya might not want to marry him, but just then, she wished she could be loyal to him.

Chapter 20

Alexander

Alex tossed the napkin-wrapped bundle of dinner out the window with a sigh. "This is getting old fast. A week is going to be long at this rate, though I guess we are down to four days at this point."

He held out his hands while Daemyn rinsed them off.

They sat at the table, and Daemyn parceled out the dried meat and camp bread Zeke had sent up. "We can leave early. They tried to curse you, and that means the whole marriage alliance ain't real."

Just a trick to lure him here. Why had he ever hoped it could be a genuine attempt at peace? Or that he could build a loving marriage out of one made for politics?

Alex picked up his camp bread, a round, almost flat roll with a thick texture. "I think I'm reaching Princess Tamya. She seemed almost guilty this afternoon."

"Or she's worried you're on to them."

"They have to already know that I know what they tried last night. It was fairly obvious." Alex took a bite, chewed, and swallowed, pondering his next words. "I'd like to try again tonight to reach her."

"Do you reckon she would turn on her sister?" Daemyn shook his head, tearing a bite from his camp bread with his fingers. "Even if she did, what would it accomplish? Princess Tamya doesn't have any real power. It ain't likely Queen Valinda would hear her out if she went against her plan, whatever it is."

Queen Valinda wouldn't be swayed. Alex had seen it in her last night.

What was he hoping to gain? The Tuckawassee apparently didn't want peace as much as Alex did. Even if he convinced Princess Tamya to be sympathetic to peace, she didn't have the power to make decisions for Tuckawassee.

It might offend Tuckawassee if Alex left early. But what would it matter? They wouldn't dare start an outright war.

Yet things would remain as they were. Tense. On the brink of war. Alex always fearing that he would be poisoned or stabbed in the back or otherwise assassinated.

"I need to try one more night. I need to give this my best possible effort before I can walk away knowing there was nothing more I could do." Alex reached for the canteen but didn't uncap it.

Something inside him went cold as he heard his own words. Was he doing just what he had in Pohatomie? Dismissing Daemyn's advice?

He set down the canteen and met Daemyn's gaze. "But what do you suggest? Do you reckon it would be best to leave now?"

Daemyn leaned back in his chair, staring at the ceiling for a long moment. "It would probably be safer and wiser to leave now. But nothing about this trip has been safe or wise. I reckon, if you want to stay one more night, then we ought to. Besides, our best time to escape the castle will be at dawn. Everyone will expect us to sleep the morning away, giving us a head start."

"You think they'll chase after us? Wouldn't Queen Valinda just let me go? She knows if she kills me, she'll bring the rest of the kingdoms down on her."

"Maybe. We don't know that. The other kingdoms might think that a war over a dead high king isn't worth the deaths." Daemyn shook his head, reaching for another piece of dried meat. "I don't reckon Queen Valinda will take kindly to you slipping through her fingers. If she can't curse you, she may try to kill you."

"Right." Alex stuffed a piece of bread in his mouth and chewed.

"This all depends on you avoiding getting cursed again." Daemyn's gaze knifed into him.

Alex wouldn't help anyone if he got himself cursed that night. Was peace for Tallahatchia worth risking himself again?

What did the Highest King want him to do? Was Alex supposed to go now or stay for one more night?

A breeze curled through the open window, cool with the hint of coming night, and all Alex felt deep in his chest was the conviction he needed to stay. "With the Highest King's strength, I won't be."

Daemyn gave a sharp nod, as if that's all the confirmation he needed. "I'll sneak down tonight, but I'll have to leave early like I did last night. I'll have everything packed by the time you return."

Not that they had much to pack. Just a few sets of clothes and that was about it. But it meant Alex would be on his own once again.

Though, he wouldn't be alone. Not truly. And the Highest King had much more power and control over curses than Daemyn did.

They cleaned up their meal, then took turns stuffing napkins Daemyn had swiped down the back of their shirts. As they finished, the expected knock rapped on the door.

Alex pasted on a smile and opened the door to Queen Valinda and Princess Tamya wearing equally false smiles and carrying a decanter of wine. Did Queen Valinda really think he and Daemyn wouldn't be wise to the whole drugged wine by now? This was now the third night in a row they had shown up on their door looking all suspicious. But, Alex played along anyway. "Queen Valinda, Princess Tamya. Here to bring me wine to help me sleep yet again? It doesn't seem to help me, though my manservant has slept quite well for the past two nights."

Queen Valinda's smile had all the friendliness of a water moccasin snake. "He does seem to enjoy it."

"Ain't that the truth." Daemyn's grin looked even more backwoods bumpkin than it had the nights before. When Princess Tamya handed him a glass, Daemyn took it and appeared to toss it back in a single swig.

Alex shook his head and leaned in to mutter conspiratorially to Queen Valinda, "I never should have hired a manservant from the backwoods. I'd have tossed him back to the hills a long time ago, but he's just so terribly loyal."

If Daemyn was going to use the prejudice many held toward the mountain folk to make the Tuckawassee underestimate him, then Alex would play along. He'd once held those same prejudices, before he'd come to respect Daemyn and his family so much.

Queen Valinda held out a glass of wine to him. "Ah, yes. Good help is so hard to find."

Alex tipped his head back and pretended to sip in a dignified manner, letting the wine trickle along the side of his face and down onto his neck, keeping his head tilted away from Queen Valinda and Princess Tamya as Daemyn had taught him the day before.

Daemyn presented Alex with the lone napkin they hadn't stuffed down their backs. "Your Majesty."

Alex took it and dabbed at his mouth, as if he were dining at a fine event. He handed the glass back to Queen Valinda with the last of the wine still sloshing on the bottom. "Thank you, but I don't believe I will need the rest of this. I won't be sleeping much tonight, will I?"

Queen Valinda smiled but didn't say anything. As if she wasn't sure if she should pretend ignorance or acknowledge what had happened the previous night. Behind her, Princess Tamya shifted and looked away.

Did that mean Alex was getting through to her? He gave another smile. "Very well. I'm sure we'd all appreciate catching a short nap before dancing the night away."

Once again, Alex shut the door in their faces. It was hardly polite, but he could feel wine soaking through the napkins to trickle down his back. It was taking everything in him to keep himself from squirming.

As soon as the door was locked, Alex yanked off his shirt and shook out the napkins. Thankfully, the napkins had caught most of the wine, leaving Alex's shirt showing only a couple of spots near his middle back.

Daemyn's shirt had a few more stains, but far less than it had sustained the first night. Daemyn wiped at the wine residue between his shoulder blades. "That was a good idea to use napkins to soak up most of the wine."

"I need to use my gift of intelligence occasionally." Alex pulled on a new shirt, the one he'd worn the night before that had now dried stiff and crinkly. "Probably would be wise to try to catch a nap before they come back to roust me out of bed."

Daemyn nodded and tossed the entire pile of wine-stained napkins out the window.

Alex crawled into the bed and lay down under the covers. But like last time, he struggled to fall asleep. The sunset blazed outside the window, pouring light into the room.

Daemyn settled onto his cot, turning his face to the wall this time. It would make his back vulnerable when Queen Valinda and her sisters returned for Alex, but it probably would be easier to pretend to be asleep that way.

The sunlight slowly faded outside, night seeping the brilliance out of the sky.

As the sun touched the horizon, the pounding of foot-steps sounded in the hall outside, punctuated with talking and giggling.

Alex didn't bother waiting for the knock. He strode to the door, slid the bolt open, and yanked the door open to find himself face to face with Princess Tamya, her hand raised to knock.

He put on his most dashing smile and held out his arm. "Time to dance the night away?"

Her expression was something between a smile and a scowl, and Alex couldn't tell which was forced and which was breaking through her façade. She took his arm, and he stepped into the hallway, closing the door behind him. Better to keep them from getting a good look at Daemyn pretending to sleep.

In the hallway, Kira skipped up to him, and he held out his arm to her as well. She gripped his forearm with both hands and kept pace with him. "Can you play cornhole with Moriah, Leigha, and me tonight?"

"Of course." Alex grinned down at her. Cornhole sounded a lot more fun than spending the entire night dancing and wondering when Queen Valinda was going to try to curse him again.

The tight dark stairway remained the same, and yet Alex caught his breath as they turned the corner and the glittering forest of gold and silver and gems spread before him. This truly was an impressive place, for all its dangers.

Time to face a third night and hope it didn't end with a curse.

CHAPTER 21

DAEMYN

Daemyn didn't want to leave, but he needed to return to meet Zeke. At the side of the dancing pavilion, Alex had gone back to playing another round of cornhole. After spending several hours tossing the small sack of dried corn at the boards, trying to sink it into the hole, he was getting better. He at least hit the board occasionally now. At the start of the night, Daemyn had struggled to hold in his chuckles as Alex hit several of the surrounding trees and would have hit Queen Valinda if Princess Ranielle hadn't caught the sack.

As much as Daemyn wanted to stay and keep an eye on Alex in case Queen Valinda tried to curse him again, he couldn't.

Daemyn didn't have any trouble sneaking back up the stairs into the room. Once there, he opened the window, dug the rope out from under the floorboards where he'd stashed it, tied to the bed, and tossed it out the window.

He leaned into the darkness and gave an owl hoot. He waited but didn't hear the answering mourning dove call.

After waiting for several moments, he tried again. Nothing.

Where was Zeke? Had something happened? Or was he still communicating with Rosanna and Isi?

Daemyn climbed down the rope, the cold night wrapped around him. As he dropped from the end of the rope to the ground, he sensed he was alone. The darkness felt empty, still. Cloth napkins littered the ground, left where he and Alex had tossed them out the window that evening.

That was unusual. Zeke should have picked them up by now.

"Zeke?" Daemyn whispered, waiting.

Still nothing.

He shifted, peering into the darkness. Something hard crunched beneath his moccasin.

He knelt, inspecting what he'd stepped on. Two halves of an arrow lay on the ground, cracked and laid across each other. In the faint light from the castle, he could just make out the goose-feather fletching, recognizing Zeke's hand in its construction.

This was one of Zeke's arrows. Daemyn's muscles tensed, his blood running cold. This was a distress signal. Had Zeke been discovered and had to leave? Had he been hurt? Daemyn examined the ground as best he could but couldn't see or feel any blood mixed with the dirt.

Would Zeke have had the time to leave an arrow here if he had been on the run from the Tuckawassee?

If Zeke wasn't the one in trouble, then who was?

Rosanna. Daemyn's chest hurt, his stomach churning. If she was in trouble...hurt...

Everything in him itched to leave right now. But he couldn't abandon Alex here. They had to leave together.

Was Alex in danger? Well, more danger than he'd already been in? Were the Tuckawassee working to cut off Alex from outside help? What was their plan?

After grabbing the arrow, Daemyn heaved himself up the rope, rolling over the windowsill into the room. He quickly hauled in the rope and tucked it under the bed, untying it. Even though he would end up tossing it back out the window in less than an hour when Alex returned, he didn't dare risk a guard stumbling across it on a patrol down below or one of the princesses seeing it when Alex returned.

It only took moments to pack. Then, he had to wait. And wonder.

CHAPTER 22

ALEXANDER

Alex tossed a corn sack toward the slanted board several long paces away. The sack arced through the air in a graceful curve and landed several inches short of the board.

"So close." Kira, his teammate, grinned as if his effort was noteworthy.

Dancing in place next to him, Moriah smirked, hefted her corn sack, and tossed it underhand. It flew through the air and plunked straight into the hole.

Even after practicing all night, Alex's aim wasn't as good as theirs, even though they were dancing while they played. Then again, they probably had nights upon nights of practice, while cornhole wasn't a game Alex had played before this.

Alex tossed his last corn sack and this time managed to hit the board, even if he didn't get the sack in the hole.

Queen Valinda glided over to them, a sickly false smile pasted onto her face. "We only have a few minutes of the evening left. Come dance with Tamya, Your Majesty."

Alex had been trying to avoid dancing all evening, hoping that would keep his mind clear. But he probably couldn't refuse. He'd stayed this night to try to convince Princess Tamya to turn against her sister and push for peace.

"Thank you for the rounds of cornhole." Alex bowed to the three youngest girls, bowing to Kira last. "And thank you, Princess Kira, for being a patient partner and losing gracefully alongside me."

Princess Kira bobbed a curtsy, grinning.

Alex faced the dancing pavilion, squaring his shoulders. Hopefully the Highest King would give Alex the words to reach Princess Tamya—to reach all of the Tuckawassee. He held out his hand as Princess Tamya twirled toward him. "Would you like to dance, Your Highness?"

With a glance toward Queen Valinda, Princess Tamya took Alex's hand. He stepped into the dance with her.

As they danced, he caught sight of one of the princesses, Princess Shandra, dancing with one of the vacant-eyed servants, a young man who moved stiffly.

Alex nodded his head in their direction. "What's the story there? Who is he?"

"That's Neill. He and Shandra were close. He sneaked down here and..." Princess Tamya shrugged, pressing her mouth into a thin line as if realizing she couldn't say more without openly acknowledging that Alex had nearly been cursed the night before. "Let's just say he's stuck in our curse with us now."

"Don't give up hope. Curses can be broken. I should know." Alex had to stifle a yawn. His eyes were growing heavier, his feet dragging.

Princess Tamya opened her mouth, as if to say something, but Valinda was there as well, dancing in twirling, graceful moves.

Alex blinked, trying to keep his eyes open. If only he could return to the room and sleep. After sleeping for a hundred years, he'd never thought he'd ever crave sleep like this again.

Was the air thickening? Queen Valinda and Princess Tamya were now both blurs. Were his ears ringing? The ringing built into a melody, wrapping around him, seeping into his bones.

A silver tree trailed its branches over his shoulder, silver leaves fluttering. *Take me. You will never have hardships. Never have burdens. Never have doubts.*

No more doubts. He would never have to make life-or-death decisions again. He wouldn't have to struggle with this bone-deep weariness.

His fingers reached out, brushing the silver branch, then grasping, snapping it off. The cool metal slid against his palm.

He wouldn't have to be the high king.

A whisper of breeze shoved aside the eerie notes, instead carrying the faint remembrance of the true melody Alex had heard on the threshold of Beyond. For that moment, he could think. He could breathe.

Being the high king was Alex's burden to carry. It was the work the Highest King had given him to do, and he couldn't shirk it.

He needed the Highest King's strength. The assurance of the Highest Prince standing before him in the throne room, telling him to come.

The breeze built, filling Alex from his toes to his finger-tips, blasting the haunting melody to silence.

Around him, the princesses continued to dance.

Princess Tamya gaped, eyes wide while Queen Valinda glared, her movements stilted and furious.

Alex bent the silver branch, more difficult than it had been with the gold branch, into a crown and presented it to Princess Leigha with a flourishing bow. "A crown for the princess who scored the most points in our games of cornhole tonight. Your aim and focus are impressive."

Princess Leigha burst into a broad smile and placed the crown on her head, wedging it between the two puffs into which her curls had been styled. "Thank you. For the crown and for playing with us."

"I'm glad I could make the night pass enjoyably." Alex bowed again. He might be failing at securing a marriage alliance with Princess Tamya, but he would at least walk away not hating this family, for all they had tried to curse him. Twice.

The culvert above the waterfall brightened. Sunrise. All around him the princesses stopped dancing, and Alex breathed a sigh. He'd survived another night.

This time, Daemyn's footsteps had dried, and Alex didn't have to throw himself into the lake. Though, without the shock of the cold water waking him, Alex trudged up the stairs, barely able to keep his eyes open. He covered a yawn as he stumbled from the trapdoor into the corridor.

A soft bed awaited him. Sleep. After staying up all night for three nights in a row, it was all he could do to trudge forward. Around him, the sisters were yawning and blinking, the energy draining from them with each step.

At his door, he forced himself to pause, turn, and smile. "Thank you for another interesting night."

Without waiting for a response, he stepped inside his room, locking the door behind him. He closed his eyes, leaned against the door, and said in a low enough tone anyone listening outside wouldn't be able to hear, "Can we catch a few hours sleep before we leave? I'm not in any shape for castle escapes at the moment."

When he glanced up, Daemyn had climbed to his feet, his mouth tight. He held out the two halves of a broken arrow. "Zeke wasn't there this morning, but he left this. The family's signal for danger. I climbed the mountain and tried to signal Rosanna but didn't receive an answer."

That might as well have been lake water dumped over Alex's head. He wasn't tired now. He straightened and pushed off from the door. "All right."

Daemyn tossed Alex's pack to him. "Reckon we ought to wait a few minutes. Don't want any of the princesses peering out their windows and spotting us."

As tired as the princesses were, they wouldn't have to wait long.

While Daemyn retrieved the rope from under the bed, Alex hefted his pack onto his back, letting the weight settle between his shoulder blades. His pack mostly contained clothes, and, if they were desperate, he could abandon it. But, for now, he'd take it along in case spare clothes became handy.

As Daemyn tied the rope around the bedpost, Alex picked up Daemyn's pack. "She's all right, Daemyn. If the Tuckawassee had attacked, then why would they leave us alone?"

Daemyn gave two hard tugs on the rope, checking it was securely tied to the bedpost. "They could be moving to cut us off from help."

"Captain Taum, Captain Degotaga, and Rosanna are very capable. Even if they were attacked, they most likely escaped." Alex rested a hand on Daemyn's shoulder.

Daemyn had sacrificed a hundred years. Surely he wouldn't lose Rosanna too. Alex would do everything in his power to prevent that from happening. "We'd best—how would you say it—light a shuck on out of here."

Daemyn's shoulders relaxed, and he braced himself on the windowsill. "Your mountain accent really is terrible."

"I know. But it took your mind off fretting for a moment." Alex scrubbed his palms on his leggings. He wasn't looking forward to climbing down the wall of the castle. Feats of strength and agility were not his talents.

But it was either climb down the castle wall or stay here with Queen Valinda.

The wall didn't look so bad after all.

CHAPTER 23

TAMYA

As the afternoon sunlight streamed through her window, Mya lay in bed, unable to force herself to get up.

How had High King Alexander resisted the curse a second time? This time, the silver branch had barely started twining around his wrist before it stopped. What kind of man was he that he could resist?

Was it possible their curse could be broken? Before Valinda had interrupted with the dance, High King Alexander had been about to tell Mya more about curse-breakers. What if there was hope for Shandra and Neill? If Mya could rescue Neill, she could bring happiness to one of her sisters, at least.

But doing so would be treason in Valinda's eyes. Valinda wouldn't want their curse broken. She enjoyed the power it gave them. Her plan hinged on being able to control all the kingdoms of Tallahatchia through this curse.

Did Mya want this curse broken? What would her life look like if she wasn't forced to dance through the night?

No, more importantly, what would life be like for her sisters? The younger girls seemed all right now, but would they become just as hardened as Valinda and Mya? Would they be as desperate as Uma? Heartbroken as Shandra?

If High King Alexander could show Mya how to break this curse, then Mya needed to figure out a way to ask. Without Valinda finding out. Valinda would be furious if Mya ruined her plans, but if Mya could free all of her sisters, it would be worth it.

She pushed out of bed, but as she reached for a dress to change out of her nightgown, a knock sounded on her door. "Who is it?"

The door swung open, and Valinda marched in, already dressed in a bright purple gown. "High King Alexander snuck out of the castle this morning."

What? Mya froze, gripping her dress, as any hope of asking the high king's help to break the curse vanishing. "What are you going to do?"

"Track him down." Valinda crossed her arms, glaring past Mya toward the window. "I've already sent soldiers after him. With Colonel Beshko between him and the border, he won't get far."

"Do you think that's wise? What will the other kingdoms do if we forcibly haul him back?" Mya hurriedly changed out of her nightgown into the pink dress she'd grabbed. "We can't afford another war with the other kingdoms. We need to focus on rebuilding. Maybe it would be best to let him go."

"Let him go?" Valinda took a step forward, her jaw tightening. "Father died for this cause, Mya. Our ancestor King Hakan willingly fell into the cursed sleep with the high king for the good of Tuckawassee. Don't you get it?

We can't give up now. We have to push toward victory for
our kingdom."

"But what about our family, Valinda? Do you really
think pushing us toward arranged marriages to conquer
Tallahatchia is what is best for us?" Mya jabbed a finger at
Valinda. "Maybe now is the time for peace. Perhaps
Tuckawassee would find more prosperity in peace than we
have in war."

"You've gone soft." Valinda's mouth curled, her eyes
sharp. "Instead of you controlling the high king, he's
turned you against your kingdom and against your family."

"It's not like that, and you know it." Mya clenched her
fists at her sides, matching her sister glare for glare. "Our
family means everything to me. We're sisters. You know
how much I'd do for all of you."

"How far will you go?" Valinda shook her head. "Seems
to me your love for us has limits. There are things you
aren't willing to do."

Yes. Because there was such a thing as right and wrong,
even if Mya wasn't sure which was which at the moment.

The high king wasn't the man Father and Valinda had
made him out to be. He wasn't a power-hungry tyrant.
Maybe the high kings had once been that, but no longer.
High King Alexander was someone who would listen to all
the kingdoms of Tallahatchia and would make changes that
would benefit Tuckawassee.

But she didn't dare say that out loud to Valinda. Was
Valinda right? Was Mya turning traitor against her family
and her kingdom if she supported the high king? What was
truly best for their family?

Valinda rested her hands on Mya's shoulders, squeezing
gently. "I know this hasn't gone as we planned. But rulers
have to make tough choices and do things that normally

would seem deplorable, for the good of the kingdom. When you become high queen, you'll understand."

Mya gave a snort. "Do you really think that's an option now? He knows this was all a trap. He knows we tried to lure him into a curse, and now he's fled. There isn't anything more we can do."

She tried to keep the hope from her voice. If High King Alexander escaped, Mya wouldn't have to marry him. He wouldn't be cursed, and Valinda couldn't force their sisters into arranged marriages without the weight of the high queen behind her to make the other kingdoms want to ally themselves with Tuckawassee. Perhaps then Valinda would try for genuine peace, once all her options for war and subtle conquering were out of her reach.

Valinda smiled, patting Mya's shoulders before stepping back. "Oh, don't you worry about that. By the time we capture him, he will have no choice. Mark my words. I will make you high queen one way or the other."

CHAPTER 24

ALEXANDER

Alex groaned as he came awake due to someone's persistent shaking. It had taken him far too long to get to sleep curled on the hard ground, even though he'd been exhausted. "It can't be time to move. We just stopped for a rest."

"It has been three hours." Daemyn's voice was roughened with his own exhaustion. "We need to keep moving."

Alex peeled his eyes open and pushed into a sitting position. "Remind me again what the Tuckawassee will do if they catch us?"

"Probably kill both of us. Colonel Beshko will definitely torture me." Daemyn's voice was rather dry and flat considering he was talking about torture.

But it was the motivation Alex needed to shove the rest of the way to his feet. His muscles ached from the miles he'd hiked since dawn. His hands throbbed from the times he'd slid on the rope lowering himself out the window and down the castle wall. His bones hurt from sleeping on the ground in the few hours of rest Daemyn had allowed. And, to top it all off, his eyes scratched from lack of sleep.

Daemyn had done all the same things, though he hadn't gotten rope burns on his hands, and he'd had just as little sleep as Alex. Yet he was unflagging.

Alex no longer had a pack. They'd sent those down the river in a canoe shortly after escaping Castle Greenbrier. Maybe the Tuckawassee would find the wreckage at the bottom of Rantahala Falls and assume they'd died.

He fell into step behind Daemyn as they trudged along the side of the mountains sloping down to the Tuckawassee River below. "Maybe we've lost them."

"Ain't likely." Daemyn glanced over his shoulder as he skirted around a boulder. "Not with the trail you're leaving."

Alex glanced behind him, but he didn't know what he was looking for. He'd been trying to walk carefully, but apparently it wasn't enough. "What am I doing wrong?"

Daemyn grimaced. "Too much. We ain't got the time to learn you proper."

He was going full on mountain in his speech. That wasn't good. Daemyn must be more worried about the Tuckawassee tracking them than he was letting on.

Alex slid in Daemyn's wake down the side of a gorge. A small creek filled the bottom, and Daemyn hopped from the slick rocks and crossed. Alex managed the first couple of rocks, but when he jumped to a third, his foot slipped into the creek.

As they hiked up the other side of the gorge, Alex huffed and tried to keep up. The truth was Alex was slowing Daemyn down. Daemyn could probably have disappeared without a trace if Alex wasn't with him.

Alex and Daemyn were currently headed toward the

cabin where Rosanna and the guards had been holed up. Would Alex's trail lead the Tuckawassee right to them? If Rosanna hadn't already been in danger, she would be after Daemyn and Alex arrived.

Alex drew in another panting breath as they reached the top. "Maybe we should head for the border with Neskahana. It's closer, and it would avoid bringing danger to those we left at that hidden cabin."

Daemyn's shoulders were hunched as he hiked up the next ridge. "It would be closer. But the terrain is rough between Tuckawassee and Neskahana. We would have to hike a long way into Neskahana before we would reach the nearest border post. The cabin isn't far from a border fort, and my family should be gathering nearby."

"And you want to make sure Rosanna is all right."

"That too." Daemyn wasn't even breathing hard as they climbed.

Alex couldn't blame Daemyn for his worry. Rosanna, Isi, and Zeke were Alex's friends. Some of the few friends he had in the entire kingdom. If they had been put in danger because of him...

He concentrated on climbing the ridge, panting loudly enough he couldn't even hear the tramping of his own feet. He was in better shape than he'd been before he'd started shooting the Gaulee rapids in the mornings with Daemyn, Rosanna, and the others, but he still wasn't as fit as Daemyn.

Ahead, Daemyn froze, going still as the trees around him. It took Alex a second to process that he should freeze as well. He tried to gain control of his breathing, his heart pounding too fast in the silence.

Daemyn lowered himself to a crouch, eyes flicking over

the forest farther up the ridge to their left, the area between them and the far-off border with Neskahana.

Alex eased forward to crouch beside him. "What is it?"

"Someone's up there. Probably the Tuckawassee cutting us off." Daemyn gripped his quarterstaff in one hand, his long knife with the other, though he didn't draw it. "There's a stream ahead. If we can get to it, we may be able to slip past them."

That didn't sound encouraging. Alex rested a hand on the dagger he wore at his belt. Perhaps it was an odd choice of weapon, since it was the same dagger King Hakan had used a hundred years ago to send Alex into his cursed sleep.

But Alex carried it as a reminder of his own weaknesses. Of how easily he could fall.

Besides, at this point, it was just a dagger. It had always been just a dagger. How its previous owner had put it to use was not its fault, and, maybe, Alex could turn its legacy into something better by using it to defend himself if necessary. A dagger was, after all, the one weapon he had trained himself to use, hoping that training would spare him the cursed sleep.

If that was a war party of Tuckawassee on the mountain above them, Alex's dagger wasn't going to do him much good.

Daemyn crept forward, stopped behind a boulder, and gestured. Alex followed as quietly as he could, each footstep still crunching far too loudly on the layer of dead leaves blanketing the forest floor.

They worked their way along the ridgeline. Alex struggled to keep his breathing even and quiet, as his heart raced.

A loud chattering, screeching sound burst through the quiet, coming from above Alex's head. He flinched and glanced up to see a squirrel perched on a branch far above him, tail swishing in time with its warning chatters.

Daemyn grimaced but didn't glance at the squirrel. He didn't have to say it. Thanks to that squirrel, everyone in the area knew exactly where they were. As if Alex's footsteps hadn't been enough noise already.

Alex swallowed, but his mouth remained dry. His underarms felt sticky, his shirt clinging to his sweaty skin. He trailed Daemyn, trying to match his footsteps as precisely as possible.

Daemyn halted behind a rock outcropping. "The stream is just ahead."

Alex nodded, not trusting himself to speak. Even if they reached the stream, would it be enough? How could the two of them outdistance the Tuckawassee? Especially with Alex slowing them down so much.

If he had been braver, he would have told Daemyn to go on without him. To escape while he still could.

But Alex wasn't brave enough for that. Nor did he think Daemyn would listen. Daemyn was awfully stubborn like that.

Daemyn set off along the rock outcropping, keeping low. Alex stayed right on his heels. From the rock outcropping, they crossed a section of forest, headed for a pile of brush collected around a fallen tree at the edge of a steep downhill that probably led to the stream.

The stream was so close. Only a few more yards. A few more feet.

Daemyn crouched behind the pile of brush. His back went rigid.

What was it? Alex knelt next to him and peered through the tangle of brush and fallen branches. His stomach dropped into his toes.

A squad of Tuckawassee warriors had pulled their canoes onto the bank. They were alert, spears at the ready, gems glittering in their hair. Packs of provisions mounded on the shoreline near a boulder.

As they watched, more Tuckawassee came around the bend in the river and pulled their canoes onto the bank. Colonel Beshko splashed to the bank and spoke in a low voice with one of the men scanning the hillside with narrowed eyes.

Searching for Alex and Daemyn, now that she had been alerted to their escape. Alex resisted the urge to scrunch deeper into the pile of brush, knowing the movement would make noise and draw the eye of the watchers below. Alex's mouth was drier than the dead leaves around him. He tasted a sour, bitter something that reminded him of bile and sweat. His chest ached from the pounding of his heart against his ribcage.

Tromping feet rustled the forest farther up the ridge behind them. Daemyn eased deeper into the brush, shoving Alex into the shelter of a fallen branch.

Down below, one of the Tuckawassee gave a whooping yell. An answering yell came from the mountainside above, and again straight behind them.

They were surrounded. Alex glanced at Daemyn. Even Daemyn might not be able to get them out of this one.

A slow smile crossed Colonel Beshko's face, visible even from Alex's hiding spot. "Daemyn Rand. I know you're cornered on that mountainside. You might as well turn yourself in."

Daemyn remained perfectly still, as if he were a stone on the mountainside.

Alex barely kept himself from flinching. What were

they going to do now? They had no hope of fighting their way out of this.

Did that mean they should march down there and surrender? Was that any better of an option? That would just get both of them hauled back to the Tuckawassee where they would most likely be killed.

Colonel Beshko gestured, and one of her soldiers reached behind the boulder by the shore and hauled something into view.

Not something. Someone. Princess Rosanna stumbled forward, hair tousled from her long, black braid. Her right arm dangled limply at her side while her left hand pressed to a large, red splotch over her right shoulder. Red soaked the front of her buckskin shirt.

"Well, Daemyn Rand? Did you really think I wouldn't search for your hideaway after you escaped from me last time?" Colonel Beshko waved at Rosanna. "It would be a pity if she bled to death."

"Don't do it, Daemyn! Get out of here!" Rosanna struggled against the Tuckawassee soldiers holding her. The Tuckawassee stuffed a rag into her mouth.

Daemyn muttered under his breath, his muscles tense. His gaze remained locked on Rosanna. "Your Highness, I'm going to turn myself in. I'll cause enough of a ruckus it will draw the rest of the Tuckawassee there. You should be able to escape. Head north for the Neskahana border."

Alex glanced from Rosanna to Daemyn, torn. That was Rosanna down there, and she was hurt. He got that. He wanted to march down there and help her as well.

But Daemyn turning himself in wouldn't help her. It would just get Daemyn killed along with her. Surely there had to be a better plan than that.

"Daemyn, think for a minute." Alex gripped Daemyn's

arm, though he wouldn't be able to stop Daemyn if he got it in his head to walk down there no matter what. "They aren't going to let Rosanna die. She's a princess of Neskahana. My death might lead to war, but her death definitely would. We're better off escaping and helping her later."

Daemyn's gaze flicked briefly to Alex before focusing, pained, on Rosanna again. Rosanna sagged against the Tuckawassee warrior holding her, head hanging, blood soaking her buckskin shirt. "Alex, she don't have long. She's lost a lot of blood."

"I understand. But we don't know they'll even let you help her. We need to get out of here." Alex tried to keep his tone reasonable even as he whispered. Daemyn was supposed to be the calm, calculating one in dangerous situations, not Alex.

"We ain't both getting past those warriors up the mountain. You go. I'll distract them." Daemyn didn't even bother glancing at Alex that time.

That all sounded well and good. Noble even. If Alex didn't know the real reason Daemyn was doing it. "I'm not you. I can't escape by myself. I don't have the skills. You know as well as I do that I'll end up getting myself hopelessly lost before the day is out. So don't pretend to be all heroic right now when you're really being foolish."

For the first time, Daemyn was choosing something other than his duty to Alex. This wasn't a choice Alex wanted to force him to make. He knew once Daemyn married Rosanna, she would have to come first.

But there were times Alex's safety would still be important. As long as Alex had a duty to rule Tallahatchia, then Daemyn had a duty to protect him. Until Alex officially released him or Daemyn resigned,

Daemyn was still his bodyguard, sworn to guard him with his life.

Down below, Rosanna had sagged to her knees. She lunged at the legs of the Tuckawassee, but her lunge was more a tottering sway.

Colonel Beshko gripped Rosanna's braid and yanked her head up. "This wound will start to fester if that arrowhead isn't removed soon."

Daemyn glared at Alex.

Alex glared right back.

Daemyn's gaze didn't waver. "It ain't a great plan, but it's all we got. You ain't getting past those warriors up there with or without me. Not without a distraction. And I ain't leaving Rosanna down there alone. Colonel Beshko ain't shy of roughing people up some, even if she don't plan to kill them. Better she get her fill of torture on me than Rosanna. So I'm going down there whether you like it or not."

There wasn't any budging him, not when he was this set on it. Alex would just have to do his best not to fall off a cliff or wander in circles until he starved to death.

"Fine. What way is north?" Alex huffed out a breath. Daemyn's family was supposedly gathering in these mountains somewhere. Hopefully Alex would run into a few of them before he had to wander too far by himself.

Daemyn jabbed a finger in the direction of the steep mountain slope. "That way. Hunker down here until the Tuckawassee are past you, then do your level best to hightail it as quietly as you can."

Alex nodded. That sounded like something he could, hopefully, handle.

Daemyn met his gaze, returned the nod, and crept along the fallen log until he'd put several yards between him and Alex. Even Alex lost sight of him as he ducked behind a large stand of trees.

Alex didn't spot him again until Daemyn stepped from behind a tree halfway down the steep slope.

Daemyn had his hands resting on the top of his head as he strode toward the Tuckawassee, though his wooden staff was balanced across his shoulders, held in place with his arms. "Very well, Colonel Beshko. You have me. Just let me help her."

Alex turned away. He didn't want to watch. He needed to keep himself focused on his mission. Escape.

Daemyn's steady tread was joined by the rustling of several pairs of feet rushing him. Then the sounds of a scuffle. The whistling, then whack of Daemyn's wooden staff slamming into a body.

Alex faced north, muscles tensing, ducking low in the brush. On the ridge above him, the Tuckawassee stepped out of hiding, hurrying toward the fight.

This was Alex's chance. If he could just bide his time, slip past them...he glanced over his shoulder.

The Tuckawassee had Daemyn on his knees, Daemyn still struggled, his movements growing more and more frantic, desperate, as he fought to reach Rosanna's side. "Just let me help her. Please. She's hurt." His voice deepened into a growl. "Let me help her."

Alex sighed, hanging his head. He couldn't leave. His chances of making it alive to the Neskahana border on his own were slim to none, even if he made it past all the Tuckawassee. Odds were, he would just end up getting an arrow in the back rather than successfully escaping.

There was nothing for it. With a deep breath, Alex stood, holding his hands above his head. "Let him go to her, Colonel Beshko. You can hold a knife to my neck if you're worried he will try to escape. He won't try anything while you have both me and Princess Rosanna."

Colonel Beshko didn't move, as if she still wasn't going to allow Daemyn to help Rosanna. How hard-hearted was she? Even Alex could see Rosanna was in bad shape.

Alex held her gaze, staying where he was. Behind him, feet tromped on the leaves, coming to apprehend him. Time for him to apply his intelligence and a little logic. "Princess Rosanna needs care. Your queen might decide to kill her, but that decision isn't up to you. You need to keep the princess alive, and unless you have someone else trained and willing to provide her the care she needs, than you had best allow Daemyn Rand to aid her."

Colonel Beshko flicked her fingers. "Release him."

As soon as the soldiers let go, Daemyn was at Rosanna's side. The guards gripping her released her, and she sagged against Daemyn. He cradled her as he lowered both of them to the ground.

Alex's view of them was cut off as the Tuckawassee surrounded him. He didn't resist as they grabbed his arms, hauling him forward.

Queen Valinda might kill him, but Alex couldn't regret turning himself in. Not when Rosanna lay pale in Daemyn's arms, blood soaking her shirt and now Daemyn's. Apparently Colonel Beshko was hard-hearted and cruel enough to deny care even when she logically should give it.

Alex had been there a year ago when Daemyn had died of old age in Rosanna's arms, and Alex had asked the Highest Prince for Daemyn to live. Now, Alex found himself asking again.

Rosanna needed to be all right. Over the past year,

she'd become one of Alex's few friends. He cared what happened to her.

One of the Tuckawassee reached for Alex's dagger to disarm him, but Alex shook off the hands that gripped him and glared at Colonel Beshko. "There's no need to tie us or disarm us yet. We aren't going anywhere while she's hurt, and we'll need our knives to help her."

Colonel Beshko must have realized Alex was right. Or she didn't want to have to deal with Rosanna's wounds herself.

Alex knelt next to Daemyn and Rosanna. "What do you need me to do?"

"I..." Daemyn's hand was pressed to Rosanna's wound, but even Alex could see the tremble in his fingers. "Water. We'll need boiling water. Supplies."

Alex patted Daemyn's shoulder. "I'll take care of it. You take care of Rosanna."

When Daemyn nodded, Alex stood and faced Colonel Beshko. "Please see to lighting a fire and boiling water."

Colonel Beshko crossed her arms. "You wished to assist. You have my permission to make a fire, Your Majesty."

Years ago, Alex would have been offended. He would have seen making a fire beneath him. Not to mention he wouldn't have known how.

Now, Alex let out a long exhale and bowed his head. "As we sent our supplies over the Rantahala Falls, I would appreciate the use of tinder and flint."

First a fire. He couldn't handle escaping by himself, but he could do this.

CHAPTER 25

DAEMYN

Daemyn's hands shook. Rosanna's blood was warm on his fingers, her breaths shuddering against him.

She was hurt, and he couldn't take away her pain. Even helping her would cause her more agony.

Rosanna's hand gripped his sleeve, leaving bloody fingerprints on the buckskin. "You shouldn't have turned yourself in. They'll kill you."

"Don't fret none about me." Daemyn eased her to the ground, then unsheathed his long knife. "That arrow has to come out."

"I know." Rosanna's teeth were gritted, even as she met Daemyn's gaze. "I can tough it out."

He smoothed her hair from her face, feeling the sweaty warmth of her skin. A result of the pain. "Hold on, Ro, love." He cut the shoulder of her buckskin shirt, widening the opening to get a better look at the injury.

"A nickname. The wound must look bad." Rosanna squeezed her eyes shut.

The broken end of the arrow shaft stuck from the wound. Daemyn swallowed back the heat in his chest. Colonel Beshko hadn't even taken the time to remove the arrowhead from Rosanna's shoulder. Then again, Colonel Beshko was much better at putting arrows into people than taking them out in a medically-sound manner. Daemyn wouldn't trust her to take out this arrow without hurting Rosanna more.

If this injury didn't heal properly, Rosanna would never have the strength in her shoulder that she once had, making paddling and steering a canoe difficult, taking away something she loved dearly.

If only Zeke were here. Daemyn knew enough about wounds to tend Rosanna's, but he was more experienced with yanking arrows out of himself during the hundred years when it hadn't mattered if he caused more damage. But this was Rosanna. She deserved far better care than he could give her.

"Would you prefer I spoke in bear puns?" Daemyn picked out a few scraps of her shirt from her wound. Rosanna's brothers Willem and Berend used bear puns all the time, one of the first things Daemyn had learned when he'd started courting Rosanna.

Rosanna sucked in a breath, but she gave an attempt at a laugh. "Please, no bear puns. I'm in enough pain as it is."

At least he'd gotten a smile on her face.

Alex knelt and held out what looked like the remnants of someone's linen shirt. Hopefully it was clean. It wasn't Alex's, at least, which was sweat and dirt streaked. "Here are some clean rags you can use for bandages. I set water to boiling, but it will be a few minutes."

"Thanks." Daemyn took one of the rags and pressed it

to the wound. He gestured to the dagger Alex still wore belted to his waist. The dagger's thinner tip would work better for digging out the arrow than the thicker long knife Daemyn had. "Hold your dagger over the flames to heat it. That should cleanse it."

What Daemyn wouldn't give for some of Frennie's moonshine. Nothing cleaned out a wound like her moonshine. The stuff was not fit for drinking and volatile enough to be downright dangerous around a fire. But it served well to stop infections.

Alex drew his dagger and retreated to the fire he'd built. The Tuckawassee stood in a circle around them, spears pointed at them, but not interfering. Colonel Beshko had her arms crossed, ready to fill them full of arrows or spears if one of them made a wrong move.

With one hand still pressed to Rosanna's wound, Daemyn unbuckled his belt and held it out to her. "Here. Bite this."

She did as she was told, biting down on the leather.

He ran his fingers over the back of her shoulder. No blood. The arrow hadn't gone all the way through. That would be both a good thing and a bad thing. The arrow hadn't gone too deep, but it wouldn't be as easy as pushing the arrowhead the rest of the way through to get it out.

"I need to..." Daemyn swallowed. His hand was shaking again as he probed the wound, feeling how the arrowhead lodged against her collarbone.

Rosanna's body went rigid, eyes squeezing shut, a moan in the back of her throat.

"I'm sorry." He smoothed her hair back again. "I know it hurts."

Drawing in a shaking breath, Rosanna peeked up at

him and managed a smile around the belt she clamped between her teeth. She reached up and squeezed his hand.

She was strong. She would get through this, if Daemyn was strong enough to do what needed to be done.

Alex knelt next to him and held out the dagger, its blade glowing. "The water is ready."

"Fetch it here." Daemyn held up the dagger, letting it cool. Hopefully he wouldn't have to cauterize the wound.

Alex returned lugging a bowl and a kettle of water. He poured some of the boiling water into the bowl and dropped in one of the rags. "Where do you need me?"

Daemyn couldn't put this off any longer. Time to get that arrowhead out. "I need you to hold her down, especially her right arm."

This would hurt. Daemyn didn't want to do this. He'd rather be the person lying there, arrow-shot. He'd take whatever pain necessary, if he could've spared her.

Rosanna pulled the belt from her mouth with her good hand. "Do what you need to, Daemyn. You've had worse."

"I had a lot of practice." Daemyn touched her cheek. "It's going to hurt something fierce."

She grimaced at him. "Stop shillyshallying and get this arrow out of me already." She stuck the belt back in her mouth and bit down.

Alex pinned Rosanna's right arm to the ground, then he reached over and held out his other hand. "I know I'm not Daemyn, but he's going to need both of his hands free."

Rosanna gripped Alex's hand, squeezing tight enough Alex winced.

Daemyn drew in a deep breath, trying to steady his hands. He eased the tip of the knife into the wound, using it along with his fingers to ease the broadhead from

Rosanna's shoulder. Blood slicked warm and sticky against his fingers, making it difficult to get a grip on the arrowhead.

Rosanna stiffened and gave a small cry in the back of her throat, but she didn't scream.

"You're mighty brave. Almost done." Daemyn eased the arrowhead the rest of the way out.

Rosanna wrinkled her nose, showing she knew he was lying through his teeth about being almost done.

After tossing the arrowhead aside, he swished the rag in the now cooling water, wrung it out, then washed the wound. Rosanna arched her back and moaned as he washed inside the gash, searching for any fibers or dirt.

He kept up his soothing reassurances, as much to keep himself calm as her.

When it was as clean as he could make it, he reached for the pile of supplies Alex had left laid out on a blanket. He located a needle and thread, bandages, herbs. Everything he'd need.

He stitched the wound, put on a poultice of mountain laurel, and wrapped her shoulder with a secure bandage.

"All done." He breathed out a long breath and washed his bloody fingers in the water before drying them on one of the last, clean rags. He still had dried blood crusted around his fingernails, but at least the sticky warmth of her blood was gone.

Rosanna turned her head and spat out his belt, releasing Alex's hand.

Alex slumped back, shaking his hand. "I think you broke my fingers."

"Sorry." Both Rosanna's voice and smile were shaky, but she managed them.

Daemyn swiped away the lone tear that trickled down

her cheek. She hadn't burst into tears. She hadn't screamed or begged him to stop. She'd been brave, far braver than he'd felt seeing her hurt and bleeding.

The point of a spear prodded his back. "Hand over your knife. It's time to move."

Daemyn pinched his long knife between two fingers to make it obvious he wasn't going to resist and held it out.

But when two of the Tuckawassee moved past him and reached for Rosanna, he shoved them back. "Don't touch her." His voice had a growl to it. Something in his chest felt feral and about ready to bite any hand that reached for her. "I'll carry her."

Alex stood, brushed off his knees, and faced Colonel Beshko with his head high. Even without a crown, dressed in dusty buckskin pants and a blue linen shirt that had seen better days, Alex managed to look every inch a high king. "We turned ourselves in peacefully. There's no need to tie us. We can't go far, and Daemyn won't be able to attempt an escape while carrying the princess."

Colonel Beshko held Alex's gaze for a moment, then turned and started barking orders.

Daemyn never thought he would've been thankful for Alex's presence. Apparently Daemyn needed Alex to be the clear-headed one at the moment. He'd been planning to lecture Alex on the foolishness of not escaping when he had the chance, but perhaps in this case, Alex knew what he was doing.

Not that any of their chances of survival were that great at the moment.

Colonel Beshko organized her force of warriors, sending those with canoes on ahead while the rest gathered packs to make the march back to Castle Greenbrier. Based on the orders Daemyn could overhear, Colonel Beshko figured she could keep a better guard on Alex, Daemyn, and Rosanna if they were hiking than if they were in canoes. A good swimmer might risk a jump over the side of a canoe and successfully evade capture. But none of them could avoid the Tuckawassee archers if they made a run for it in the forest.

Rosanna was struggling to push herself to a sitting position while keeping her right arm tucked close to her body.

"I got you." Daemyn eased his arms beneath her knees and around her back, hefting her from the ground.

"I can walk." Rosanna's teeth were gritted, her breathing ragged. But she was alert, muscles poised.

"I know." With her in his arms, he could murmur into her ear in a low enough tone the surrounding Tuckawassee wouldn't be able to hear. "Save your strength for when it's needed most."

She gave a small nod and leaned her head against his shoulder, gripping his shirt with her good hand to keep herself steady in his arms.

Right now, she probably felt strong enough to walk. But they had miles to hike to reach Castle Greenbrier. Attempting such a hike would set Rosanna's injury to bleeding, and the blood she'd already lost would tire her.

If she risked tearing the stitches, it had best be for an escape attempt with a good chance of success. Not for this hike.

Daemyn straightened, Rosanna's added weight burning through his muscles. Hopefully his own strength wouldn't give out carrying her.

Alex stepped closer, whispering. "We can take turns. You need to conserve your strength as well."

"Thanks." Hopefully Alex realized the gratitude was

for more than the offer to help carry Rosanna. For a hundred and twelve years, from the moment Daemyn turned ten and became Alex's manservant, Daemyn had looked out for Alex the best he could. It was strange to have the roles reversed as Alex looked out for him and Rosanna. For the past year, they'd called themselves friends. But in that moment, Daemyn finally felt how true it was.

The spear was back, prodding Daemyn's lower back. "Move."

Daemyn glanced around at the assembled Tuckawassee forming a tight squad surrounding them. No hope of escape anytime soon. Not that he, Rosanna, and Alex could get far even if the Tuckawassee left them an opening.

As the spear prodded again, Daemyn strode forward, cradling Rosanna to him as gently as he could as he trudged over the rough terrain. Alex was dragged into line behind the Tuckawassee menacing Daemyn with the spear.

Rosanna's eyes were closed, but she murmured in a low voice even the Tuckawassee behind them wouldn't be able to hear. "The others got away."

Daemyn ducked under a thin branch, using the movement to put his mouth close to her ear. "What happened?"

She held so still, no one would be able to tell she was talking to him unless they looked directly at her. "They jumped Isi and me yesterday evening as we hiked to the top of the mountain to wait to signal Zeke once it got dark. Reckon they were aiming for Isi, but I shoved her out of the way and distracted the Tuckawassee long enough for her to get away and warn the others. Captain Degotaga is going to be furious."

At himself more than anybody. He took his duty to protect Rosanna very seriously. To the point Daemyn suspected Captain Degotaga would continue to see himself as Rosanna's bodyguard even after she and Daemyn were married.

Daemyn bent to slip beneath another branch. "At least they got away."

That was fifteen people out there who could help. Sixteen counting Zeke. He would have hightailed it toward the cabin the moment he couldn't contact Rosanna and Isi as planned.

"My brother Berend showed up at the cabin yesterday. Apparently he wandered into Tuckawassee while Father was marching Neskahana's army toward the border just in case we got into trouble. Father must be furious." Rosanna's breathing hitched as he jostled her while dodging a branch the Tuckawassee in front of him had let whip toward his face.

That meant there were seventeen people who would be coming to help, though it was debatable how much help Berend would be even if he was a bear at night.

But at least Neskahana's army was poised at the border. If the Tuckawassee intended to kill Alex, Daemyn, and Rosanna, Neskahana's army wouldn't arrive in time, but at least they would have the comfort of knowing vengeance for their deaths wouldn't have to wait long. If knowing a war would be sparked by their deaths could be considered a comfort.

"And Josiah reported to us that most of your relatives have gathered at Aunt Frennie's. Zeke will report to them what happened." Rosanna shifted her head against his shoulder.

In the hundred years Alex had been sleeping, Daemyn had never needed of the family quite like this. They'd rallied to his call, but what would they be able to do against the Tuckawassee warriors and the might of Castle Greenbrier's walls?

Still, it was a comfort knowing help was coming.

If only it would arrive in time.

CHAPTER 26

ALEXANDER

Alex's whole body ached by the time Castle Greenbrier appeared on the next mountain ridge, its square tower and straight walls framed by the setting sun hanging low on the horizon.

Daemyn carried Rosanna once again, though Alex had done his best to take a few turns. She rested her head on his shoulder. After all the jostling her shoulder had taken, her eyes were squeezed shut, mouth pressed tightly in a line.

Alex straightened his shoulders as they were directed into canoes waiting for them on the bank. The Tuckawassee must feel secure hauling them across the river here, knowing it would be foolish to jump into the river now with the Rantahala Falls only a short way downstream.

Daemyn laid Rosanna into the center of a canoe before he was separated from her at spear point and forced into a different canoe. Alex was forced into a third canoe.

The Tuckawassee crossed the river, then disembarked

on the far side below the castle, dragging Daemyn, Rosanna, and Alex along with them.

Once again, Alex found himself hiking the switchback trail from the river to the castle. Last time, he'd wondered if he'd ever leave the castle alive. Well, he'd left. But here he was, getting dragged back. This time, he definitely wouldn't leave this castle alive if the Tuckawassee had any say in it.

He glanced over his shoulder. Daemyn carried Rosanna in his arms again. None of them were likely to make it out alive.

The door into Castle Greenbrier creaked open, its darkness closing around Alex before the gates slammed shut behind them, as if all of Castle Greenbrier was their prison.

Most of the soldiers remained behind, but Colonel Beshko and what appeared to be her handpicked soldiers marched Alex and Daemyn carrying Rosanna straight to the royal wing, arriving as Queen Valinda and her sisters were gathering in the hall to make their nightly trek to their underground dancing pavilion.

Queen Valinda took one look at them and smiled. "Excellent. Bring them below."

A spear jabbed the small of Alex's back. Forcing him to walk down those stairs to what would probably be his death.

As he made the final turn in the stairs, the forest of gold and silver trees glittered just as brilliantly in the light of the mirrored lamps. The gemstone leaves and gravel shimmered. So much light and beauty for a place so deadly.

The princesses crowded onto three of the barges while Colonel Beshko and her four handpicked soldiers shoved Daemyn, Rosanna, and Alex onto the fourth barge. They barely had room to pole across the lake, the barges sinking so low in the water they were in danger of going under if anyone shifted their weight in the wrong direction.

On the other side, Alex was shoved from the barge onto the gemstone shore and marched down the path. He tried to take in the forest, the danger, his own weariness pressing in on him. But a part of him was just numb. Detached. The strangeness of eleven princesses and one queen bursting into dance amid shining, otherworldly trees while he was surrounded by warriors with their spears trained toward him buzzed in his head.

At the dancing pavilion, Daemyn set Rosanna down next to one of the trees. Fresh blood marred the bandage at her shoulder while sweat dotted her forehead. The hike hadn't been easy on her. He touched her cheek, murmuring to her.

Alex stepped forward to see if he could help, but a spear blocked his path. He glared at Queen Valinda. "She needs care. It will not go well for Tuckawassee if the princess of Neskahana dies in your castle."

Queen Valinda raised her eyebrows as she twirled past him, smirking as if she didn't care that Rosanna's death would cause a war. She flicked her fingers as a gold tree reached with its branches and wrapped around Rosanna's waist, pinning her to the smooth trunk.

The silver tree next to it grasped Daemyn's arms. He struggled, fighting to stay at Rosanna's side, even as the tree dragged him back against its trunk.

Alex expected one of the other trees to grab him, but none of them did. Instead, Queen Valinda motioned, and Colonel Beshko gave the order for her soldiers to take up positions at the edge of the pavilion, spears still at the ready.

At the far side of the pavilion, Princess Tamya had gathered the rest of her sisters, hugging Kira to her even as all of them danced in place. "Valinda. What are you doing? The younger girls shouldn't have to see this."

"Shouldn't they? Why shouldn't they witness the rise of our kingdom?" Queen Valinda's smirk never wavered as she approached Alex, dancing in a circle around him. "They should know this is what our father wanted. They are orphans because he gave his life for this."

Moriah and Leigha hugged Princess Uma while Kira glanced between Alex and Valinda, her eyes wide. "He's our friend."

"Don't you see what you're doing?" Princess Shandra had her fingers clenched. She sent a pained look toward the young man in the guard's uniform that stood with the cursed servants. "Wasn't Neill enough?"

Queen Valinda huffed and flicked her fingers in her sisters' direction.

Colonel Beshko marched around the dancing pavilion until she and two of her soldiers stood near the princesses, as if prepared to restrain their own royalty if Queen Valinda gave the order.

Alex gestured toward Daemyn and Rosanna. "Let them go. Your quarrel is with me."

"Is it? That's Daemyn Rand. He killed our father. And Princess Rosanna aided him. We have plenty of reasons to want both of them dead along with you." Queen Valinda continued her slow, dancing circle around him.

"Is that what you plan to do to me? Kill me?" Alex planted his feet rather than follow her circling. He didn't want to end up dizzy. "How will that help Tuckawassee? All you'll get is more war."

"Will the other kingdoms go to war over you? Or will

they see avenging an already dead high king too much of a cost after a hundred years of war?" Her voice was sharp as the glittering lamplight around them.

"You'll be risking your kingdom's future on that chance. And, even if the kingdoms wouldn't go to war over me, they would go to war over them." Alex pointed to Daemyn and Rosanna again. Rosanna rested against the tree, face pale and drawn, while Daemyn still struggled, though the thin silver might as well have been iron.

Queen Valinda's mouth turned twisted, her eyes widening, into such a fake expression of innocent shock Alex nearly gagged. "Where am I to blame in this? You are, after all, the one who refused my generous hospitality and left Castle Greenbrier, slighting all of the Tuckawassee. And after you had claimed your only intention was an honorable, peaceful mission."

"Cut the act. There's no one here who doesn't already know your true intentions." Alex had been up for thirty-six hours with only a few naps to keep him going. He didn't have the patience for her word-twisting. "I know you had no intentions of peace. For the past two nights, you've tried to drag me into your curse." He pointed toward the five servants standing by the refreshment table, staring off into the distance, ignoring the scene playing out before them. "You tried to turn me into your mindless puppet. Hate to break it to you, but you failed."

"How? No one has ever been able to resist for long. No one who has taken a branch has shaken it off." Queen Valinda's dancing steps turned into a stalking prowl around him.

The air pressed down on him, carrying a heavy, sweet smell. Strains of music crowded around him, eerie and lilting. The room blurred as he struggled to breathe through the music.

A tree branch fashioned of twining gold and silver with diamonds for leaves reached out to him, tenderly, invitingly. *Take me, and you won't have to die tonight. Take me, and you'll live. You'll be happy. Content. You'll have peace.*

He found himself reaching, his fingers brushing the diamonds. Peace was everything he wanted, except...

A puff of breeze wafted against his cheek, brushing against his fingers. He withdrew his hand, focusing instead on the breeze and the different music it carried. The music he'd heard while standing on the threshold of Beyond.

What the curse promised wasn't peace. Peace wasn't mindlessness. It wasn't abdicating his responsibilities and duties.

Peace was kneeling before the throne of the Highest King and being heard, rather than turned away. It was trembling in awe rather than stark terror. Peace was knowing he'd failed and still having the Highest Prince reach a hand to him and pull him to his feet.

With the music of Beyond filling his ears and the fresh, light scent of forest in his chest, Alex reached for the branch again. Not for himself. Not to abandon his burdens and duty. But to prove to those watching that the Highest King's strength flowing in him was stronger than their cursed dance.

The gold and silver snapped in his hand, the diamond leaves tinkling against each other. But the branch was just a branch. It didn't move, even as he held it out to Queen Valinda. "I resist because the Highest Prince is with me. The strength of the Highest King sustains me. And the Breath of all Breezes fills me."

Queen Valinda snatched the branch with a tiny,

growling shriek and tossed it to the ground before dance-stomping a few steps away.

If the breeze hadn't still been so strong around him, Alex might have felt more fear seeing her fury. The pretense was gone. All that was left was for her to decide how she wanted to kill them.

Queen Valinda's shoulders straightened, and she whirled in her dance to face him, her far-too-sweet smile back on her face. Her purple dress swished around her, complemented by the gold of her crown and the amethysts and jet woven into the pile of her hair on her head. "If that is how you wish to play this, then fine."

She gestured to the servants. Daemyn's blank-eyed nephew Ted grabbed a decanter of wine, poured it into a glass, and marched it over to Queen Valinda.

Queen Valinda pulled on a pair of gloves, then removed a tiny leather pouch from a pocket of her dress. She dumped a portion of the contents, an orange-white powder made from what looked like a ground root of some kind, into the wine and swirled it around for a few moments.

"Valinda..." Princess Tamya stepped forward, but she was blocked by Colonel Beshko and her spear. All five of the soldiers were now standing by the princesses, holding them back.

Then, with a smile, Queen Valinda presented the glass to Alex. "This wine is poisoned with water hemlock. One sip will kill you. But I will give you a choice. Either you drink this and die a horrible and painful death or..."

"Or..." Alex stared at the goblet. Whatever peace he'd felt a moment ago fled, and he had to clasp his hands behind his back to hide their shaking.

"Or you give this to your manservant and he dies. But you will be free to go."

Alex could see right through that to Queen Valinda's scheme. "I'll be free, but you'll blackmail me with my choice whenever you want me to do something for you."

"Of course. You wouldn't want Buckhannock and Neskahana, your closest allies, to find out that their precious high king made such a choice." Queen Valinda waved her hand, as if that was a small thing. "But you'll be alive and will have more freedom than under the curse as I had originally planned. You can tell the kingdoms whatever story you wish about what happens here, and I will only ask a few favors now and then. A good compromise."

A good compromise that would leave both Daemyn and Rosanna dead, since that was the only way this blackmail plan would work.

"Valinda, don't do this." Princess Tamya still danced even as she squirmed against Colonel Beshko's restraining grip. "This isn't the way to achieve peace or prosperity for Tuckawassee."

"Father poisoned a high king. I am just following his footsteps. I am always his perfect little girl." Queen Valinda glared at her sister, her posture straight.

"Father was wrong. This is wrong." Princess Tamya struggled, but she couldn't break free of Colonel Beshko.

"You've already done enough harm." Princess Shandra broke away from the other girls to stand next to the still cursed young guard. "This needs to stop."

Princess Uma had all three of the youngest girls pressed against her, holding them close with the rest of the girls crowding in close behind them. Princess Ranielle danced, fists clenched in front of them. The Tuckawassee guard facing her held Ranielle's confiscated spear.

Alex glanced over his shoulder to Daemyn.

Daemyn's face twisted, pained, as he glanced at Rosanna before his shoulders slumped. "I'll drink it."

Alex's chest ached. Daemyn. Always the perfect manservant to the bitter end. He'd died—well, mostly died —nine times in order to rescue Alex from the cursed sleep. No matter how much it had cost him, he had never shirked his duty. Never turned away because something was too hard or too painful.

"Let him drink it." Queen Valinda's purring confidence was back in her voice. "You can't save him regardless. I've promised Colonel Beshko she can kill him. You might even be doing him a favor by letting the poison kill him. I can guarantee Colonel Beshko's method will not be any quicker or less painful. One of you has to die. Why should both of you?"

"I'll drink it." Rosanna struggled to sit more upright against the tree, her eyes glassy with pain.

"No, Rosanna." Daemyn shook his head, meeting Alex's gaze. "It has to be me. You know it does, Your Highness. Your life is worth more than mine."

Was it? Alex was the high king. The last of his line. If he died, all of Tallahatchia would fall apart.

But Daemyn was the one with something to live for. He had Rosanna, a future, his large extended family. He had done far more to hold Tallahatchia together in the past hundred years than Alex ever had. If Alex died, Daemyn would see to it that Tallahatchia didn't fall.

No, the truth was, neither of them was worth any more or any less than the other. Before the throne of the Highest King, they were both worthless. And, yet, they had both walked where only the worthy were allowed to walk because the Highest Prince, the only true worthy one, had claimed them as his.

Alex's stomach clenched, his hands shaking. He knew what he had to do. Everything in him shook, bile threatening to climb up his throat. It wouldn't do any good to pour out this glass of wine. Queen Valinda had more poison. She had enough guards she could force them to their knees, force Alex to choose.

She was right. One of them had to drink that poison, and Alex knew exactly which of them it had to be.

He reached out with trembling fingers and took the cup of poisoned wine from Queen Valinda. He strode toward Daemyn, earning a broad smile from Queen Valinda.

Daemyn held his gaze, his expression pained. When Alex halted a few feet away, Daemyn drew in a deep breath and spoke in a low tone. "Make sure Rosanna gets out of here alive. Please."

Alex held up the glass, the crystal winking in the lamplight, the wine dark as blood. "You have already sacrificed so much for me. It's about time I sacrificed for you."

"What do you..." Daemyn stared, brow furrowed.

Alex lifted the glass toward his mouth. His hand shook so violently wine sloshed over the rim and spilled onto the marble floor of the dancing pavilion.

Daemyn's eyes widened. "Alex. No. Don't."

The glass was cold against Alex's mouth. He steeled himself, trying to gather the courage to drink his own execution.

"Alex!" Daemyn struggled against the silver tree holding him. Frantic. Wild. "Don't you dare! Alex!"

He couldn't think about it. Just one swallow. That's it.

Footsteps scuffed on the marble behind him. Queen

Valinda, perhaps, racing as fast as she could while dancing to try to stop him. This wouldn't have been her plan. She would've been sure he would choose any option other than dying himself. If he had been the selfish, arrogant high king she'd believed him to be—as he'd once been—then she would've been right.

But thanks to the Highest King, Alex was not that man any longer. Even as his stomach heaved, his body fighting against the thought of drinking that poison, Alex had never been more certain that this was the right thing to do. This cup of poison belonged to him. Had always been meant for him.

Perhaps the line of the high kings was always meant to die out like this. Alex would die just like his father had. Poisoned with water hemlock by the Tuckawassee.

Drawing on every scrap of courage the breeze had given him, Alex tipped the glass back. And drank.

The wine was sweet, cold, but held a hint of a bitter, carrot-flavored aftertaste.

The footsteps grew louder. As he tipped the glass for a second mouthful, it was dashed from his hand. Glass shattered, crystal shards and blood-red wine spilling across the white marble.

Queen Valinda faced him, glaring. "What have you done?"

Alex wiped his mouth on his sleeve. "I did as you ordered. I made my choice."

She gaped at him, her feet and arms still moving in her dance, as if she couldn't comprehend the thought of anyone—especially a high king—willingly choosing to die to spare someone else.

Behind her, Daemyn stared at Alex as well, still as the tree keeping him captive.

Maybe, by doing this, Alex could buy Daemyn and Rosanna time. Enough time for Daemyn's family to figure out what had happened and stage a rescue. Colonel Beshko's torture might be slow, but torture was survivable when rescued.

A rescue Alex wouldn't live to see.

He was going to die. Alex swallowed, the bitter taste of the poison lingering on his tongue. There was no antidote for water hemlock. No cure. In all likelihood within two hours or less, he would inevitably be dead.

For all his courage, his hands were still shaking. His heart pounding.

Even now, he didn't want to die. He didn't.

He didn't have a choice about it now. Somehow, he'd have to endure the agony of the next two hours.

Just two hours. Two excruciating hours.

Focus on the threshold. On the WaterVeil separating this life and Beyond. Think about it parting, the Highest Prince taking his hand, pulling him through. Stepping into the throne room without the last Veil drawn between him and the Highest King.

Beyond awaited, no matter what the next two hours held.

Alex drew in a deep breath and straightened his shoulders. This would be his last act as high king. To die with as much dignity as he could muster.

He pushed past Queen Valinda and strode across the dancing pavilion. As he approached where Colonel Beshko still restrained Princess Tamya, he motioned toward the soldiers. "Release them."

Perhaps they were stunned by what had just happened, but even Colonel Beshko obeyed him, her fingers sliding almost numbly from Princess Tamya's arm.

Alex forced his hands and legs to steady. He swept into a bow. "Princess Tamya, would you do me the honor of dancing with me?"

She took his offered hand, studying him. "Dancing will just make the poison move through your system faster."

"I know." He pulled her onto the pavilion, matching his dancing steps to hers.

Faster or slower, it wouldn't matter. He had drunk the poison. He was dead already.

Chapter 27

Tamya

Mya had never seen anything as brave as High King Alexander taking that goblet and drinking that poisoned wine. Why had he done it? He could have easily ordered his manservant to die instead. It's what Valinda would have done.

But not the high king. In that moment, Mya had seen a glimpse of those old stories about honorable, self-sacrificing kings who truly cared about the people they ruled.

A hint of a breeze stirred the hair by her face. If a legend like a noble king could be true, then were the stories about cursebreakers true as well? Was there hope?

She held on to him as he whirled them through a dance, feeling all eyes in the room focused on them. She needed to ask, while she still had the chance. His time was running out, and her chance at saving her sisters and rescuing Shandra's Neill along with him.

Valinda had retreated to her throne, dancing in front of it as if content to wait to make her next move until after the high king succumbed to the poison. Perhaps Valinda had enough sense not to give Colonel Beshko the order to start torturing Daemyn Rand right then and there while Kira, Leigha, and the rest of the younger girls were watching.

For the sake of her sisters, especially Shandra, Mya needed to find out if the high king knew of any kind of hope to break their curse.

"You broke your curse." Would he even tell her anything, after what her sister had done to him? How he must hate their whole family. And she couldn't blame him. Up until a few minutes ago, she'd gone alone with Valinda's plan. She'd drawn the line at murder, but that didn't excuse her for not stopping it sooner at entrapping him in a curse.

But when she lifted her gaze to his, she didn't find hatred. Or even anger. A bit of tired resignation, maybe. Even a hint of fear.

His mouth tipped into a smile. "The Highest King used Princess Rosanna to break the curse. I didn't do anything."

"Cursebreakers are real?" She so desperately needed him to say yes. She'd thought she'd recognized how trapped she and her sisters were in this curse, but now this place felt suffocating.

"Yes. They are real because they point to the true Cursebreaker. That's how curses work. They are given so that they can be broken." High King Alexander spun her outward, before pulling her in to face him once again. "There is a cursebreaker for you and your sisters. I know that because the Highest King has promised it, and he never fails his promises."

A cursebreaker. Hope. Mya wasn't even sure how to take it in.

That waft of breeze stirred again, brushing aside the jangling notes Mya had always danced to.

Wasn't that what Mya's mother had told them in the whispered stories before bedtime? Stories about promised cursebreakers and the Highest King's gifts?

For all these years, Mya and her sisters had always focused on the curse to dance all night. The curse had ruled their life. Somewhere along the way, they had seen the curse as a gift that made them powerful.

Yet, that wasn't how it should be. The curse wasn't the gift. Dance itself had been their gift. A gift they had never focused on using the way it ought. They had embraced the curse when they should have clung to the gift.

The breeze built around her feet, ruffling her skirt, carrying with it a new melody unlike anything Mya had heard before.

Right now, they danced because they were forced to. Or because it gave them power.

Simply dancing for themselves wasn't enough. Perhaps it wasn't as obviously evil as dancing to trap people, but it still wasn't what the gift of dance was meant to be.

If Mother's long-forgotten stories were right, if High King Alexander was right, then the gift of dance was meant to be used for the Highest King.

The breeze swirled around her now, from the worn soles of her dancing slippers to the tips of her fingers. The music it carried shivered through Mya, something of unearthly notes and strains she shouldn't be able to hear.

She stepped from High King Alexander's grip, closing her eyes. This was the music her fingers and toes had been longing to dance to all her life, even if she'd never realized it. It filled all the cracks and crevices inside her, as if this music was made of light itself.

She launched into a dance unlike anything she'd ever danced before, following the lead of the breeze and the music it carried.

This was the gift of dance. It was something that demonstrated the beauty in the way the body moved, glorifying the one who'd designed such strength and elegance in muscles and joints. It bared the soul for those watching, asking their hearts to glorify the Highest King along with the dancer.

Mya tipped back her head and laughed as she spun and leaped into the air. Even if her curse was never broken, this was freedom and peace and everything she'd wanted for her sisters.

As she spun again, she opened her eyes and found herself facing High King Alexander. He had picked up the branch with leaves of diamonds that Valinda had discarded. A sheen of sweat coated his forehead, his breathing coming far too rapidly. But his hand only trembled slightly as he formed the branch into a crown and held it out to her. "I trust that your curse will be broken, even if I won't live to see it."

Why did a lump fill her throat at that? She hadn't managed to fall in love with High King Alexander or even find a way to be attracted to him.

But he was a good man and a noble high king. He shouldn't have to die.

She slowed her dance. The compulsion to dance was still there, but the heaviness and darkness to it had been pushed aside. She bowed her head to let the high king place the makeshift crown on her hair as he had her little sisters. She didn't care if it was a disrespectful move to Valinda, as if Mya were the queen of Tuckawassee receiving her crown from the high king as it had been in the days of old.

The weight of the gold and silver branch settled against her hair, and, in that moment, Mya felt something shift and shatter.

For the first night in her life, her feet slowed to a halt, and she stopped dancing.

In front of her throne, Valinda stood still, fists clenched, eyes widening. "No. Impossible."

Mya glanced over her shoulder. Her sisters were standing still, glancing at each other as if in shock or disbelief or confusion at what to do. Beside them, the five servants blinked, staring about as if stepping from a dark cave into an unexpectedly bright day.

"Neill!" Shandra dashed forward and threw herself at Neill.

For his part, Neill caught her and held her close, though he was still blinking and glancing about as if trying to figure out what had just happened.

"The curse is broken." Mya stared at her unmoving, not-dancing feet before lifting her gaze to High King Alexander. "You were our cursebreaker."

"I'm a cursebreaker." High King Alexander gave a laugh, closing his eyes for a moment and tipping his face upward, as he pressed his arms to his stomach. His voice came out strained, even with his light-hearted tone. "That's something I never thought I'd hear. I thought I was better at stumbling into them than breaking them. But I guess the Highest King is pleased to use even me to…"

The high king trailed off, his face twisting, going a shade of gray-green. He took a few stumbling steps to the side before he collapsed to his knees, vomiting.

"Alex!" Now that the curse was broken, Daemyn Rand was straining to bend the silver branches enough to free himself. Even injured, Princess Rosanna worked with her good arm to bend the gold branches holding her.

"Uncle Daemyn." One of the servants rushed across the room to yank on the silver branches.

Colonel Beshko raced after him, raising her staff. The servant spun on his heels, broke a branch off a nearby tree, and swung it up in time to block Colonel Beshko's strike. Daemyn Rand broke the last of the silver branches restraining him and surged to his feet. After planting himself between Colonel Beshko and Princess Rosanna, Daemyn swung one of the broken branches at the colonel's head.

What should she do now? Mya glanced from Daemyn Rand and the servant fighting Colonel Beshko and her guards to Valinda shouting orders. Their sisters huddled with wide eyes while High King Alexander still hunched on the ground, vomiting as if he was trying to hurl out his internal organs.

"We should give him this." Uma stepped forward, carrying a glass of water. She pulled a pouch similar to Valinda's from her pocket and poured gray ash into the glass, stirring with her finger.

"You brought some of the charcoal?" Mya glanced from the glass to Uma. The specially heated and powdered charcoal was the only thing the Tuckawassee healers had discovered that helped give someone poisoned with water hemlock a chance of surviving. "Why?"

"I had a hunch Valinda might do something like this and I just..." Uma shrugged and looked away, holding out the glass to Mya. "It just seemed better to be prepared."

Sweet Uma, of all of them, had been prepared to stand up to Valinda. Perhaps Mya had underestimated her sister, not seeing the depths she had beneath her agreeable, motherly nature.

Taking the glass, Mya approached High King Alexander, avoiding the splattered vomit as best she could. "Here. Drink this."

"What is it?" High King Alexander gasped between panting breaths, one arm clutched over his stomach, the other bracing himself against the floor. Sweat beaded on his forehead, his face pale as the marble beneath him.

"It isn't more poison, I promise." Mya forced herself to crouch next to him, fighting her gag reflex at the stench of vomit. "It's charcoal. Try to drink and keep down as much as you can. As far as we can tell, the charcoal helps absorb the poison. It may give you a slim chance of surviving this."

He took the glass with shaking fingers, barely able to bring it to his mouth. But he chugged it down, grimacing. He gagged, swallowed, and hunched over, breathing hard.

"What are you doing?"

Mya turned to find Valinda marching toward her. "Trying to save his life."

"He needs to be dead. Father wanted him dead." Valinda's fingers curled a moment before she lunged, as if intending to strangle the high king with her bare hands.

Mya tackled her. They landed on the marble, and Mya struggled to pin her sister down. "This isn't right. This isn't what Mother would have wanted."

"Let go of me." Valinda shrieked and grabbed Mya's hair, yanking, clawing, and screeching. "Guards!"

Mya dug her nails into Valinda's hands, trying to force her sister to let go. Pain flared along Mya's scalp, hot tears filling her eyes. Her own savage scream came from her throat as she fought back, biting her sister's hand hard enough that Valinda hissed and let go of Mya's hair.

Several of the soldiers rushed over, but Ranielle jumped between them and Mya, wielding the spear she must have reclaimed in the initial confusion.

Mya rolled out of her sister's reach and scrambled to her feet. "Valinda, it doesn't have to be like this."

"Traitor." Valinda hissed, her muscles tensing to spring at Mya again. The skirt of Valinda's purple dress hung in tatters at the hem while her large, gold crown lay discarded on its side at the base of the throne. "Guards, kill her."

The four guards hesitated, shifting as they glanced from Valinda to Mya. They were loyal, yet even they hesitated at the order to kill a princess of Tuckawassee.

Beside Mya, Ranielle faced all four of them, spear at the ready. "If you want to kill Mya, you'll have to go through me."

Mya clenched her fists. Ranielle was good, but she couldn't hold off four guards by herself. Nor would Mya be a lot of help. She had always been more interested in infrastructure than fighting.

"You'll have to go through me too." Uma joined Mya on her other side, standing tall.

"And me." Quinna crossed her arms and stepped up beside Uma.

"And us." Shandra and Neill stood on Ranielle's other side.

Then all of Mya's other sisters were with her. Panya, Octavia, Nakeisha, Moriah, and Leigha stood around Mya with glares and crossed arms. Even eight-year-old Kira had her fists clenched.

"Traitors! You're all traitors!" Valinda screeched. She hurled a handful of gems from the ground in their direction.

The guards shifted and backed away, as if fearing she

would give an order to kill them all. Behind them, Daemyn Rand and the servant held off Colonel Beshko. Off to the side, Rosanna knelt beside High King Alexander, her injured arm tucked to her side while she gripped a silver branch in her other hand, looking prepared to defend the high king. High King Alexander had fallen to the ground and now curled in a fetal position.

"We're not traitors. We're standing for Tuckawassee." Mya straightened her spine and stared her sister down.

Valinda shrieked and launched herself forward. Ranielle lashed out with the end of her spear and knocked Valinda aside right as Daemyn and the servant tossed Colonel Beshko backwards.

Valinda and Colonel Beshko went down in a heap at the edge of the pavilion.

"I smell something weird." Kira tugged on Mya's sleeve.

Mya sniffed. Now that Kira mentioned it, there was a strange stench to the air. Like really strong alcohol. And something else she couldn't put her finger on.

Across the pavilion, Daemyn Rand stiffened. His gaze snagged on something, though Mya couldn't tell exactly what he was looking at. His gaze snapped back down to the rest of them. "We need to get out of here."

Colonel Beshko climbed to her feet and brandished her spear at Daemyn. "You aren't going anywhere."

"No, we really need to get out of here." Daemyn glanced somewhere above Mya's head, then he threw himself at Rosanna, taking both of them to the ground. Daemyn shielded both Rosanna and High King Alexander with his body.

Mya turned, searching the wall behind them. What was—

A whump vibrated into the ground. Fire jetted from the culvert above the waterfall, heat flashing across Mya's face.

Then the wall exploded.

Chapter 28

Daemyn

Daemyn protected Rosanna and Alex as stone and water burst into the underground room. A wave of cold water crashed over Daemyn's back, a few stones pounding into him.

They couldn't stay here. That wall was holding back the might of the Tuckawassee River. Now that the upper wall had been breached, the river would spill over the top, flooding this entire room in minutes.

With an arm around Rosanna's waist, he clambered to his feet, dragging her upright along with him.

Alex staggered to his feet for a moment before collapsing back to his knees in the water, dry heaving and shaking.

The initial burst of water had receded, but the waterfall now gushed in over the wall of bedrock. Several inches of water sloshed around the sides of the dancing pavilion. The ground vibrated, cracks appearing in the upper part of the wall and the ceiling.

If the water didn't get them, the ceiling caving in would. The entire castle courtyard and walls could collapse on top of them.

A few yards away, Colonel Beshko grabbed Queen Valinda and dragged her toward the forest of gemstone trees. At the tree line, Queen Valinda paused, glancing back at her sisters.

A rumble filled the air as the river pushed aside a few more of the foundation stones of the castle on either side of the culvert. Another wall of water slammed into Daemyn's knees, and he reached out to steady Rosanna. The younger princesses tumbled, swept away in the flood, while Alex tumbled and crashed against Daemyn's legs.

Queen Valinda turned and dashed into the gold and silver trees, leaving her sisters behind. In all the chaos, Daemyn wasn't sure anyone but him had even noticed her departure.

Chunks of the ceiling crashed down, splashing into the water covering the floor, cracking through the forest of gold and silver trees. Terrified screams filled the air.

Daemyn gripped Rosanna's elbow. Her stance remained shaky, her eyes too bright. Blood soaked her shirt all the way to her waist.

He needed to get both her and Alex out of there. They should be his priority.

And yet, he hesitated to leave while the young princesses dashed about screaming and cowering beneath the gold and silver trees as if those would be strong enough to save them. Someone needed to stay and help get everyone out.

"We need to get everyone out of here." Rosanna pulled out of his grip to stand on her own. "I'll get Alex out.

Wounded as we are, we won't be much help. You concentrate on everyone else."

It went against everything in him to leave her and Alex's side at a time like this, especially when both of them were so weak.

But he had to trust Rosanna. She wouldn't offer if she didn't believe she could get herself and Alex out in one piece.

"All right." Daemyn lifted Alex from the ground. "Rosanna will get you out of here, Your Highness.

"Leave me." Alex shuddered, his voice strained. "I'm dying anyway. Get the others out of here."

"Daemyn will get the others out." Rosanna took Alex's arm over her good shoulder. "And I'll get you out. Don't try to protest. I'm not leaving you behind. So either you do your best to come with me, or all of us are dying down here."

That seemed to give Alex the strength. He and Rosanna staggered a few steps toward the path through the forest toward the lake and the stairs.

The whole center of the ceiling gave way, the stone splintering through the forest, rubble blocking the paths. More of the wall collapsed, flooding into the lake.

Rosanna and Alex skidded to a halt. The few princesses who had dashed into the forest now raced out of it again, though Queen Valinda and Colonel Beshko didn't reappear. Daemyn tried to get a head count of the remaining guards, servants, and princesses but everyone was moving and screaming.

Reaching the stairs on the far side of the lake would be nearly impossible now. Were they trapped? Would they have to wait for the water to rise until it was level with the river and hope they weren't crushed or swept downriver?

Ted appeared at Daemyn's side, his black curls dripping water and a cut across his temple. "Uncle Daemyn, I have a back way out of here. There's a hidden door in the back wall where we servants have been going in and out."

Daemyn didn't waste time questioning Ted on what he remembered from when he was under the curse. That back way probably led into that locked door in the kitchen the cook had disappeared into when Daemyn was scouting. "Go. Get the door open."

Ted nodded and raced away, headed toward the inside wall with a large painting of mountains.

With one last glance at Daemyn, Rosanna hurried after Ted, dragging Alex along with her. Alex gamely hobbled alongside her.

Daemyn forced himself to turn away. He trusted Rosanna, with her life and with Alex's.

Turning to the nearest group of servants and guards, Daemyn gave one a shove in Ted's direction. "Follow him. He has the way out."

The guards nodded, and together they and the two servants raced for the exit.

A large crack split the ceiling above them, pebbles raining onto their shoulders. The younger princesses scattered once again, running, screaming. They were terrified, several of them running toward the ruined forest. Colonel Beshko and Valinda might have made it through, but it wasn't a safe route now.

The floor shook. Another wave of water.

Daemyn dashed through the knee-deep water to the first group of princesses. Princess Uma had Princess Moriah, and both of them were shaking as they stood frozen next to one of the pavilion columns. Daemyn pointed toward the door Ted had pulled open, leaving a black opening where a painting of a mountain had once been. "That direction. Go."

Another rumble and cascade of rubble. A cry of pain.

Daemyn waded toward the sound. Princess Ranielle tugged on Princess Shandra where she had been partially pinned beneath one of the pillars on the other side of the dancing pavilion. The last servant, a young man in a guard uniform, was attempting to lift the stone by himself.

Reaching their side, Daemyn helped the young man heave on the stone, rocking it enough to free Shandra.

When Ranielle dragged her sister to her feet, Daemyn pointed. "Get out of here. Go. That way."

The water was nearly at his waist. He pushed through, fighting a growing current.

More debris splashed into the water around him. Everything shook. Walls collapsing. More screams of pain and terror.

Two of the Tuckawassee soldiers floundered past with Princesses Leigha and Nakeisha. Both girls were crying. Princesses Quinna, Panya, and Octavia rushed toward the door.

The water was past Daemyn's waist. A fist-sized rock smashed into his shoulder, sending him stumbling into the water, his arm going numb before pain shot through his body.

He forced himself to his feet. They were still missing Princess Tamya and Princess Kira.

"Princess Tamya! Princess Kira!" He wasn't sure his shout would even be heard over the roar of water and grinding stone.

"Here!" Princess Tamya's voice came from the other side of a pile of rubble.

Daemyn scrambled over the pile before splashing back into water that reached his chest.

Princess Tamya held Princess Kira to her as she struggled to slog through the rising water. The little girl was sobbing, face pressed to her sister's shoulder.

Daemyn reached their side. "This way."

He helped them around the pile of rubble. The current strengthened, the water now at Daemyn's shoulders. Princess Tamya stumbled and plunged underwater. When Daemyn yanked them to the surface, Kira shrieked between coughs, hugging her sister tighter.

Daemyn kept a hold of Princess Tamya, keeping her and her sister from being swept away. "Get her on my back." He had to shout above the roar of water, the rumble of collapsing stone.

Tamya tried to pry Kira from her, but Kira was too scared to be reasonable. Her tight grip could drown both of them if something wasn't done.

There wasn't time to be gentle. Daemyn dragged Kira from Princess Tamya, slinging the girl onto his back. She wrapped her arms around his neck, clinging to him by instinct.

Beside him, Princess Tamya was working at the laces of her gown, letting it drop so she was clad in her chemise. Good. She probably would've drowned in that gown, and Daemyn was thankful she'd thought of it before he'd had to embarrass both of them to point it out.

Where was the exit? With the rising water, piles of rubble, and spray and dust filling the air, it would be easy to become lost.

There. Daemyn caught sight of the back wall, the only wall still fully standing. None of the door remained visible above the water, but the tip of the mountain in the mural jutted above the rising water.

He tugged Princess Tamya forward, swimming with Kira on his back. The water roiled with collapsing walls and swirling currents, threatening to drag them under.

If they didn't make it to the door in time, they would be trapped until the water level rose high enough someone from the ground level could reach them. By that time, the water current would probably have dragged them over the far wall and into the Tuckawassee River, where they would have to fight to get to shore before they were dragged over the Rantahala Falls just downstream of the castle.

Giant cracking sounds split the air. Pebbles rained onto Daemyn's head. He glanced up, catching sight of the remnants of the ceiling splitting apart overhead. "Move!"

He stroked through the water as fast as he could. Tamya matched his pace, thankfully a strong swimmer.

Chunks of rock splashed into the water behind them, showering them with spray. The undertow dragged Daemyn under, and Kira near choked him in panic. He shoved his way upward, gasping a breath of air as soon as his head broke into air.

Princess Tamya was treading water ahead, waiting, the tense set of her jaw relaxing as her gaze snapped to him.

"Go!" He motioned her forward, swimming at her heels.

The wall was just ahead. More of the ceiling came down. Farther away, a mighty groan of rock and whoosh of water sounded as something large collapsed.

His fingertips brushed the wall, then he gave one last stroke and pressed himself against the shelter it provided. Princess Tamya pressed her back to the wall, gasping for breath. Next to her, the top of the mountain in the painting was only a few inches above the water. The doorway was fully submerged.

"How far does this stay level before it rises into stairs?" Daemyn pointed at the door. If it stretched in a long corridor before reaching a set of stairs, they probably wouldn't be able to hold their breath long enough before they found the surface again. Kira certainly wouldn't.

Princess Tamya's face scrunched. "I only took these back stairs once when I was little. The servants would set up for us before we arrived and disappear after we left. But I think it turns into stairs right away before it levels out at the servants' quarters beneath the main part of the castle."

Hopefully she was right. If not, they would have to wait here as the water continued to rise and hope they survived the collapsing ceiling and walls. "All right. You go first, and I'll be right behind you. If I reckon we won't make it, I'll grab your ankle, and we'll turn around."

She nodded, her face set. She reached over Daemyn's shoulder and patted Kira's back. "You need to be brave, all right, Kira? Hold your breath and hold on to Daemyn Rand. He's going to get you out of here."

Daemyn felt Kira's nod against the back of his neck. He squeezed her hands where they were clutching him around his neck. "It's going to be just fine, princess. Just fine."

With one last look at her sister, Princess Tamya heaved in a deep breath and dove through the doorway, now fully covered by water.

"Take a deep breath." Daemyn felt Kira's body expand against his back before he gulped in a breath and dove beneath the churning, brown water.

The doorway was black in front of him. He pushed toward it, grasping the edges of the doorframe and propelling himself inside.

He reached forward as he swam, feeling the swirling disturbance in the water from Tamya's kicking ahead of him. His fingers brushed stone, feeling its contour.

A stair step.

He peered upward. Was that a faint light far above? It had to be, since he could see Tamya's silhouette as she pushed through the water toward it.

He followed, the light growing brighter, brighter, until his head broke the surface. Kira coughed and gasped in a breath, her weight warm against his back in the cold water.

"Valinda? Is Valinda up here?" Tamya's voice came from ahead by the cluster of people holding lamps and candles.

She must have received a negative response because she turned and prepared to dive back under the water.

Daemyn caught her just in time. "You can't go back."

"Let go of me." She struggled, shoving at him, nearly sending all three of them plunging underwater. "Valinda's still down there."

"You don't know that. I saw her and Colonel Beshko head for the main entrance just before everything started collapsing. They probably made it out on that end of the castle." Daemyn gripped Tamya around the waist with one arm and stroked toward the people on the landing with the other. "It's too dangerous to go back there now. And you ain't likely to find her. Not in that chaos. You would do her more good by organizing the guards on the surface to search using ropes and canoes."

If Queen Valinda hadn't gotten out already, then she wasn't going to. If she was still back there, Daemyn highly doubted she was still alive.

But his alternate plan seemed to reassure Princess

Tamya, and she stopped fighting him and started swimming.

His knees bumped into the stairs. He crawled his way out of the water as hands lifted Princess Kira from his back. People helped Princess Tamya to her feet, wrapping her in a blanket and leading her away.

A hand reached down, offering to help Daemyn up. Still panting, he took it and let the person pull him, staggering, to his feet.

He found himself face-to-face with Asa Rand, Zeke's older brother. Perhaps it was the cold. Or the exhaustion. But all he could do was blink at him. "What are you doing here?"

Asa shrugged and held out a blanket. "Zeke rallied the relatives. Told you we'd tear the castle apart to get to you. It took a heap of Aunt Frennie's moonshine and this saltpeter concoction cousin Jericho has been whomping up. We stuffed it all with sawdust, and it went up even better than we'd reckoned."

Daemyn huffed out a laugh, letting Asa steer him away from the edge toward another set of stairs. He'd always known Frennie's moonshine was strong enough to kill a body, but he hadn't figured on it being deadly enough to take out a castle. "Next time, make sure we ain't under the castle before you bring it down on our heads."

"There's going to be a next time?" Asa cocked an eyebrow at him.

"Reckon so." Daemyn shrugged as he staggered up the last few steps.

"Then I reckon we'd better have Jericho refine the mixture. We only planned to blow up part of the wall as a distraction, not take down the whole castle." Asa grimaced.

"Zeke told us you were under that courtyard. It had us all a heap worried."

Daemyn couldn't think of a response for that. As they reached the top of the stairs, they turned and entered the grand entry hall with its banks of windows overlooking what had once been the courtyard and river.

The entire lower half of the courtyard was gone. Only the upper terrace garden beside the broad wall of windows in the great hall had been spared. A large chunk of the outer wall was gone, along with the towers flanking it. Even the end of the family wing of the castle had collapsed into what was now a lake extending inside the castle from the rushing Tuckawassee River. The early morning starlight reflected on the roiling, crashing water as the last few chunks of the courtyard gave way around the edges.

Castle Greenbrier had stood for hundreds of years and withstood a hundred years of warfare, but it had been breached in a single night by a very determined horde of mountain folk and a few kegs of moonshine. At that moment, Daemyn wasn't sure if he should be saddened at the loss of life it had probably caused or proud at what the Rand clan could accomplish when riled.

When he turned his back to the windows, he finally took in the bustle around him. His relatives were everywhere, organizing the surviving Tuckawassee soldiers, handing out blankets, directing people to the great hall to receive medical care. They may have destroyed the castle, but now that they had it, they set to cleaning up their mess with a vengeance.

Josiah and a few of his older brothers worked along with Zeke and a few more of Zeke and Asa's siblings to pull people from the river. Hezekiah Boda led a bunch of the Neskahana and Kanawhee cousins to subdue the remnants of the Tuckawassee army. Stefan Vinzen, the seneschal of Pohatomie was there with a few of the scattered Pohatomie relatives, working alongside the pack of nieces and nephews from Guyangahela to help the wounded. Frennie and Ted were organizing the rowdy branch of the family to distribute blankets and food.

Finally, all Daemyn could think to do was clap Asa on the back. "Thank you."

Chapter 29

Daemyn

Daemyn gripped Rosanna's good hand, kneeling at her side. She lay on the floor of Castle Greenbrier's great hall, grimacing, as Zeke eased the bandage from her shoulder.

Around them, wounded men and women lay in rows on the floor, most of them Tuckawassee soldiers who had been in the courtyard, patrolling the wall, or in the towers that had collapsed, though a few Tuckawassee servants had been injured as well during the collapse of the courtyard and royal wing.

Daemyn's family members were moving among the injured, providing medical attention. Asa wrapped a bandage around a Tuckawassee soldier's leg. Frennie cleansed wounds with moonshine while Ted and their older children bandaged lesser wounds.

Captain Degotaga leaned against the wall a few feet away, guarding Rosanna with an icy determination, as if he blamed himself for her getting hurt. Rosanna's other guards were patrolling the perimeter with more of Daemyn's relatives, guarding the uninjured Tuckawassee.

Isi hurried to Rosanna's side, carrying a bowl. "I have the boiling water. Laced with moonshine for good measure."

"Sounds pleasant." Rosanna muttered between her gritted teeth.

Daemyn smoothed her hair back from her face, squeezing her hand. "Zeke will patch you up real good."

Zeke eased off the last of the bandages, revealing the gaping wound. Most of Daemyn's stitches had torn free, mangling the gash and causing fresh bleeding.

"How bad does it look?" Rosanna craned her neck. From experience, Daemyn knew she'd have trouble getting a good angle to see into the wound. At least she had help tending it. Patching up one's own wounded shoulder wasn't easy.

"It ain't pretty." Zeke claimed the bowl from Isi. "I need to pick out the other stitches before I stitch it up proper again."

"Just do it." Rosanna squeezed Daemyn's hand tighter.

Isi squeezed in next to Zeke and patted Rosanna's other hand. "We'll be right here. Don't you fret."

As Zeke laid out the supplied he would need, Captain Taum, the captain of Alex's guard, approached and faced Daemyn. "The high king is asking for you."

Alex. Daemyn's muscles tightened. "How is he?"

Under Princess Tamya's orders, the Tuckawassee healers had taken Alex into a side room, saying they would their best to help him.

"It isn't looking good." Lines etched into Captain Taum's face.

Rosanna took Daemyn's belt, then patted his arm. "Go. He needs you more than I do."

"Rosanna..." He was being torn in two directions. Rosanna was here, bleeding.

But Alex was dying. He didn't have friends and family surrounding him like Rosanna did. All he had was Daemyn.

"Go." Rosanna gave him a small shove. "I'm in good hands."

"We'll take care good care of her." Isi met Daemyn's gaze, held it.

Zeke and Isi would take care of Rosanna. She was right. In this moment, Alex needed him more.

With one last kiss to her knuckles, Daemyn stood and followed Captain Taum, weaving around the injured lying on the floor. Behind him, he heard Rosanna, her voice tight and determined. "Quick. Get those stitches out before he gets back."

It would have made him smile in other circumstances. But the door to the side room was just ahead.

Captain Taum pushed the door open, Daemyn at his heels. Inside, a pallet had been set on the floor, and Alex lay on it. His whole body shuddered, his breathing ragged. The rest of his guards stood along the wall, staying out of the way of the healers. One of the Tuckawassee healers was stirring more powdered charcoal into a glass while another laid out a variety of instruments on a table. What were they preparing to do?

Daemyn hurried across the room and knelt beside Alex's pallet. He reached out a gripped Alex's hand. "I'm here, Your Highness."

Alex's eyes flickered open, and he blinked up at Daemyn, as if it was a struggle to focus on him. He squeezed Daemyn's hand, moaning as he curled on his side.

Princess Ranielle stepped forward, her face just as drawn as the rest of them. As far as Daemyn had heard, Princess Tamya and her guards hadn't found Queen Valinda yet. Still, Princess Ranielle was here, following Tamya's orders to see what she could do for the high king. "We need you to make a few decisions for the high king."

"Why me? Shouldn't he make the decisions?" Daemyn glanced from Princess Ranielle down to Alex. Only then did he notice the layers of leather Alex was biting.

One of the healers knelt at Alex's other side. "His muscles are seizing. We managed to get the leather between his teeth before his jaws locked, so he won't break his teeth. But he's in no condition to be making medical decisions."

"What decisions?" Daemyn glanced from Alex's shaking form to the healer and back. What decisions had to be made? Alex was dying of water hemlock. He had already been made to drink as much powdered charcoal as he was going to keep down. There's wasn't anything more they could do except beg the Highest King to spare him.

Alex gave another cry of pain. His hand spasmed in Daemyn's grip, fingers going stiff.

The healer's face was drawn in lines, and she rested a hand on Alex's shoulder, not flinching away as he shook. "Water hemlock causes muscles to contract, sometimes hard enough to break bones. Suffocation is, in the end, what kills a person poisoned with water hemlock more often than not."

Daemyn gritted his teeth, forcing himself to be patient. This explanation would be important, even if all he wanted to do was hurry up to the part where she told him what they needed to do to try to save Alex's life. Water hemlock grew as a weed here in Tuckawassee. Their healers would have methods to help since accidental poisonings happened occasionally.

"In past poisoning cases, we've had success in putting a gold tube down a poisoning victim's throat to hold it open and using a bellows to keep them breathing. Sometimes even then, the patient dies from other organs shutting down, but this method has saved people who otherwise would have suffocated." The healer met Daemyn's gaze. "But, to insert the tube, we would need to cut his throat. Around here." She traced the spot on herself.

Daemyn understood then why they needed someone to make this decision. Alex was curled on the pallet, unable to talk besides moans and nods of his head. But that wouldn't be enough for the Tuckawassee to dare take a knife to the high king's throat. If the procedure didn't work, everyone would blame them for slitting his throat and murdering him twice over. If they wanted a chance at peace, then the blame for his murder needed to rest solely on the currently missing Queen Valinda.

Daemyn glanced to where Captain Taum stood beside the door. "You're his guard captain. Shouldn't you be the one to make this choice?"

The captain was already shaking his head. "I'm just a captain. You're his friend and advisor. Everyone in the seven kingdoms knows the depth of your loyalty. If you make this decision, no one will question if it was the right one."

Alex's shaking hand bumped Daemyn's, though Alex's eyes were squeezed shut. Daemyn wasn't sure if the movement was a nudge or a convulsion.

Would this save Alex's life? Or would it just hurry along his death? Daemyn swallowed, remembering the feel of a knife slicing through his own throat, the pain of choking and suffocating and dying there on the forest floor before the Highest King's power had restored him to face another two decades searching for the princess to wake Alex.

Yet here Alex was dying. After all they'd been through together. After everything Daemyn had done to protect him, they had still ended up here.

Daemyn couldn't let Alex die like this. Not when he was finally becoming the high king he was always meant to be. One who was on the verge of uniting the kingdoms and bringing about a peace Tallahatchia hadn't seen in over a hundred years. He was pointing the people toward the Highest King in a way that had been nearly forgotten by all but a faithful few.

It couldn't end here. Not like this.

Spare his life. Please. Daemyn clenched his fists, everything in him aching with the memories of kneeling before the throne of the Highest King, the wonders he'd seen there. In his mind, he was there again, pleading.

"You need to make a decision soon. Once he goes into convulsions, it will be that much harder to insert the tube and keep him breathing." The healer's voice broke into the memories, dragging him back to the tiny room, kneeling there in wet clothes.

Alex was dying. Would it matter if they tried the procedure and failed? Alex's chances weren't good without it. Perhaps the risk would be worth it.

But if it went wrong, there would be no hope of saving him. He'd choke to death on his own blood or suffocate because his throat had been cut.

With a choking sound, Alex's eyes rolled back in his head. His body writhed, convulsing spasmodically. His breathing went tight, then disappeared into a choking, gagging sound.

"Hold him down." The healer shouted, even as the other healers and assistants in the room rushed to Alex's side, holding him down so he didn't hurt himself in his thrashing. "It's now or never."

"Do it." Daemyn pinned Alex's shoulder down, his own breathing ragged past the tightness in his chest.

As the healer snatched a thin, sharp knife from the table where the supplies had been laid out, Daemyn could only hope with everything in him that he'd made the right choice.

🍷

DAEMYN LEANED AGAINST THE WALL, staring as the healer worked the bellows that kept Alex breathing. Alex's shuddering had reduced to a mild trembling, through his body remained contorted from his tight muscles.

The door opened, and Rosanna stepped inside, her right arm resting in a sling. Her gaze swept over the space before she crossed the room and slid down the wall to a seat next to Daemyn. She nodded toward Alex. "How is he?"

"Alive." That was about all the healers were saying at the moment. "Right now, all we can do is wait and hope his body ain't going to give up on us." Daemyn reached out and took her good hand. "And you?"

"Zeke got me fixed up proper." She leaned her head against his shoulder.

Daemyn shifted to better cradle her against him, wrapping his arm around her shoulders. "I'm sorry I didn't come back to you."

"You were needed here." Rosanna gripped his hand,

closing her eyes. "I've known since the day I met you that your duty to the high king will always be a burden you carry close. And I'm here to help you carry it. I might fall asleep, but I'm going to stay right here all night with you."

Daemyn held her close and kissed her temple. "Thank you."

CHAPTER 30

TAMYA

The first rays of the sun spilled over the far horizon, sending shafts of weak light across the black water that filled what had once been the courtyard of Castle Greenbrier.

Mya sat in the middle of a large canoe, surrounded by a flotilla of guards as they scoured the water, fishing out bodies. So far during the dark hours of the night, they had recovered the bodies of eleven castle guards who had been killed when the walls and towers collapsed.

The upheaval had calmed, leaving behind a still lake extending from the side of the Tuckawassee River, broken up by jutting mounds of rubble and hemmed in by the upper terrace garden and the remains of the walls.

Guards dug through the piles of rubble, searching for those who had been trapped or killed beneath the stones. Others worked pumps to try to lower the water level in the flooded underground room, a thankless task as the river continued to pour inside and would do so until a wall could be constructed on top of what remained of the bedrock riverbank that had formed the foundation of the outer wall.

So much destruction. Mya struggled to take in the ruins of what had once been her family's home. The underground dancing pavilion where she and her sisters had spent so much of their waking, nighttime hours was utterly destroyed, swept away by the river or buried under tons of stone.

Right now, they were at the mercy of the people who had breached their wall and conquered their castle. If they wished, the Neskahana, Buckhannock, or Kanawhee armies could march into Tuckawassee and conquer it with little resistance.

And her sister was still missing.

It had been too long. If Valinda had been alive, she would have been found by now.

And yet, Mya's chest ached with hope she couldn't quench, no matter how logic told her it was impossible.

Mya forced down the churning in her stomach, keeping her emotions cold and her voice steady. With Uma comforting the younger girls, that left Mya in charge as temporary queen. She had assigned Shandra to organize the relief efforts in the castle and Ranielle to oversee the efforts to save the high king, leaving the task of retrieving dead bodies and searching for Valinda for herself.

"There's another one!" One of the guards in a canoe to her left pointed while the rest of the men in his canoe paddled furiously.

Without being told, the soldiers in Mya's canoe turned in that direction, getting closer. Close enough Mya could make out the puffy skin and bulging eyes above the drenched buckskin pants, black linen shirt, and leather tunic that served as the uniform for the Tuckawassee army.

Even before the corpse was fished from the water and proclaimed dead, everyone knew the verdict already.

Another soldier found dead. Another family suffering a loss. On top of the losses their army had suffered a year ago in Kanawhee, it was yet another blow that spelled the end to any hope Tuckawassee had ever had to rise to the greatness her father and grandfather and great-grandfather had envisioned. More than that, they would be at the mercy of the other kingdoms.

"Princess!" One of the soldiers digging through a pile of rubble waved his arm and raised his lamp higher to help dispel the last lingering shadows as the sun still struggled to rise.

Mya turned and motioned for her guards to turn her canoe in that direction. Next to the mound of rubble, purple silk undulated in the ripples, glinting in the weak sunlight.

The same purple as the dress Valinda had been wearing last night.

"Go. Hurry." Mya clenched her fingers against the top rail of the canoe, willing the canoes to converge on the spot faster. Everything inside her twisted, ached, knowing what she'd find and yet hoping...hoping...it wasn't true.

One of the canoes of guards reached the pile of rubble first. Assisting the soldiers already there, they tossed aside stones, which fell with wet plunks into the water. Several of them dove beneath the water, disappearing for several seconds before surfacing with grim expressions.

More stone shifted, and more purple silk floated to the surface, along with one moccasin-clad foot.

The guards froze. One turned and frantically motioned to her oncoming canoe. "Stay back, Your Highness."

"If that's my sister, then I want to see her." Mya

clenched her hands, straightening. She could face this. Someone had to be strong today, and it looked like that someone had to be her.

"No, you don't, Your Highness. Believe me, you don't." The soldier's face was ashen. "She didn't drown. It looks like she was struck by falling rubble and died instantly. Please, Your Highness. You don't want to remember her like this."

How was Mya supposed to remember her? In their last minutes together, they had been fighting. Not just fighting, but clawing and tearing at each other as if they intended to kill each other.

And now Valinda was dead. Mya would never have a chance to make this right. Never have a chance to hug her sister ever again.

Mya forced her shoulders back, her expression to remain blank. When she spoke, her voice didn't waver. "I have to see her. Either me or one of my sisters needs to identify her in order for the crown to pass to Princess Uma, and that is not a task I will assign to anyone else."

The guard studied her face, then nodded. "Very well. But please wait a moment." He gestured to one of the other canoes. "Bring a sheet to cover the queen."

Mya hunched in the canoe, staring numbly at the bustle of soldiers. A sheet was passed to them, and they leaned out of Mya's sight, presumably dragging Valinda's body onto the rubble pile under which she had been trapped and tucking the fabric over the worst of her wounds.

Valinda had died in the center of what would have been the underground room. To be killed here, Valinda would have had to race down one of the paths almost as soon as the first explosion happened. Had Valinda run to save herself, leaving all of her sisters behind without a thought?

No, Valinda had been manipulative, scheming, enraged there at the end. But she loved her sisters. She wouldn't have left them behind. Not on purpose. Right?

If Mya squeezed her eyes shut, replaying those terrifying moments as the water poured in and they scrambled for safety, she vaguely remembered Colonel Beshko hustling Valinda past her. Getting the queen to safety would have been Colonel Beshko's primary concern, and she wouldn't have known about the backway in. That was only revealed to the servants after they were cursed so that they could deliver refreshments secretly.

They had yet to find Colonel Beshko's body in this mess. Perhaps she was buried in another part of this pile of rubble. Without voluminous skirts to tear and float to the surface, the guards wouldn't know where to dig, as they had with Valinda. Maybe Colonel Beshko's body would turn up weeks later with all the other bodies that floated down the river and over the Rantahala Falls. They might never find it.

But at least Mya could lay to rest that gnawing guilt in her stomach that if she'd only turned back instead of letting Daemyn Rand persuade her otherwise, she might have saved her sister.

Daemyn Rand had been right. Valinda had already been long dead at that point. Mya would've only become another one of the floating bodies to be retrieved, leaving her sisters mourning two sisters instead of only one.

One was already too many.

The soldier straightened and motioned to Mya. "Your Highness, she's ready, if you wish to see her."

Mya drew in a deep breath and nodded. "Yes."

The other guards on the mound of rocks held the canoe steady as Mya clambered out. She picked her way over the rubble, hopping from stone to stone until she reached the soldier's side.

Valinda lay on her back, the remnants of her dress in tatters around her. A sheet covered her left arm, shoulder, and side of her face, red soaking into the white fabric.

But it was definitely Valinda. Mya could see enough of Valinda's face that there was no doubt.

Her sister was dead. Cold and dead and gone forever. Mya caught her breath, pain searing through any numbness the long night had worn into her. She braced herself against one of the tilting stones, gasping for breath against a rush of tears.

She couldn't cry. Not now. Valinda was dead, and the Tuckawassee needed someone to act the role of queen until Uma could take on that role.

Inch by inch, Mya forced her back to straighten. Her voice to steady. Her face to harden. "Place her in my canoe."

"Are you sure, Your Highness?" The soldier studied her with concern.

She wasn't backing down on this. She needed to stay at her sister's side for this last journey. "Yes."

While one of the soldiers helped Mya back to her canoe, the others took another sheet and wrapped Valinda's body. Then, they lifted the sheet-wrapped bundle. Purple skirts spilled from the bottom while Valinda's hair stuck from the wrapping.

Mya scooted closer toward the guard paddling in the stern, giving more room in the center. The soldiers eased Valinda's body into the canoe with her head toward Mya.

Mya tried to ignore the growing red spot on the sheet covering Valinda's head.

"Thank you." Mya met the soldier's gaze, the one who had found Valinda and seen to covering her wounds. "What's your name, soldier?"

"Fess Ramey, Your Highness." He gave her a bow.

She returned it with a nod and motioned for the guards in the canoe to shove off. She'd remember that soldier's name. He had shown good sense and loyalty tonight. Mya would recommend him to Uma as a soldier to promote once things calmed and Uma took the throne.

As her canoe was turned toward the remains of the castle, Mya reached a shaky hand forward and touched Valinda's hand. It was cold, clammy. So obviously dead that Mya's skin crawled and it took everything in her not to snatch her hand back.

She was touching a dead body. Prickles creeped up her back, but she swallowed the feeling back. This was all she had left of her sister. For all the pain of their last few minutes fighting each other, Valinda deserved Mya to remain at her side.

Time dragged as the guards navigated around the mounds of rubble. At last, they reached the stairs from the upper courtyard that now ended in the water and provided the best way from the new lake into the castle.

Mya stood to the side as the guards lifted her sister's body from the canoe and carried it up the stairs. "Please lay her out in the throne room with the rest of the dead. She can lie in state with her people."

As the soldiers wound their way through the crowd, the whispered news was spreading. Mya needed to find her sisters and tell them before they heard the news second-hand. They should hear it from her.

Inside the entry hall, she located Shandra and Neill kneeling next to a wounded soldier. Mya touched Shandra's arm. "I need you to join Uma and the others."

Shandra's jaw tightened, her gaze started to stray toward the windows. Mya turned her away before she caught sight of the guards passing below with Valinda's sheet-wrapped body.

Neill glanced out the window, his jaw tightening. He clasped Shandra's hand. "Go with your sister. I'll be here when you need me."

Shandra still hesitated, as if she already sensed what neither of them were telling her.

Mya steered Shandra in the direction of the study. "Go on. I'm going to fetch Ranielle, and then we'll join you."

Her eyes wide, Shandra nodded and hurried down the hall that led to the study.

Mya squared her shoulders and headed for the room where she'd sent Ranielle with High King Alexander. In front of the door she paused, bracing herself. What would she find inside? She hadn't seen any indication that the high king had died, but she'd been busy searching for Valinda. She pushed the door open and stepped inside.

The high king lay on a pallet on the floor, limbs trembling, though not violently. His face was obscured by the bellows and apparatus hooked up to the end of the gold tube sticking out of a wad of bandages over the high king's neck.

The high king's manservant was kneeling beside him, helping one of the healers operate the bellows. Princess Rosanna lay sleeping on a pallet near the wall, a blanket over her so that Mya couldn't see any bandages from the princess's injury.

An injury caused by a Tuckawassee arrow. Another

reason for Neskahana to take advantage of their weakness and attack.

Ranielle eased along the edge of the room and joined Mya beside the door. Mya stayed focused on the high king, not yet ready to meet her sister's gaze, and waved toward the high king. "How is he?"

"Holding steady. For now." Ranielle shrugged. "There's nothing more we can do but wait and see."

It had been about three and a half hours since he'd been poisoned. In the normal course of the poison, he would have been dead already. But not being dead didn't mean he would recover. There was still a chance his body would shut down under the strain or he would simply never wake and breathe on his own.

"Thanks for taking care of this for me." Mya squared her shoulders, her muscles aching under the strain of everything she carried. "Looks like the healers and Daemyn Rand have everything in hand for the moment. Can you step away?"

"Yes. What's wrong?"

Mya couldn't meet Ranielle's gaze, even if she felt it searching her expression. She needed to tell this once, to all of them. She'd break if she had to tell it over and over. "The others are waiting for us in the study."

Ranielle followed Mya from the room without another word.

Mya walked through the entry hall again, forcing herself to smile and nod at those who greeted her. She couldn't let her people see her break.

Without letting herself hesitate, Mya pushed the door open and stepped into the darkly paneled room with its desk in the center and paintings of past kings lining the walls. The scent of Valinda's favorite perfumed soap still lingered.

Her sisters clustered around the room, all looking up or turning to face her. Moriah, Leigha, Nakeisha, and Quinna had been playing a board game on the floor. Panya and Octavia were sitting in a couple of the chairs, talking quietly while Uma sat in the chair, hugging Kira to her.

Shandra had positioned herself by the window. Ranielle stepped around Mya to kneel next to the younger girls on the floor.

They were all there. All except Valinda. And she was never coming back. For the rest of their lives, they would always be eleven sisters mourning their missing twelfth.

Mya clenched her fingers, squeezing her eyes shut. Valinda, who had always tried so hard to be the heir their father had wanted. Valinda, who had died trying to bring their father's vision for Tuckawassee to pass. Valinda, who had become as cold and distant and ruthless as their father until the bonds of sisterhood had stretched thin.

Like with their father a year ago, Mya didn't know how to mourn. There was so much hurt and pain and those angry, unresolved moments. Valinda had died trying to murder the high king. She'd died in the wrong. And, yet, she was Mya's sister. They'd hugged and laughed and cried together.

Mya opened her eyes, facing her remaining sisters. She pried her mouth open, but the words lodged in her throat. How could she tell them? How could she meet Kira's large, trusting eyes and give her this news? There wasn't a way to blunt its raw, painful edges.

"We...we found Valinda's body." Mya swallowed, her eyes growing hot with tears she refused to shed. Not now.

She needed to be the strong shoulder to bear her sisters' grief. "She was killed when the ceiling collapsed."

Silence stretched for a long moment, as if everyone was hoping those words weren't real.

Then, the tears. The hugs. The questions Mya didn't want to answer. The questions she couldn't answer.

Another person ripped from their lives. They'd lost their mother, then their father. And now Valinda. How much more loss would they have to suffer?

After long hours of soothing and tears, Mya leaned against the wall, Leigha sleeping against her shoulder. Ranielle had gone with Moriah, Nakeisha, Panya, and Quinna to see that they went to bed. Shandra had long since left, probably to cry on Neill's shoulder. For all Shandra's anger at Valinda over cursing Neill, she'd still cried at Valinda's death.

Uma crossed the room, holding a now sleeping Kira, and eased down next to Mya. "How are you holding up?"

"I'm fine." She had to be. She glanced over at Uma. "You don't have to marry King Cassius now. You'll be queen of Tuckawassee."

But Uma shook her head even before Mya finished. "The betrothal has been promised already, and Tuckawassee is in too precarious a situation to go back on our word to King Cassius. I've abdicated my place in the line of succession."

"Not officially yet. You're still next in line until you officially announce your abdication. You don't have to do this." Mya held Leigha tighter. She'd already lost one sister. She didn't want to lose another.

"This is what I want, Mya. Don't you see? I don't want to be queen of Tuckawassee. Not as the sole ruler. I'd much rather be the queen of Pohatomie where my responsibilities will be raising my children and supporting King Cassius at his side." Uma met Mya's gaze, holding it steadily. "Those are the duties my personality and dreams are suited for. It's the life I want."

Mya bit her lip against another protest. This was Uma's choice. There wasn't anyone forcing her into it any longer. She seemed to firmly believe that marriage to King Cassius was what would make her fulfilled, and there wasn't anything Mya could say to sway her. All that was left was to ask of the Highest King that her sister's choice was the right one.

Uma rested a hand on Mya's arm. "Besides, you are the one who should be queen. Look at how you handled today. I froze. I was relieved to retreat and huddle in here with our sisters. You were the one who took charge and organized everything from the high king's care to finding Valinda's body to seeing to the needs of the wounded. You're the queen Tuckawassee needs right now."

"Are you sure, Uma? I don't want any hard feelings that I stole the crown that rightfully belongs to you." Mya wasn't sure why her heart was beating in her chest. As if in hope for the future. As if this was what she'd always wanted and yet never dared even admit, even to herself.

"It's a crown I'm willingly—happily—giving to you." Uma squeezed Mya's arm, her voice and eyes soft. "You've always been a leader. I think, deep down, Valinda might have even feared you. She saw the leader you could become, and she decided to use it to her advantage by making you high queen rather than leaving you in a position to eventually challenge her crown."

"I never would have..." Mya trailed off. She couldn't finish that sentence. Not truthfully. Because, in the end, she had challenged Valinda. She'd refused to follow

Valinda's orders because Valinda had been wrong. Mya had to do the right thing, even if meant disobeying her sister's and her queen's commands.

Even if it had cost her sister her life.

Perhaps Mya hadn't been the one to kill Valinda. If any blame was to be had, it fell on the ones who had breached Castle Greenbrier's walls.

But she wasn't going to demand vengeance. Instead, she was going to make peace with the very people who had killed both her father and her sister. Because they had been in the right while her sister had been wrong.

Not everyone in Tuckawassee would agree. She would have a fight on her hands with many of her own people if she took the kingdom down this path.

But, for the first time that day, she felt the same peace as she had when using her gift of dance for the Highest King. No matter how hard, this was the right thing to do.

CHAPTER 31

ALEXANDER

Alex knelt on the gemstone grass, one hand pressed to the ground, the other wrapped around his stomach. Somewhere, far away, his body still ached. His lungs struggled to draw in breath.

But here, that pain was only a distant memory, fading the longer he knelt there. Water thundered before him, showering his face with a soothing spray. A breeze wrapped around him, warm and filled with the fresh, forest scent that spoke to the heart.

The light embraced him, soothing the lingering ache of his distant, struggling body. Massive, burnished tree trunks surrounded him. Before him, the WaterVeil separating this life from Beyond plunged into a turquoise pool that never seemed to fill.

He was at the threshold of Beyond. He'd been here before and yet, this time, when the music from behind the WaterVeil wafted around him, he felt a tugging deep inside his chest so strong he reached out and traced his fingers through the water.

"If I opened the door, would you wish to enter?" The Highest Prince's voice washed over Alex.

Alex drew in the steadying sound before he lifted his eyes to the Highest Prince standing beside him. For a moment, all Alex could do was rest there in the Highest Prince's presence.

Was this his death? He'd been poisoned with water hemlock. That was rarely survivable. Was the Highest Prince telling him that the door was about to open?

Alex wasn't dead already. If he was, he wouldn't be able to feel his aching, struggling body. The moment Alex died, the WaterVeil would've been opened, and the Highest Prince would have taken his hand and pulled him through.

He wanted to go. He did.

And yet...

"If you opened the door, I would step through and not look back. But I'm not ready. Not yet." He let out a long exhale and hung his head. Another failure on his part. He should want to step through without looking back. It should be the greatest longing in his heart.

But what about his mother, who had already lost so much? Daemyn, who had sacrificed for a hundred years, only to have Alex get himself killed a year after waking? All the people of Tallahatchia who were depending on him to bring about peace after decades of suffering?

He'd only begun to make progress in restoring Tallahatchia. He felt like he had work yet to do.

More, he longed to truly *do* something that mattered. Not something great as people measured greatness. But something that mattered. Like building a life, whether with a wife and children or single with friendships and nieces and nephews.

Not because he wanted to earn anything. He knew he

was here because of nothing he'd done. But he wanted to live a life that showed how much it meant that he had done nothing and yet was here at the threshold.

When he finally could bring himself to lift his gaze to the Highest Prince, he met eyes filled with compassion. "Is it wrong that I am not ready?"

"It is not your time." The Highest Prince's voice eased the tightness in Alex's chest. "I have more work yet for you to do, my faithful servant."

Alex wasn't sure if he wanted to smile or laugh or what. Because he understood. Finally. The work wasn't a burden. All the weight he carried as high king. All the responsibilities. They were light. Nothing. Because it was a gift to do the work the Highest Prince planned for him.

More than that, even the *wanting* to do the work was a gift.

And yet, the Highest King had called Alex faithful.

"Thank you." Alex drew in a deep breath, peace filling him. He wasn't going to die today. But that didn't mean he was ready to wake up to the pain just yet. "Can I stay here a while longer?"

"This threshold is a promise of the things to come." The Highest Prince swept a hand at the thick forest of otherworldly trees, the suggestion of a palace rising into the clouds filled with rainbow light. "This is my rest. Stay. Drink of the water. Be refreshed."

Alex dipped his hand into the turquoise pool and sipped the water. It tasted like sunlight and a sweetness he couldn't name. Its coolness slid down his throat and settled into his stomach, easing the pain.

He closed his eyes. He would have to return to his life and burdens eventually, but, for now, he bathed in the light of this place so that he could carry it with him into whatever he would face.

I

HE WAS CHOKING, his lungs aching. He tried to breathe deeper, but sharp pain stabbed through his throat. Something was tight and restricting around his neck.

What was going on? He needed air. He reached to claw the thing from his throat.

Hands pinned him down, strong as iron.

"Alex. Listen. I need you to stay calm." Daemyn's voice, soothing. "Breathe slowly."

Alex forced himself to slow his breathing, trying to relax. Daemyn was here. Daemyn wouldn't allow them to harm him.

He peeled his eyes open, blinking several times before he could bring Daemyn into focus.

Alex opened his mouth, but the pain stabbed through his throat again. His breathing surged in his chest again, rasping faster and faster.

"Steady." Daemyn gave Alex a small shake. Not hard, but it was enough to break the panic.

Alex would've nodded, but something held his neck stiff.

"Listen. The Tuckawassee had to insert a tube into your throat to keep you breathing." Daemyn's grip was tight on Alex's shoulder. "Now that you're breathing on your own, they removed it. You're going to be fine, but the cut in your neck needs time to heal. The bandages are thick to keep you from moving."

At least he had been unconscious for all of that. Alex

forced himself to relax. Of course, he'd be all right. The Highest Prince told him he had more work to do.

As if sensing he was calm, Daemyn sat back on his heels before settling back into a more comfortable sitting position against the wall. "You had us fretting there for a while."

Alex gathered as deep a breath as he managed. It hurt as he forced it out, but he managed to murmur, "How...long?"

The words weren't very clear, but thankfully Daemyn seemed to understand. "It is the middle of the night right now. About a day since you've been poisoned."

Alex closed his eyes for a minute, taking that in. He'd been out a full day.

He hurt like he never had before. His entire body throbbed. Sharp pain came from one of his fingers while his insides ached as if he'd taken a beating. Honestly, if he'd known how badly this would hurt, he might not have gathered the courage to take that poison and drink.

"Rosanna?" Alex forced her name out, even though it hurt in his throat, in his jaw. Even his teeth ached.

"Rosanna's fine. She's sleeping now." Daemyn pointed to the other side of the room.

Alex eased his head over enough to spot Rosanna curled on a pallet against the wall, the blanket rising and falling with her steady breathing. Some of his last, pain-filled memories were of her dragging him across the underground room as debris rained down on them. He'd fallen to his knees several times, retching and telling her to go on without him.

She hadn't. Instead, she hauled him to his feet and kept him moving, even as her wound reopened and blood soaked her shirt. Once she was awake and Alex could talk properly, he'd have to thank her. All he could manage now was one word. "Brave."

"Yes, she is." Daemyn's gaze softened as he focused on Rosanna. "We've been taking turns staying with you."

"What...happened?" With three syllables, that second word ended up so mangled, even Alex could barely recognize it. But he needed to know.

"Castle Greenbrier is a ruin. Turns out my family blew up the wall with moonshine, a mess of saltpeter, and sawdust." Daemyn shook his head, dark circles beneath his eyes. "Quite a few soldiers were killed. As was Queen Valinda."

Queen Valinda was dead. She had poisoned him and yet, his stomach sank at the news. He hadn't wanted her dead. He'd wanted peace.

Was Princess Uma next in line? Or had she already abdicated for the betrothal? Did that mean Princess Tamya would become the next queen of Tuckawassee?

Daemyn rested his head against the wall behind him. "They buried her and the rest of the dead this afternoon, but they are waiting on a coronation until you're more recovered. Reckon there's a few details to straighten out yet."

Did Princess Tamya still plan for a marriage alliance to Alex? If so, then her next sister Shandra would be the one taking the crown.

Were they waiting on him to perform the ceremony? It used to be the high king's duty to crown the other kings and queens of Tallahatchia, but, so far, the only coronation since Alex had awakened from his cursed sleep had been Queen Valinda's, and she certainly hadn't wanted to be crowned by the high king. That would signal her loyalty to him, after all.

The weariness pressed into Alex. He tried to swallow, and pain shot through his throat. He couldn't help a moan.

"Easy." Daemyn rested a hand on his shoulder. "I can fetch you some water, if you'd like."

Alex managed a small nod. It would hurt, but his mouth felt coated in sand. His eyes scratched when he blinked.

Daemyn disappeared from Alex's line of sight for a moment before he returned with a tin cup. His mouth quirked as he knelt next to Alex. "Don't fret. This ain't poisoned."

Alex felt an answering smile tug on his face. How long would it take before he felt safe putting food or water in his mouth anywhere besides in the safety of the threshold?

Daemyn lifted Alex's head and pressed the cup to his mouth.

The tin was cold against Alex's mouth, the water colder still as he sipped. While it tasted fresh, it held nothing of the pure sweetness of the water Beyond.

He held it in his mouth for a moment before he gathered the courage to swallow. It was harder than it should for something he'd been doing since he was a baby. But he forced himself to take several more swallows before he turned his face away.

As Daemyn set the cup of water aside, he rested his arms on his knees. "You drank that poison instead of me."

"Had to." Alex dug his fingers into the straw pallet beneath him. What else was he supposed to do? One of them had to drink it, and Alex never would have been able to get everyone out if he had let Daemyn drink the poison in his stead.

"I never thought..." Daemyn hung his head before shifting his gaze to stare past Alex to where Rosanna still slept. "Never thought you'd do something like that for me."

Alex would have felt hurt by that, but he knew what Daemyn meant. Alex had been the type to always expect everyone else to take the pain and suffering for him. Even when he'd started to be better, he wasn't exactly the person known for heroic acts. "Would not...if knew how...it would hurt."

"The healers told me you'll be sore for a while. Your own muscles gave you bruises and dislocated a few joints that had to be popped back into place." Daemyn's gaze dropped to Alex. "Thank you."

This gratitude wasn't something Alex ever thought he'd hear. He never expected he would do something self-sacrificing enough. Daemyn was usually the one doing all the saving.

A yawn built in Alex's chest, but he tried to suppress it. Yawning would probably hurt.

He yawned. It hurt. A lot. Alex grimaced, squeezing his eyes shut.

"Rest." Daemyn leaned back against the wall, closing his own eyes. "It has been a long few days for all of us."

Rest. Alex let his eyes fall closed, falling back into peaceful rest.

CHAPTER 32

TAMYA

A week had passed since the high king was poisoned, the wall was breached, and her sister was killed. Tomorrow, Tamya would be crowned queen of Tuckawassee.

Assuming, of course, this next conversation went as planned.

Mya squared her shoulders and crossed the entry hall. The bank of windows streamed morning sunlight onto the patterned floor, now cleared of the wounded. Most were recovering with family outside of the castle or had minor injuries. The seriously injured now rested in rooms to finish their recovery.

She strode outside, glancing around the garden before she located the person she sought.

High King Alexander sat in one of the overstuffed chairs hauled outside into a spot under one of the grape arbors. A footstool rested under his feet while his lap was covered with a blanket. The morning sunlight cast shadows over his gaunt cheeks and sunken eyes. A bandage wrapped around his neck where his throat was still healing.

But he had managed to walk that far this morning. A feat for someone who had survived poisoning by water hemlock only a week ago.

His captain of the guard along with four soldiers were stationed in various posts a few yards away while Prince Josiah and his bodyguard loitered nearby.

By the edge of the water, Daemyn Rand sat next to Princess Rosanna, quietly talking. They must have returned from their morning walk to Rantahala Falls. Occasionally, Daemyn would glance over his shoulder toward Alex. Keeping a watchful eye on the high king.

Mya couldn't blame them for their watchfulness. Even though she'd done her best to provide hospitality to those who had taken the castle, tensions still ran deep. On both sides. Many of the Tuckawassee soldiers weren't happy that Mya was being so cooperative with those who had technically conquered Tuckawassee. And the high king's friends were wary as they were still in what they considered to be enemy territory.

Mya shifted her gaze to the riverbank below the castle. There, contingents from the Neskahana and Kanawhee armies were camped, having arrived yesterday. They were preparing to provide an escort to the high king to the safety of either Neskahana or Kanawhee. Mya hadn't been privy to his exact plans.

She reached for one of the wooden chairs set next to a table beneath one of the grape arbors, but one of her guards beat her to it, silently moving it to a spot next to the high king.

Mya nodded her thanks and took the seat. The attention of the guards was going to take some getting used to.

The guards had been thoughtful when she'd been third in line to the throne, but now that she was the queen-to-be, they hovered. Perhaps they felt some guilt that Valinda had been killed under their watch.

Not that it was their fault. The castle had collapsed, and the one guard who had been there, Colonel Beshko, had yet to be found, either dead or alive.

Mya sat stiff and straight in her chair, gathering her courage. This conversation might become uncomfortable. Her stomach churned, her chest tight. She forced a smile onto her face. "You are looking well this morning, Your Majesty."

High King Alexander had his face tipped toward the morning sun, his eyes closed. "I feel fine as long as I don't move."

His voice was still a little rough and scratchy from his healing throat.

"So, I've been meaning to talk with you..." Mya swallowed. Was there a tactful way to go about this conversation? "I know my sister had been in the process of arranging a betrothal between me and you, and I know nothing was official. But before I'm crowned tomorrow, I need to know if you intend to honor that contract. I would need to abdicate if a marriage alliance is what it takes to secure peace."

Mya had no intention of forcing any of her sisters to marry against their will. Uma made her choice to honor her marriage alliance. If High King Alexander wanted Tuckawassee to honor the verbal offer Valinda had made to him, then Mya would do it herself. Hopefully Shandra would be up to the task of ruling Tuckawassee in that case.

At least she would have Neill by her side. He wasn't holding Valinda's actions against Shandra, and the two of them were now inseparable. Their wedding would probably be the next big event in Tuckawassee after the coronation.

High King Alexander stiffened and straightened. When he swung his gaze toward her, his posture and expression were stiff. Formal. "Do you wish to marry me?"

This was the tricky part. Had High King Alexander started to fall for her? How was she supposed to let him down gently? She didn't want to risk offending him and sending Tallahatchia straight back into war. "Please don't take this the wrong way, Your Majesty. But, no, I have no wish to marry you. It is my hope that my pledge of loyalty to you will suffice. Peace can be better accomplished if you have an ally as queen of Tuckawassee."

She held her breath, everything in her wound painfully tight. After all this, would she still be forced to marry him? He had become someone she respected. A high king she would willingly serve as queen of Tuckawassee.

But she really, really didn't want to marry him.

High King Alexander rested his head against the back of his chair. Then, of all things, he burst into short, raspy chuckles. After a moment, he caught his breath, resting a hand over the bandage on his throat. When he met her gaze, his mouth was tilted into a smile. "You sound about as eager to marry me as I am to marry you. Don't misunderstand. You're nice. Nothing wrong with you."

"Or you either." Mya quickly added.

"But, you're right. I believe we will make much better colleagues than husband and wife." High King Alexander shook his head, the smile still creasing his sallow face.

Mya breathed out a long sigh of relief. Who knew she could feel so good about someone breaking it off with her?

But she and High King Alexander had been the most

relaxed with each other when they were talking policy and rebuilding projects. Not as romantic partners, but as two leaders discussing similar goals.

With him as high king and her as queen of Tuckawassee, they could both accomplish the peace and building projects that they dreamed about. This was what was best for both of them and Tallahatchia.

Now that the cloud of the marriage alliance wasn't hanging over her, Mya felt free enough to pat his arm. "If there is a high queen out there for you, I'm sure she will be a much better fit for you than I am."

It was the kind of reassurance Mya was sick of hearing herself. The reassurance that there must be someone out there for her. But it was all she could think to say to High King Alexander. Perhaps he was the type who would appreciate it.

He tipped his face toward the sun, the smile still on his face. "Maybe, eventually. But right now, I am content with the place I have been given. And, what about you? I know from experience that a crown is a heavy thing to carry alone."

"I have my sisters and, hopefully, nieces and nephews someday." Mya shrugged, staring out over the ruined section of castle.

The water had receded enough that the foundation of the outer wall was now visible over the water, though what had once been the underground room and courtyard remained about half-filled with water.

"Maybe, someday, if someone comes along who can change my mind, then I'll marry him. But, right now, I don't think I'll ever marry. I've never dreamed about a husband and children. This..." She swept a hand over the castle, the people bustling back and forth from the town of

Greenbrier, the guards moving rubble. "This is what I've always dreamed about. I have an entire kingdom to nurture with my leadership."

So many ideas. Improvements she could make. Sewage systems to dig. Lives she could make better.

She paused, the echoes of her own excitement stabbing into her. How could she sound so thrilled about this when the only reason she was queen was because one of her sisters had died and another was honoring a marriage contract to a stranger?

She hung her head, gripping the sides of her chair. "I shouldn't sound so happy about this. My sister died a week ago."

High King Alexander lifted his head. "Don't feel guilty about finding the work satisfying, and definitely don't hold yourself back from ruling whole-heartedly. The thing about inheriting a crown is that it usually happens after a death of someone you love."

"Still. I shouldn't—" Mya blinked at the tears gathering at the corners of her eyes. How disloyal was she to her sister? The ache rushed back into her chest at the thought of Valinda.

"Don't." High King Alexander shook his head, his gaze steady, for all the weakness in his movements. "You aren't to blame for your sister's death. You didn't take the crown from your sister by any of your own doing whatsoever, so don't act as if you did. Queen Valinda died because of her own choices, namely her choice to capture me. She was killed in my rescue. None of the guilt belongs to you. It's your duty to embrace your new role and give it your best."

She let out a long breath, finding herself surprisingly thankful for his wisdom. He had probably gone through similar thoughts, having also inherited his crown young after his father's murder.

Without a husband and children, Tuckawassee would be her sole responsibility. Perhaps that was why the Highest King had given her the personality he had. This was the calling he had placed on her, one he had given her the talents to pursue.

For the first time since Valinda had died, Mya felt again the peace she had when dancing for the Highest King. This was where she was meant to be.

Tomorrow, High King Alexander would crown her queen of Tuckawassee, as the high king had done of old. As Valinda's crown had yet to be found and was assumed to have been destroyed, Mya would wear a new crown, fashioned from the three branches High King Alexander had broken in the underground dancing pavilion without succumbing to the curse. Kira and Leigha had both saved their crowns from the two earlier nights, and, during the chaos, Uma had saved the final crown, the one that had broken their curse.

Mya would wear that crown as a reminder of the strength of the Highest King who provided the strength to overcome to the even the weakest of his servants and who kept his promise to send a cursebreaker, just as the stories said.

Tomorrow, Mya would set Tuckawassee on a new path. One of loyalty and peace. One that would, hopefully, make whole and united the once broken Tallahatchia.

EPILOGUE

TWO WEEKS LATER...

Daemyn streaked the black grease across his face, three stripes across each cheek. For good measure, he swiped some across his forehead. Grabbing the buffalo spear his family had decorated for the occasion, he turned to face Alex where he sat in a padded chair by the window. "How do I look?"

Alex's eyebrows shot up. "Like one of the mountain folk about to kill something with his bare hands. The buffalo are going to keel over in terror at the sight of you."

That was about the look he was going for. Daemyn forced a grin. "I believe that would be *bear* hands."

Alex huffed and shook his head. "Those bear puns really are terrible."

"Yes, they are." Daemyn shrugged. As his soon-to-be brother-in-law Berend turned into a black bear at night, it was apparently Berend and Willem's inside joke. "But I'm going to be stuck with them so I need to practice."

"I don't think practice will make them better." Alex leaned his head against the back of the chair.

Daemyn drew in a deep breath, taking in the room at Castle Deeling in Neskahana that he currently shared with Alex. The door to Alex's bedroom was closed while Daemyn's and Zeke's straw mattresses on the floor had been pushed aside to give floor space during the day.

This was the last night Daemyn would spend on his usual pallet on the floor of the high king's room. It had been his place since the day he'd turned ten and become Alex's manservant, though he'd spent more time sleeping in the forest during the hundred years searching for Alex's cursebreaker.

But, starting tomorrow, Alex's guards would take turns sleeping in the sitting room to guard him, both when he was traveling and at Castle Eyota.

And, starting tomorrow, Daemyn would be married. With an entire suite he'd share with Rosanna at Castle Eyota.

"I can still make you a baron." Alex gestured at the room around them. "If you're still worried about your differences in rank..."

"Thanks, but no." Daemyn suppressed a shudder. If he became a baron, his children would inherit a title...and would be gifted and cursed on their eighth day like every other child of the nobility and royalty. No way was Daemyn ever going to afflict his children with that. "We'll be more than fine. Between my position as your chief advisor and Rosanna's position as Neskahana's ambassador, we'll have more than enough."

Nor did the differences in their rank bother him as it once had. Rosanna had long ago convinced him it didn't matter to her.

She was Rosanna. His princess. And in a few hours, they would be married. Finally.

A knock sounded on the door a moment before Zeke stuck his head inside. Grease paint streaked across his face. "Ready, Uncle Daemyn? Everyone's gathered outside the castle gates."

"I'll be right there." Daemyn turned back to Alex. Alex had settled back against his padded chair where he would have a view of the mountains bathed in morning sunlight. "Sure you don't want to come?"

"And take part in another buffalo hunt?" Alex gave an exaggerated shudder. "No, thanks. Besides, I'd just slow you down. I'm getting along better than I was, but my strength and stamina aren't up for a day-long hunt. With most of the royalty of Tallahatchia here, I'm going to spend my day in meetings."

For once, Daemyn was more than happy to ditch his duties and spend the day in the forest rather than being stuck indoors at Alex's side.

"Enjoy the meetings." Daemyn gripped his spear and strode out the door. He found Rosanna waiting for him at the base of the stairs, her right arm still in a sling as her shoulder healed.

She leaned forward, as if to kiss his cheek, but switched to patting his chest with her good hand, probably once she noticed the grease paint. "Have fun and stay safe."

"I will." He kissed her forehead, careful not to smear grease into her hair. Holding his spear out of the way, he cradled Rosanna against him, careful of her arm. "We can postpone, you know. You're still injured and—"

She placed a finger over his mouth. "I'm fine. I'm not about to let a little arrow to the shoulder mess with my wedding plans. Besides, all your family is already here. It would be a hassle to round them all up again. Just so you know, I'm going to marry you tomorrow no matter what. So if you get yourself injured or gored by a buffalo or trampled, I'll have Zeke drag you to the wedding in whatever state you're in."

"It's doubtful I'll get within spitting distance of a buffalo today. Not when I have fifty of my nephews and even a few of my nieces along with me." Daemyn suppressed a sigh.

They'd come back with a buffalo or two or three. That wasn't the problem.

The problem was that, on the day before his wedding, all his pack of relatives had gone mighty protective. In the old tradition, it was the duty of the groom's men to help him in the ceremonial hunt to prove he could provide for his bride. If any of the men bagged an animal, it counted as the groom's catch.

Nowadays, most people, outside of the mountain folk, didn't go on an actual hunt, and the groom presented something else as proof he could provide, like a loom if he was a weaver or an axe to show he could work with his hands.

But where Daemyn came from, a hunt was still the tradition. And, since this was Daemyn's family, just about everyone from ages seventeen to seventy wanted to partake in the hunt, including a bunch of the nieces. It wasn't exactly traditional for the groom's men to consist of some women, but Daemyn wasn't going to say no. His sisters had always hunted right alongside him and his brothers. If they could wield a spear or shoot a bow, they were welcome.

"I'm glad you have them keeping you safe." Rosanna patted his chest again before stepping back. "Now go on before your family gets impatient and blows up another castle."

As he was rather found of Castle Deeling, since it was Rosanna's home, Daemyn grinned, snatched one last kiss, this time to her mouth, and hurried out the doors of the keep. Several of Neskahana's soldiers nodded or greeted him as he passed, but he didn't slow his stride.

When he stepped outside Castle Deeling's gates, he faced a crowd of young men and women dressed in buckskin and carrying spears or bows and arrows. Somewhere in the back, one of them let out a whoop. Within seconds, all of them were whooping and hollering.

Zeke grabbed Daemyn by the elbow and yanked him into the crowd.

Daemyn swept a glance over the crowd and raised his voice to be heard. "Remember, we're after buffalo today. Maybe elk if we run across them. But no bear whatsoever."

At the back of the crowd, Rosanna's brother Berend jumped up and down and gave a whooping snarl, waving his spear in a way that was more likely to hurt himself than anything they were hunting.

Josiah stepped forward, black grease paint smeared in messy lines across his face. "Come on, Uncle Daemyn. You ain't one of them stuffy old folks yet. Give us your best yell."

For today, Daemyn didn't have to remember to be the high king's dignified advisor. Or the wise leader of a clan stretching across Tallahatchia. He didn't have to be what living in a castle for so many years had turned him into.

Today, he was all mountain folk. He could give in to the wildness thrilling through his blood. He could be the warrior who had walked these mountain paths before any of the people surrounding him had even been born.

Gripping his spear, Daemyn let out a whoop to echo off the mountains and leapt into a ground-eating lope, racing for the nearest trail. With more hollers and yells, the small army of his great-great grandnieces and nephews sprinted behind him.

☙

DAEMYN STRAIGHTENED his fringed shirt once again, trying not to appear nervous as he paced inside the tree line on his side of the large glade he and Rosanna had picked out for the wedding. The sky above curved in a solid blue dome without a single cloud while a wisp of a breeze cooled the spring warmth.

His relatives were finding their seats in the glade, each of them taking a moment to find him to wish him well or impart one last bit of marriage advice.

And there seemed to be a lot of marriage advice. He couldn't count the number of times a niece or a nephew would come up to him and tell him some version of, "My great-grandfather Luke told the family to tell you once you finally got married that..."

Even though his siblings couldn't be with him today, it was as if they were reaching out through their descendants. Daemyn didn't lack for family.

King Omri of Buckhannock strode toward him through the trees, still steady and spry for an eighty-year-old. His face was worn into wrinkles, especially around his eyes, and his hair was pure white and thinning. But his gaze remained sharp, his smile quick.

Daemyn reached out and shook his hand. "I'm glad you could come. I wasn't sure you'd be able to."

King Omri clapped him on the shoulder. "Of course I came. I ain't that old. You still got me beat by forty years."

That brought a smile, and Daemyn shook his head. Even at eighty, it seemed some nephews never grew out of teasing him. "Still, I'm thankful you and everyone else could come. Nearly the entire family is here. I wasn't sure so many would take the time."

King Omri's expression sobered, settling into the lines around his mouth. "You have meant a lot to this family over the years. You are the one who shaped the Rand clan into the close-knit group that we are. You have always been there for every birth, every death, every marriage, every joy, every sorrow. We always knew we could count on our Uncle Daemyn being there. Today, we ain't about to miss this chance to stand at your side and celebrate with you."

Daemyn stared at the gathering crowd, a lump gathering in his throat. He couldn't find the words to express what their loyalty meant to him.

"I know you must miss your parents and siblings on today of all days." King Omri's gaze met Daemyn's, and in their depths, Daemyn could read the wealth of memories they shared. King Omri was one of the few still living who remembered Daemyn's mother and siblings, though Daemyn's father had been dead before King Omri had been born. King Omri drew Daemyn closer and hugged him. "But I am proud to stand in their place for you today."

"Thank you." Daemyn hugged King Omri, then stepped back. Yes, he missed his parents today. His father's hand on his shoulder telling him he was proud of him. His mother dabbing at her eyes as she watched her oldest son finally marry. His brother Luke teasing him while Silas and Hasil helped. His sisters Nancy and SueAnne fussing over their dresses and commenting on how pretty Rosanna was, all done up fancy.

But Daemyn wouldn't go back and change the past. He wouldn't trade the family he had now for anything.

King Omri glanced over his shoulder as a soft, haunting melody rose from the glade behind him. "Looks like its time to start."

Daemyn swiped his sweaty palms on the front of his buckskin leggings and straightened his shoulders.

King Omri led the way from the trees in time with the swooping notes of SallyMae, one of Frennie's daughters, playing a bent saw as if it was a fiddle.

Across the glade, Rosanna's parents stepped from the trees, the sunlight glittering on their crowns. Rosanna's brothers strolled behind them, both standing tall. Daemyn couldn't get a good look at Rosanna past her parents and brothers besides the flutter of white buckskin and glint of beads.

In front of the gathered people, the canoe Rosanna and Daemyn had built together rested on a fluffy buffalo hide to keep it from damage. Alex stood behind it, facing the crowd. For all his weakness and gaunt angles, he stood tall at the moment. Alex no longer wore a bandage, and the wound across his throat had healed to a red mark with raw, new skin still growing in.

King Omri halted in front of the canoe as Rosanna's parents, King Faron and Queen Erina, halted across from him.

When Alex spoke, his voice rang loud and steady over the gathering, despite his healing wound. "We are gathered here today to join in marriage Princess Rosanna of Neskahana and Daemyn Rand of Tallahatchia."

Daemyn glanced to Alex. It should have been of

Buckhannock. Or of the mountains. Probably nothing at all, really. He didn't have a title.

But Alex had added on the *of Tallahatchia* part as if he had a title. As if all of Tallahatchia belonged to him in a way it only did to Alex as the high king.

Alex caught him looking, and his mouth quirked with a suppressed grin for a moment before he schooled his features back to a regal, official expression. "Who brings this woman to this man?"

When Daemyn swung his gaze forward, Rosanna's parents and brothers had stepped aside, leaving Rosanna standing before him on the far end of the canoe.

The sunlight glittered on the beadwork of her white, buckskin shirt paired with a flowing, blue silk skirt above white moccasins. Perhaps it was an odd look—a meeting of fancy royalty and the mountains—but it fit her.

As she fit him. And he her.

She wasn't wearing her sling at the moment and carried her right arm stiffly at her side. Her hair hung loose down her back, shimmering depths of brown and black as the sunlight hit it. He'd so rarely seen her hair free of her braid, and he itched to run his fingers through it. To hold her close, kiss her as he'd longed to without the entire pack of his family watching.

Only a while longer.

Across from him, Rosanna met his gaze and grinned. No hesitation or nerves for either of them.

Daemyn only vaguely heard Rosanna's parents reply. By the time Daemyn could drag his gaze from Rosanna, her parents and brothers were taking their seats in the front row. Willem smirked while Berend grinned, showing all of his teeth.

Alex cleared his throat. "Who brings this man to this woman?"

Daemyn expected King Omri to speak. He was the one Daemyn had asked to take the role to speak for his parents and siblings.

Instead, King Omri turned to the crowd. As one, all of Daemyn's gathered nieces and nephews shouted, "We do!"

For a moment, Daemyn had to bow his head. He didn't belong just to a father and a mother and a few siblings but to this entire family, over a thousand members strong. It was humbling that, after a hundred years and even after they had fulfilled their ancestors' promise to him, they were still loyal to him. Still embraced him as family, even if the connection was distant by this point.

Daemyn could barely concentrate on the rest of the ceremony. It passed in a blur until, finally, he was kissing Rosanna, cradling her right arm for her so that she could rest it as he held her. His family was cheering far too raucously for the solemnity of the occasion, but he didn't care. She was his and he was hers, and that was exactly how it was meant to be.

ALEX WAITED in the line of well-wishers, trying to avoid being elbowed and jostled. Even two weeks later, his body still ached, and a few of the deep bruises caused by his own muscles had yet to fade. After standing for the wedding, his legs were shaking, his weakness catching up to him.

But he didn't demand a path to the front of the line. At the moment, it seemed his rank didn't afford him special privileges. Not when Daemyn's entire family was rushing to give him their well wishes.

He didn't mind. It felt good to be a part of the crowd as if, in an odd way, he belonged to this family. He was certainly indebted to them.

In the glade, Daemyn's family was busy setting up trestle tables, rearranging the chairs, and bringing out trays upon trays of food, including the buffalo meat they'd slow cooked overnight. This would be a feast to be remembered, that was for sure.

Finally, he reached Daemyn and Rosanna. She had her arm once again in a sling, and Daemyn's arm around her waist tucked her injured arm against him as if to protect her from jostling.

Something inside Alex's chest warmed with a kind of contentment and maybe a bit of satisfaction at seeing them together. Not that he could take full credit, but he was the reason they'd met. That had to count for something, right?

"Congratulations to both of you." He leaned in and gave Rosanna a short hug, careful of her arm, before he clapped Daemyn on the back. "Don't hurry back to Castle Eyota. In fact, take the next month off. No, better make that two months. I don't believe you've had a proper day off in about a hundred and eleven years."

Daemyn stared, eyebrows raised. "Two months? Reckon you'll survive without me for two whole months?"

"No." That was the truth. Alex wasn't sure how he would navigate bringing Tuckawassee back into peaceful relations with the rest of Tallahatchia without Daemyn's wisdom and advice. But he'd have to figure it out and hope he didn't mess it up too badly. It was his duty as the high king, after all. He couldn't forever lean on Daemyn to fix his messes. "But I'll be fine. Don't you dare show up at Castle Eyota any earlier than two months from now. I'll make it an order if I have to."

"In that case, I ain't going to argue." Daemyn pressed a kiss to Rosanna's temple, his gaze softening as he looked down at her. "What do you say to a trip to Buckhannock? I can show you the cabin where I was born and there are a few waterfalls I've been hankering to show you."

"Sounds perfect." The look in Rosanna's eyes was just as soft as she glanced up at Daemyn.

It sent a lance of pain into Alex's chest, but he shoved it away quickly. He'd told himself he was not going to mope through this wedding or let any thought of longing or jealousy or loneliness mar today. He was content. He was right where the Highest King had called him to be.

As others rushed to take his place, Alex quietly backed away. He needed to find a chair in the shade to sit and rest for a while. He'd stay through the feast, but then he'd slip away to return to Castle Deeling and rest. Daemyn didn't need Alex hanging around, tearing his focus between celebration and his lingering duty to look after Alex.

When he had faded far enough back in the crowd, Alex pivoted, only to crash into someone standing directly behind him. He stumbled backwards, tripping over a dip in the ground.

The young woman he'd bumped into caught him before he fell all the way backwards. With her strong grip keeping him steady, he righted himself, brushing at his shirt to gain his composure before he faced her.

What a great impression as the high king he was making. He straightened his shoulders, lifted his gaze to her face, and caught his breath.

The young woman wore her dark brown hair in a braid down her back with a few wisps flying free to frame her bronzed face. Her deep brown eyes sparkled with the warmth of her wide smile, as if she found all of life amusing.

"Sorry about that." Alex cleared his throat, ignoring the twinge of pain from his healing wound. "I'm High King Alexander."

He resisted the urge to slap his forehead. Of course, she knew he was the high king. If his crown hadn't been a giveaway, the fact that he had been standing in front of everyone and married Daemyn and Rosanna would have.

The young woman smiled back at him, nodded, then hurried away without looking back, the braid swinging back and forth with the jauntiness to her stride. Without even saying a word to him.

Alex just stood there, staring after her like the utter fool he was, wishing he'd thought to ask for her name. Where she lived. Anything to talk longer and get to know her better.

Prince Josiah ambled out of the crowd. "Uncle Daemyn sent me to see if you needed anything."

Apparently, Alex hadn't faded into the background fast enough. Daemyn was still looking out for Alex, even on his wedding day.

"No, I'm fine." Alex pointed at the young woman's retreating back. "Do you know who that is?"

"Who?"

"The girl with the red shirt and dark brown braid down her back." It was a long shot. With so many people at this wedding, Josiah likely wouldn't know her, but it was worth a try.

"That's Kezzie." Josiah studied Alex. "My sister."

Alex's stomach sank. She was one of Daemyn's nieces. Not just any niece, but one of the nieces from the

Buckhannock side of the family, the family with whom Daemyn was especially close.

Alex squeezed his eyes shut, drawing a deep breath and trying to will his heart to beat at a normal rhythm. He couldn't allow himself to be attracted to one of Daemyn's great-great grandnieces. Shortly after Alex had woken, Daemyn had said he'd rather not inflict Alex on any of his nieces. It had been said in jest, but the implication was there. Daemyn's nieces were off limits. It was the one thing Daemyn had ever asked of Alex. He couldn't let him down.

Alex glanced one more time at the crowd, unable to spot her. Why, of all people in Tallahatchia, did he have to be attracted to her?

♗

NIGHT HAD FALLEN, a chilly spring evening where breaths misted in the light of the thousands of stars crowding the clear sky overhead. Daemyn's family had built huge bonfires in the glade. On the cleared space between the fires, several of Daemyn's nieces and nephews jigged to the sawing of Asa's fiddle, the thump of the Neskahana drummers, and Frennie's brood puffing away at jugs.

Daemyn sat close to Rosanna on a makeshift bench, clapping along with the rhythm as Josiah, Frennie, Zeke, and a few others tried to out-jig each other.

Zeke collapsed onto the bench on the other side of Daemyn, panting. He gave Daemyn a shove. "Get on up there as show the relatives how its done."

"I don't..." Daemyn wasn't sure he really wanted to cut loose with the entire family watching. Nor did he want to leave Rosanna by herself. She'd danced with him earlier,

279

but her face had gone pale, her good arm cradling her wounded one.

But she nudged him. "Go on. I want to see this."

With whoops and yells of encouragement, more hands were gripping his arms, pulling him to his feet, before depositing him at the edge of the whirling dancers.

It was a night to remember he was mountain born and bred. He closed his eyes, letting the music filter into him before he stepped out onto the flattened dirt. The music seeped into his toes until he was stepping with the rhythm. He crossed his arms, high kicking in a pattern with Frennie. Frennie was quickly replaced with Josiah's sister Kezzie. Then Frennie's husband Ted faced him, matching Daemyn's movements.

Daemyn kicked it up a notch, stomping, high kicking, knees-a-flying and heels-a-pounding until Ted dipped his head and bowed out.

Next thing Daemyn knew, he was facing a bear standing on his hind legs, shuffling in an attempt at a jig. Berend gave his bear grin, one that showed every one of his pointed teeth as he patted his chest with his black-furred paw.

Maybe it was the wildness of the night flowing through his veins, but Daemyn grinned back, matching Berend step for step. He didn't even flinch when Berend thumped him on the back, claws clicking, and bowed out of the dance.

By the time Daemyn finally collapsed into his seat next to Rosanna, he was breathing hard and sweat beaded along his hairline and stuck his shirt to his chest. But his grin was so wide it hurt.

"Having fun?" Rosanna kissed his cheek, even though he was a sweaty mess.

"Yes." Daemyn swept a glance over the laughing, boisterous crowd. Zeke was now standing by Isi across the way. When Zeke caught his eye, Daemyn gave a nod. He turned back to Rosanna. "Reckon now is as good a time as any to make a sneaky retreat and get on out of here."

"Sounds like a good plan to me." Rosanna clasped his hand.

Together, they kept their heads low as they sneaked through the crowd. Thankfully, everyone was too busy cheering on the next set of dancers jigging in time to the music to notice them slipping away.

Still, Daemyn didn't breathe easy until he and Rosanna reached the stream that cut through the forest on one side of the glade.

There, Zeke already had the canoe in the water, the provisions stowed, the paddles waiting. Isi stepped forward and gave Rosanna a hug while Daemyn stepped into the river to take the canoe from Zeke. "If anyone asks, you never saw us."

A few of the wilder branches of the family still had the tradition of rousting the newlyweds out of bed with raucous music, parading them around for a while, and generally trying to embarrass them. It would all be in good fun, but it was a tradition Daemyn would rather avoid.

Zeke grinned. "Reckon they're in too high of spirits to notice you're missing for an hour or two."

Daemyn glanced over his shoulder, where the bonfires' glow flickered between the trees. "Try to keep the rowdier relatives from spiking the punch."

"There ain't a whole lot of moonshine left after blowing up Castle Greenbrier, but I'll do my best to keep them from slipping in the little they got left." Zeke shrugged, glanced at where Isi and Rosanna were still quietly talked, and shifted. "Reckon you and Rosanna can come back tomorrow? Isi and I talked it over, and my family is already here, as is her family, and it just made sense. But we didn't want to steal your thunder today, so we—"

He was interrupted by a muffled squeal from Rosanna as she leapt to give Isi another hug.

Zeke's mouth quirked. "We decided we're getting married tomorrow."

"Then we'll be there." Daemyn clapped Zeke on the back. He'd known Zeke and Isi wouldn't be that far behind him and Rosanna in tying the knot. It made him all the more grateful to be a part of the life he had now. Zeke was like a brother to him. Closer in many ways than his own brothers had been. "Going on a hunt the morning before the wedding?"

"Yep. Reckon we'll go after elk, since everyone's already full up of buffalo." Zeke glanced at him, as if he wasn't sure Daemyn would want to return that early in the morning.

For Zeke, he'd be there. Rosanna would want to be there for Isi as well.

As Rosanna strode to the stream's edge, Zeke joined Isi on the bank before the two of them disappeared into the forest, headed for the bonfires to keep an eye on the relatives.

"Where are we headed?" Rosanna slid into the prow of their canoe, her movements easy even though she only the use of one of her arms. Her right arm remained in its sling, and it would be up to Daemyn to do all the paddling for a while.

"A secluded spot near a tiny waterfall I don't reckon even Zeke knows about." Daemyn climbed into the stern of the canoe and took up his paddle. The wood slid smooth against his palms as he pushed them away from the bank. "Ready for the next adventure, Princess?"

She glanced over her shoulder, her grin flashing wide in the starlight. "Always."

With a firm paddlestroke, they were off, disappearing into the night.

Don't Miss the Next Adventure!

Tentatively Coming 2024

Goose Princess

High King Alexander promised Daemyn and Rosanna that they would have two months off from their duties. But when dangerous tidings come from Pohatomie, Alex needs to call them back before the situation in Tallahatchia grows worse.

Instead of finding Daemyn, Alex instead finds himself stuck with Daemyn's mountain family, especially his great-great grandniece who spends her days tending geese and has yet to say a word to Alex.

Don't miss this mash-up retelling of the Goose Girl and Wild Swans fairy tale.

ALSO BY TRICIA MINGERINK

†

THE BLADES OF ACKTAR

Dare

Deny

Defy

Destroy: A novella

Deliver

Decree

BEYOND THE TALES

Dagger's Sleep

Midnight's Curse

Poison's Dance

Acknowledgments

Thank you so much for reading *Poison's Dance*. I hope it touched your heart and brought a smile to your face. I appreciate each and every one of you. If you would care to take the time, reviews on Goodreads and Amazon are greatly appreciated and help spread the word to help others find the book.

Thanks once again to my parents. To my mom, who instilled in me a love of fairy tales. To my dad for helping me tweak the pacing of the book to make it so much better.

To my sisters-in-law Alyssa and Abby who fangirl over my books even to me.

To my brothers Ethan, Josh, and Andy who keep my guy characters real. Though I am glad pun wars are not our family's thing, lol.

To Bri, Paula, and Jill for being the best friends a person could ever ask for. Thanks so much for your continued encouragement and understanding when I'm pushing for a deadline.

Thanks so my writer friends Sierra, Jaye, Morgan, the whole Mitchtam crew, the Fairy Tale Facebook Group, and so many, many more. I would never be able to survive the crazy journey of writing and publishing without all of you!

Thanks to the PR writer group. It has been fun

meeting with you guys and finding a critique group! This is now the second book you have seen from start to finish, and I thank you so much for all your helpful feedback each month.

Thank you to Tom and Mindy Bergman for once again coming through when I pile on the proofreading projects!

But most of all, all glory belongs to my Heavenly Father. He has abundantly blessed me with His love and grace.

Made in the USA
Monee, IL
01 September 2023

41983650R00164